THE SON OF THE RED GOD
AND OTHER TALES OF THE
TA-AN, VOLUME 1

OTHER BOOKS IN THE ARGOSY LIBRARY:

THE BRAND OF VINDEX: THE COMPLETE
ADVENTURES OF CAPTAIN VINDEX
TRACY FRENCH

CRIMES OF THE YEAR 2000
RAY CUMMINGS

STEEL CUT STEEL
MAX BRAND

THE ASSASSIN: THE COMPLETE ADVENTURES
OF CORDIE, SOLDIER OF FORTUNE, VOLUME 6
W. WIRT

SAND IN THE SNOW
NORBERT DAVIS

THE PLUMED SERPENT
RICHARD BARRY

PROMISE OF THE NIGHT WIND
VARICK VANARDY

THE SON OF THE RED GOD AND OTHER
TALES OF THE TA-AN, VOLUME 1
PAUL L. ANDERSON

THE SCREEN OF ICE: THE COMPLETE CASES
OF GILLIAN HAZELTINE, VOLUME 2
GEORGE F. WORTS

REMEMBER TOMORROW
THEODORE ROSCOE

THE SON OF THE RED GOD
AND OTHER TALES OF THE TA-AN, VOLUME 1

PAUL L. ANDERSON

INTRODUCTION BY
RUSTY BURKE

COVER BY
C.C. SENF

POPULAR PUBLICATIONS · 2023

© 2023 Popular Publications, an imprint of Steeger Properties, LLC

First Edition—2023

PUBLISHING HISTORY
"Introduction" copyright © 2023 Rusty Burke. All rights reserved.
"The Son of the Red God" originally appeared in the January 31, 1920 issue of *Argosy* magazine (Vol. 117, No. 2). Copyright © 1920 by The Frank A. Munsey Company and assigned to Steeger Properties, LLC. All rights reserved.
"The Lord of the Winged Death" originally appeared in the March 6, 1920 issue of *Argosy* magazine (Vol. 118, No. 3). Copyright © 1920 by The Frank A. Munsey Company and assigned to Steeger Properties, LLC. All rights reserved.
"The Cave That Swims on the Water" originally appeared in the May 8, 1920 issue of *Argosy* magazine (Vol. 120, No. 4). Copyright © 1920 by The Frank A. Munsey Company and assigned to Steeger Properties, LLC. All rights reserved.

ALL RIGHTS RESERVED
No part of this book may be reproduced or utilized in any form or by any means without permission in writing from the publisher.

Visit argosymagazine.com for more books like this.

TABLE OF CONTENTS

INTRODUCTION BY RUSTY BURKE IX
TRANSLATOR'S NOTE 1
THE SON OF THE RED GOD 3
THE LORD OF THE WINGED DEATH 109
THE CAVE THAT SWIMS ON THE WATER 207

INTRODUCTION BY RUSTY BURKE

I WAS AT the Library of Congress, scrolling through microfilm reels of *Argosy* magazine as I attempted to locate possible sources for poetry Robert E. Howard had quoted or mentioned in letters. Because the magazine in the years of interest did not include poems on the contents page, I had to scroll through, page by page. This led to occasional serendipitous discoveries, such as poems that Howard had written parodies of, or had modeled other verses after, and once or twice to things I was actually looking for.

As I scrolled along in the issue for July 17, 1920, a story heading caught my eye. It was for "The Master of Magic," and the illustration showed a man with a bow and arrow on the left of the title, drawing a bead on a man who was running away, on the right. The author, Paul L. Anderson, was not familiar to me, but a quick glance at the first paragraph set my pulse racing, as it mentioned "the Ta-an, the People of the Mountain Caves."

You see, I knew that one of Robert E. Howard's earliest known writings—handwritten—was "Am-ra the Ta-an," a poem about a caveman who leaves his tribe, "[o]utlawed by the priests of the Ta-an," and enters a land where the hunting is good. He is there joined by a friend, Gaur, who apparently spent a little time stewing over Am-ra's treatment and decided to bump off the high priest and then hurry off to find his pal. We're told that Am-ra comes back from a hunt to find a bunch of black men hanging around the spring, which ticks him off, "[f]or he would not share his country | With a band of black ape-men." And there the poem breaks off.

There's also a contemporaneous fragment titled "The Tale of Am-ra," only an introductory paragraph, which tells us that "When the days are short and the nights are long in the country of the people of the caves… then the people of the caves gather about the fire of old Gaur…" to listen to him talk about the days of his youth. One supposes, given the title, that the tale being led up to was that of Am-ra, but all we learn about in this paragraph is Gaur. We learn that "Gaur was skilled in the mystery of picture making and cunning with the tools of the art.

Skilled in war also, was Gaur." And so forth.

There is also a five-line verse, "Summer Morn," with the first line "Am-ra stood on a mountain height," but it tells us nothing much, save that Am-ra was awake to watch the sunrise. There are two other prose fragments as well, though I did not know about them at the time. But, having tried and failed to come up with a source for either Am-ra or Ta-an, I'd simply thought they were Howard's own inventions.

Knowing all this, you can imagine my excitement at finding a story about a tribe of Crô-Magnons called the "Ta-an," referred to as "The People of the Mountain Caves." I quickly noted Anderson was "Author of 'The Cave That Swims on the Water' and 'The Lord of the Winged Death,' etc." Thus was necessitated a couple of days of seeking out these other stories, which led to yet others, and printing out copies on the Library's creaky old microfilm reader/printers. I found five stories right away, as all had been published in 1920, beginning with "The Son of the Red God" (January 31), and ending with "The Wings of the Snow" (August 28). It was again serendipity, as I continued my scrolling for other source material, that led to the final (as I believe) story, "Up From the Abyss," in the March 24, 1924 issue, almost four years after its predecessor.

Beyond the superficial similarity in the name of the tribe, the fact that they are called the "people of the [mountain] caves," most of the characters have hyphenated names (such as "En-ro," "Va-m'rai," "Nan-a-ta," etc.), and they are Crô-Magnons ("cavemen"), we also note some other similarities: the protagonists are generally artists, or at least creative types, as well as warriors; in at least three of the Anderson stories and the Howard Am-ra poem, the hero is exiled from the tribe due to a conflict with the priests; there is usually a rivalry over a girl; and there is an apparent similarity in writing style, which is pretty different from Howard's "natural" style. (For instance, from Howard: "Skilled in war also, was Gaur"; "But not needlessly he slew…"; "Am-ra's footprints he followed…" It calls to mind Wolcott Gibbs' criticism of *Time* magazine style: "Backward ran sentences until reeled the mind.").

I am convinced that Howard had read one or more of these stories and that they were very influential in his earliest work. We have, of course, the "Am-ra the Ta-an" poem and "Summer Morn," and three prose fragments. There is "The Tale of Am-ra," previously mentioned, which features

Gaur, who also appears in the "Am-ra the Ta-an" poem, and another in which Am-ra threatens to whip a young woman, Ah-lala, whom he accuses of having "tormented" and "provoked" him. (He is unable to bring himself to do it.) Of perhaps greatest interest here, though, is a one-page typescript describing "the land in which dwelt my people, the Ta-an." In it we find mention of "the Fear That Walks By Night," "the Hill That Walks," and "the Beast That Carries A Horn On His Nose," all of which are thus named in Anderson's "The Son of the Red God," though Howard gives them different Ta-an names ("the Fear," for instance, is "Snorr-m'rai-no" in Anderson, but Howard names it "Na-go-sa-na"). Howard also adds to the mix "the A-go-nun, the Red One, the cone [*sic*] horned monster of another age," and, intriguingly, "the E-ha-go-don, the frightful monsters of an earlier epoch—the dinosaurs." If he had ever finished that tale, no doubt it would have been a wild ride!

While Howard did not, so far as we now know, complete any of these tales of the Ta-an (the Ah-lala fragment consists of two legal-size sheets, numbered 10 and 11, but no other pages related to it have come to light), the influence of Anderson's tales did work its way into other of his works. In "Spear & Fang," his first published story, a Crô-Magnon artist, Ga-nor, must save A-aea, a young woman of his tribe, from her Neandertal abductor (she had first been accosted by a fellow tribesman, the arrogant son of an important leader, who was taking her into the woods for less-than-honorable purposes, only to be killed by the Neandertal). The story was written in response to a brief editorial by Farnsworth Wright in the December 1924 issue of *Weird Tales*, which went on sale November 1: "How would you like a tale of the warfare between a Cro-Magnon (say one of the artists who painted the pictures of reindeer and mammoths which still amaze the tourist) and one of those brutish ogres, perhaps over a girl who has taken the fancy of the Neandertaler; and the Cro-Magnon artist follows the Neandertal man to his den, and… But we have no room to tell the story in 'The Eyrie'" (the *Weird Tales* letters column). "We wish one of our author friends would write it for us." Young Robert E. Howard, aching to get a story published, almost immediately submitted a story that fit the bill perfectly, and by the end of the month he was informing his friends of the story's acceptance. I have little doubt that Howard was able to move so quickly on the suggestion because he had read, and already tried to emulate, the Ta-an stories of Paul L. Anderson.

Perhaps to a lesser extent "The Lost Race" and "Men of the Shadows" show some Anderson influence. In the latter, as an ancient shaman relates the history of the "Nameless Race" (an odd designation, since they have already been identified as Picts), Howard helpfully provides footnotes to "Sea of Silent Waters" (Pacific Ocean), "Atlanteans" (Cro-Magnons), "beast-men" (Neandertals), and "Middle Sea" (Mediterranean). Some of this seems similar to the migration of the Ta-an from their original homeland, a trek that took them toward "The Land of the Dying Sun" ("Amra the Ta-an" came "out of the land of the Morning Sun"), and into a country of "Little Hairy Men." It is Howard who adds the interesting detail that the Crô-Magnons are Atlanteans.

As Patrice Louinet explains, Howard had become

convinced, probably after reading the work of Lewis Spence, "that there was a linkage between the Crô-Magnons and Atlantis, and that the latter was historical, an empire belonging to Earth's past, not an imaginary one." In a letter to a friend, he had written, "About Atlantis—I believe something of the sort existed, though I do not especially hold any theory about a high type of civilization existing there—in fact, I doubt that. But some continent was submerged away back, or some large body of land, for practically all peoples have legends about a flood. And the Crô-Magnons appeared suddenly in Europe, developed to a high state of primitive culture; there is no trace to show that they came up the ladder of utter barbarism in Europe. Suddenly their remains are found supplanting the Neanderthal Man, to whom they have no ties of kinship whatever. Where did they originate? Nowhere in the known world, evidently. They must have originated and developed through the different basic stages of evolution in some land which is not now known to us."

It is no surprise, then, that the last we hear of Am-ra from Howard is in an untitled story, in which he and an older man named Gor-na are of the Sea Mountain tribe of Atlantis. Another character, named Kull, is an adopted member of the tribe, having been found "roaming in the woods," a "hairless ape" who "could not speak the language of men" and whose "only friends were the tigers and the wolves." The story is very slight, consisting of a fireside conversation in which Gor-na, the oldest, attempts to impress upon the younger men the importance of traditions, and a concluding incident in which Kull defies tradition to disrupt a priestly attempt to burn a young woman

INTRODUCTION xv

at the stake, and flees. Am-ra's primary role is to save Kull's life by lurching, "as if by accident," into an archer who has drawn a bead on the transgressor. It is his last appearance: from this point on in the Kull series, no Atlanteans will appear, other than Kull himself. The role of barbarians is instead taken by Picts.

"Amra," without the hyphen, would later be used by Howard in three stories: when "The Frost-Giant's Daughter" failed to sell to *Weird Tales*, he changed the name of the protagonist from Conan to "Amra of Akbitana" and sent it to a fanzine, which published it as "Gods of the North"; and in "The Scarlet Citadel" and "The Hour of the Dragon," he used it as an appellation for Conan, "the name—Amra, the Lion—by which the Cimmerian had been known to the Kushites in his piratical days." This usage of Amra seems to have no connection with the earlier Ta-an character.

Paul Lewis Anderson was born October 8, 1880 in Trenton, New Jersey. He graduated from Lehigh University in 1901 and began working in electrical engineering. In 1907, reportedly under the spell of Alfred Steiglitz's magazine *Camera Work*, he took up photography, and three years later embarked upon a career as a professional photographer, eventually running two portrait studios, teaching, and writing books and articles. Again, after a few years he began yet another new career, as an author. His first published story was "The Son of the Red God," the first of his series about the Ta-an. Over the course of the next decade, he would sell ten stories to *Argosy* (and *Argosy All-Story*), thirteen to *Boys' Life*, and, from April 1923 to September 1927, he appeared in an astonishing ninety-four issues of *Ace-High*, out of one hundred eight published during that span! He also had three stories in *Adventure*, and even had one in *Weird Tales* (May-June-July 1924). And once again, following success in this line of work, he made a switch, though this time it was just from writing stories for magazines to writing novels. He began with two novels about prep school life, then switched to historical tales, penning five novels about ancient Rome, the work for which he seems to be best remembered today. He died September 15, 1956, in Orange, New Jersey.

Paul Anderson's work has not really survived the passing years, and his posthumous reputation now seems to hinge more upon his photographic work than his writing. But while his Ta-an stories may not be Great Literature, we can be thankful for the role they played in jump-starting the career of a young writer in Cross Plains, Texas.

TRANSLATOR'S NOTE

DURING THE SUMMER of 1911 the present writer was conducting certain archaeological investigations in the Dordogne valley, and found, in a newly opened cave, a pile of skins which had been parchmentized and which bore strange markings that suggested, by their regularity and by the repetition of the figures, that they might constitute a written record. By dint of several years of close and patient application a translation was arrived at, when the record was found to be far more valuable—from an archaeological and ethnological standpoint—than had been supposed possible, since it was no less than an account, by a chieftain of a tribe of the great Cro-Magnon race, of the beginning of that vast racial replacement whereby the Cro-Magnons, for thousands of years the dominant race of Europe, first left their original home in the southern Himalayas and spread over western Europe, exterminating the former inhabitants of the country, the Neanderthal race.

This replacement, beginning in early Aurignacian times (about twenty-five thousand years ago) was one of the tremendous events in the development of humanity, and it has been suggested that some portions of the record might be of general interest. Accordingly, the present writer has prepared the following excerpt from the Cro-Magnon's manuscript, and offers it to the public.

It will, of course, be understood that the excessively archaic—almost monosyllabic—language of the prehistoric author has been modernized throughout.

THE SON OF THE RED GOD

1

THE SACRIFICE

"**GO SUMMON EN-RO**, the Carver of Tusks. He is the strongest among the tribesmen of the Ta-an."

The speaker was Men-ko, High Priest of the People of the Mountain Caves, and the priest to whom he spoke bowed, turned, and went swiftly down the long slope of the mountain, the group of skin-clad tribesmen who watched from a little distance parting to let him through.

The messenger bowed curtly as they saluted him with respect, then hurried on, and disappeared in the forest far below. Presently he returned, and with him came En-ro, a man of perhaps twenty two years, tall and straight and strong, whose wide shoulders, long limbs and muscular figure proclaimed him powerful and swift in war and in the hunt, and whose broad, high forehead, square chin and aquiline features showed him a man of high intelligence, even among the Ta-an, themselves no mean people.

The Carver of Tusks was a warrior, as was to be seen by the weapons he carried, and that he was an artist as well was shown by the exquisite carving and shaping of those same tools.

His ax, the flint head bound to the wooden shaft by thongs of deer-hide, bore at the end a little knob to keep the hand from slipping, and this knob was fashioned in the form of a bear; his throwing-stick, with shaft of wood and cup of bone, was decorated with outline drawings of mammoth, lion, and hyena, and the knob at the end was in the form of a bat, feared and worshiped by the Ta-an, who called it the Devil of the Air.

The young man was naked save for a girdle of lion's hide, into which was thrust his flint dagger, and for a leopard-skin quiver over his shoulder, to hold his darts; his ax and throwing-stick he carried in his hands.

One who knew the customs of the Ta-an might recognize En-ro for an artist by another sign as well, for his hands were unmutilated. When each boy of the tribe came to the age of fifteen he was taken before the priests, his station in the tribe, whether artist, priest, chieftain, hunter or other was determined, and one or more of his fingers—but never the thumb—solemnly cut off at the first or middle joint; artists only kept the hands entire.

So the Carver of Tusks climbed the mountain, the priest at his side trotting and panting by the effort to keep up with the young man's long, unhurried strides, and as the pair drew near the group of tribesmen parted again to give them passage, a murmur of respectful admiration following the most famous artist of the Ta-an.

En-ro came up to the priests and bowed to Men-ko with deference, yet with something of hostility showing in his eyes.

"I am here," he said.

"En-ro," spoke the High Priest, "it is known to you that the time of the Great Hunt is drawing close, that the beasts must be slain to furnish food through the winter, that the flesh of sheep and wild ass must be dried in the sun to keep

The Son of the Red God
by Paul L. Anderson

the tribesmen when the snow lies deep on the ground and the wind bites hard and we may not leave the caves. Also, do you know that the priests of Ta-an have labored long and hard to build the altar of the Great Hunt here on the roof of the world, that sacrifice may be made to bring us favor in the eyes of O-Ma-Ken, Great Father of the People of the Mountain Caves.

"But the last—the very last—of the chosen stones is held by two others, so that we cannot move it. You are the strongest of all the tribesmen; try now to move the stone. Much honor, and the favor of the Great Father shall be yours if you can loosen the stone."

En-ro smiled, a little scornfully.

"Men-ko," he said, "much honor have I already, more than any other among the Ta-an, save only yourself and Snorr, the Chieftain. Nevertheless, for the favor of the Great Father, I will try."

He turned to the stone, looked carefully at it on all sides, then laid aside his weapons, and, bending over, placed his hands beneath the rock.

Once, twice, and again he heaved, and the muscles of his arms and back and legs started out like twisting ropes, but still the stone lay fixed. Panting, the sweat trickling down his face, En-ro straightened up and looked again at the stone, while the priests shook their heads mournfully—bad fortune was sure to follow if one of the chosen stones was abandoned. But as the Carver of Tusks gazed in thought there came to him a vague, half-erased memory of something he had once seen while hunting.

Suddenly he grunted, turned from the rock, lifted his stone ax, and walked quickly down the mountain to the edge of the forest, where he cut down a young tree, a sapling, a little thicker than his arm, trimmed off the branches, and returned, the priests looking at him in wonder. Thrusting one end—the larger end—of his lever under the rock, he placed his shoulder beneath the other end and lifted.

The sapling bent and crackled, but the great rock quivered, stirred and lifted, and with a shout the priests sprang forward and turned it over, tearing it from the place where it had lain wedged, while the tribesmen, amazed at the new and strange tool invented by the artist before their very eyes, set up a cry:

"Great is En-ro, the Carver of Tusks! Great and wise and skilled and strong!"

En-ro picked up his weapons from the ground and watched the priests as they rolled and lifted and placed the stone he had conquered, while beside him Ko, one of the older priests, weary from his labor, stood and watched also.

"Tell me, Ko," said En-ro at length, "what is the sacrifice to be? The Ta-an have no captives taken in battle, nor is there among us any who has broken the laws of the tribe. Where, then, is the victim? Surely the Ta-an will not court the wrath of the Greatest One by offering him less than a man!"

The priest did not answer, and En-ro repeated his question, whereupon Ko grunted, shook his head, and replied:

"Go ask of Snorr, the Chieftain."

En-ro, his curiosity aroused by this evasion, thought a minute and saying"

"That will I do!" turned and strode down the mountain toward Snorr's cave. Straight down the slope he walked, for a mile or more, till he reached the edge of the forest, then turned sharp, to the right, and continued along a level stretch for another mile, till he came within sight of the cave where the Great Chieftain lived.

Suddenly, as En-ro was nearing the cave, a man stepped out from the forest on his left and a little ahead of him. En-ro dropped quickly out of sight and hid behind a boulder, for he had recognized Meng, the Bison, giant chief of a tribe of negroes who, wandering from their own country far to the south, had taken up their home on the mountain slopes and in the foot-hills and valleys where lived the Ta-an.

A huge man was Meng, tall even among the Ta-an, and far taller than any other among his own people, heavy-shouldered as the beast from which he took his name, his whole body covered with a thick black fell, almost a fur.

His forehead was low and slanted sharply back from his heavy eyebrows, his nose was broad and flat, his jaw protruding, his lips thick and heavy, his whole look evil and forbidding; nor was his ugliness less for the maze of scars that covered his face and chest and arms and thighs, marks of the fight in which Meng, his ax and dagger broken, had slain with his bare hands the great cave-leopard, whose skin now hung about the negro's loins.

He stooped slightly from the hips as he walked, and this, together with his hairy body and the great length of his arms, had caused the maidens of the Ta-an to nickname him "the Ape-man," a name that none of the warriors of the tribe cared to use, for Meng was terrible in battle.

En-ro scowled as he saw the Bison, for Meng was suitor for the hand of Va-m'rai, the Swift Runner, Snorr's daughter, whom the Carver of Tusks also loved and meant to have as his wife.

Meng, En-ro saw, carried a load on his shoulders, wrapped in a skin, and this he laid down a few yards from where En-ro crouched, grunting and chuckling as he undid the skin and sorted over the contents.

En-ro peered over the top of the boulder and saw that the Bison, stooping down, offered his broad back as a fair mark, and the young warrior, hatred in his soul, drew a dart from his quiver and fitted it to the cup of his throwing-stick. He raised it to his ear, his forefinger and thumb steadying the dart, and hold it poised; then lowered it, shaking his head; he could not slay an enemy from behind.

Before a month was past En-ro was to wish and wish again that he had hurled the dart, but for the present the Bison was safe—the young man could not read the future—and slowly and reluctantly the Carver of Tusks placed the dart back in his quiver and sank down in his hiding-place.

Presently the Bison took up his load and went on to Snorr's cave, En-ro slipping along behind him from rock to rock, silent as the shadow of some great bird, for no other of the tribe could move so quietly over rocks or through the forest as the warrior-artist.

At length Meng came to where the Great Chieftain sat warming himself in the sun before his home, and the Carver of Tusks grew nearer and nearer till he could hear their words, and could hear also the cracking and crunching from the flat table-rock to one side, where Snorr's wife, A-ai, the Dawn, and his daughter, Va-m'rai, were breaking and pounding bones that the sweet narrow might easily be sucked out.

Meng stopped before Snorr and laid down his pack, then, stooping, drew with his finger in the dust the three interlocking propitiatory circles, without which none might speak to the Great Chief.

Snorr looked at the mark in the dust and at Meng, then grunted and waved his hand, and the Bison sat down. After a few moments' respectful silence the Bison spoke, and En-ro heard him say:

"Oh, Snorr, Great Chief, I come to ask your daughter, Va-m'rai in marriage."

"No!" exclaimed Snorr. "You cannot have her."

"I bring gifts."

"No!"

"Rich gifts."

"No!"

"Look, Great Chief!" And Meng, opening his pack, spread out his gifts: darts and lance-heads, shells brought by the traders, the Little Hairy Men from the Land of the Dying Sun, skins of wild beasts, and even—strong magic, won only by great daring—the dried form of one of the furry, leather-winged Devils of the Air.

Snorr barely glanced at these gifts, rich enough to buy a dozen ordinary women, but shook his head, repeating "No!" and Meng, bowing, gathered his offering together, and, his face twisted with rage, took his way down the slope, passing close to the rock where En-ro, his teeth showing in an angry grin, lay gripping tight the haft of his flint ax.

The Bison was no sooner out of sight in the forest than En-ro, unseen by Snorr, slipped back from rock to rock till he in turn reached the woods, and then, his former errand forgotten, ran to his cave, where he seized something from a ledge of stone, and took his way once more, this time openly, to the Great Chief's home.

In turn the Carver of Tusks bowed before Snorr and drew in the dust, and in turn seated himself before the chieftain as Snorr waved his hand.

"Oh, Snorr, Great Chief," he said, "long have I loved your daughter, Va-m'rai, the Swift Runner, fairest of all the maidens of the Ta-an, and I come to ask her in marriage. I do not come empty-handed, but bring a gift—"

"One gift?" Snorr asked.

"One gift, but a gift that any of the tribesmen might envy you. Look, Great Chief!"

And En-ro lifted the little roll of skin he had taken from his cave, and laid it reverently at Snorr's feet. Snorr said nothing, but gazed thoughtfully past the suitor's head to where, across the wide valley, the distant hills met the sky, and it seemed to En-ro that he could read sorrow and regret on the face of the Great Chieftain.

At length Snorr raised the gift and carefully unwrapped the skin, and his eyes shone, for he held a little statuette two palms' breadth in height, carved with long and patient labor from a piece of ivory, the figure of a woman, young and slim, the star on her forehead marking her for the wife of O-Ma-Ken, Great Father of the tribe of Ta-an.

"The Star-Marked One!" he whispered, gazing with reverence at the little figure.

"True, Great Chief, the Star-Marked One. Seven months have I labored to carve this form, having traded with the Little Hairy Men for the fairest piece of the tooth of Do-m'rai, the Hill That Walks; seven long months, using my best skill, and adding thereto my prayers, that the bride of the Greatest One might bring me my bride. Is the price good?"

Snorr looked long at the figure, turning it from side to side, his eyes gleaming and his breath coming fast, but at last he wrapped it again in the skin and laid it down.

"Oh, Carver of Tusks," said Snorr, "this is indeed a gift worth far more than the flints, the shells, and skins the Bison offered, a gift that might purchase many women; never before have you wrought so skilfully, nor has any of the Ta-an carved so well. Take then the figure, and buy yourself another maiden, for never can the Swift Runner be your bride. And fortunate, indeed, shall be the one in whose cave the Star-darked One shall rest. Good fortune shall be his in battle and in the hunt, in love and in war; rich food and a soft bed, through many years. If you had come sooner!"

"Va-m'rai is then promised to another?"

"Not to you, nor to Meng, nor to any man, neither of the Ta-an or of another tribe, can she be given."

"She is destined to the gods?"

"You may ask, but I may not answer. When the time is ripe, then shall you and all the tribesmen know; but till then I may not speak." And Snorr waved his hand.

En-ro got to his feet and took the little parcel, erased the circles he had drawn in the dust, bowed, and turned away, his brown eyes troubled and his forehead knotted beneath the thick mass of unkempt hair. As he turned he looked toward Va-m'rai, and swiftly and secretly she made a sign he knew, the signal that called him to meet her at dusk under a certain tree far down the mountain.

He nodded and went on, looking back to see Snorr, his cloak of lion's hide drawn close about his shoulders—for autumn was coming, and the air was cool in the high hills—still sitting and gazing at the distant mountains that reared their crests through the blue haze, a long day's journey to the south.

That evening, as the sun was sliding down behind the hills, the Carver of Tusks took his way to the great pine where he and Va-m'rai had so often met. It grew on the edge of a deep ravine, and since the girl had not yet come, En-ro flung himself down to watch the path along which she must travel. Ten times the height of a tall man the cliff fell away in a sheer drop to where, at the bottom of the ravine, a noisy brook tumbled over the stones.

It was still light under the tree, but in the depths of the ravine the shadows were gathering, and En-ro shuddered as he heard, far down the mountain, the deep, earth-shaking, hunting roar of Snorr-m'rai-no, the Fear That Walks the Night, and saw in the growing dusk below him the flutter and swoop of the leather-winged Devils of the Air.

Presently, far down the ravine, he saw the white form of Va-m'rai hurrying along the path beside the brook, and he settled himself to wait, for he knew that she would have to pass beneath him, climb the path that led up the face of the cliff, turn, and come back to where he lay.

So the young warrior lay watching his sweetheart as she drew nearer, but suddenly she stopped, and En-ro, looking closely, could see a dark form blocking her way, a form that he knew for the Bison's, and he leaped to his feet to go to the girl's help, for he guessed why Meng was there. But even as he stood upright there was a struggle, a swift whirl of two forms, one white and one black, the girl's arm flashed, once, twice, and the giant fell.

Instantly the girl leaped over the fallen body and fled along the path toward her lover, and En-ro, watching, saw three dark forms in pursuit; Meng had not come alone.

But Va-m'rai was not called the Swift Runner for nothing, and En-ro saw the distance between her and her pursuers widen slowly, and he knew the negroes could not overtake the flying girl. At length two gave over and returned to their chief, and as the third still came on En-ro lifted a great stone, larger than his head, poised it carefully, and when the negro was almost beneath him he hurled it. Full and square and true, right where the neck and shoulder join, the great rock struck the negro—he fell as though struck by a thunderbolt—and the chase was over.

The young warrior hurried down the path to meet the girl, who, stumbling, panting, staggered into his arms, and as he held her he saw that her right arm was red with blood and spots and splashes of blood marked her white body.

"Va-m'rai!" he cried, frightened. "Are you wounded? Where?" And he looked anxiously for the hurt. But the girl, leaning back against his arm, her hands on his shoulder, shook her head.

"Not—mine!" she gasped. "The Bison's." And as she felt her lover's muscles tighten in anger, "Wait!"

Presently her trembling grew fainter and her breath came more easily, and she seated herself on the earth, her lover beside her.

"Meng stopped me," she said, "and asked me to go with him, to be his wife, and when I scorned him he seized my arm and tied to drag me, but I snatched the dagger from his belt and struck him with it and fled."

"I saw! I saw!" cried En-ro. "Indeed and indeed, Va-m'rai, for strength and courage you are fit mate for a warrior of the Ta-an. But is the Bison slain?"

She shook her head.

"But wounded. And now we have his vengeance to fear as well."

"We need not fear the Bison. You have but to tell the tribesmen, and they will hunt down and slay the man who dared to raise his hand against a chieftain's daughter of the Ta-an."

"Indeed, Carver of Tusks, my love, there is more than the Bison to fear. Last night Men-ko, the High Priest, came to the cave of Snorr and talked long with my father. I could not hear what they said—too far was I, and feared to go nearer—but they looked often toward me, and I saw my father bow his head in his hands."

"You think, then, that Men-ko has claimed you for the sacrifice? Would your father give you?"

"What can a tribesman do, even the Great Chief, when the gods call? Can he refuse, though they demand his own child?"

"It is true that the great Sacrifice of the Hunt is at hand," said En-ro thoughtfully. "The altar was finished to-day. And it is true also that Snorr refused gifts of great value, both from me and from the Bison, and, though he might refuse the Bison because he is black of skin and evil of soul, he could have no reason to deny me."

"That makes it sure. Oh, my love, and we had thought to spend so many happy years together. But if the gods call, what can we mortals do? But it is hard to say good-by. And it is hard to die when life has just begun. En-ro, my love"—and she clung about his neck and looked wistfully into his eyes—"En-ro, my love, will you think sometimes of me in future years, when another woman has my place at your side, after my soul is with the gods and my body has been thrown to the wild beasts?"

The young warrior shuddered and ground his teeth and clasped the girl in his arms, then sprang to his feet and shook his fists at the sky.

"It will not be!" he cried. "Not though I tear the altar in pieces with my own hands! It is not the gods who call for you! Could the Star-Marked One see lovers wrenched apart? It is but the priests. Oh, Greatest One, that I should have helped to build the altar! And Men-ko hates me because I have more honor in the tribe than his son; he has claimed you to strike through you at me. But you shall not die on the altar! Let me think."

"But what can we do? If the priests claim me for the sacrifice we two cannot stand against the whole tribe of the Ta-an!"

En-ro seated himself again on the earth and drew the girl close to him, his arm about her shoulders, and her warm, young body pressed against his own. Her head was thrown back against his arm, and her eyes looked into his; her long, brown hair fell in waves about them both, and he felt her sweet breath against his cheek. At last he spoke.

"Listen, Va-m'rai," he said. "When I bargained with the Little Hairy Man for the tooth of Do-m'rai, that I might carve the figure of the Star-Marked One, to him I showed still other figures that I had carved, daggers and ax-heads that I had chipped from flint, and the tools I had made for my carving.

"He said to me then that great honor awaited me in the Land of the Dying Sun; that none among his people could carve the tooth of Do-m'rai or chip the flint so skilfully as I, and he asked me to return with him.

"I but laughed and refused, for I thought that long life and great honor and happiness would be mine among the Ta-an. But now—but now, if Men-ko seeks you for the altar, why shall we not go together? Indeed, I think the Little Hairy Man spoke truth, for the flints he and his mates carry are but poor things beside my own."

"Oh, Carver of Tusks, it is a long journey to the Land of the Dying Sun."

"Not so long a journey as into the Long Dark."

"And a perilous one."

"More perilous than to stay?"

"No-o. But to live; always among the Little Hairy Men."

"I shall be there with you."

The girl flung her arms around her lover's neck and kissed him full on the lips, then leaped to her feet, saying:

"Come; we will go."

"Not yet, Swift Runner. First must I go to my cave for my weapons; we cannot start with empty hands—there are beasts to bar the way, and food we must have on the journey. You must spend this night in your father's cave, and to-morrow we will slip away to the Land of the Dying Sun—and I cannot leave the Star-Marked One; she will bring us good fortune on the journey and in our new home."

"But En-ro, my love, if they take me to-night? You know the victim must pass seven days and seven nights in the Cave of Purification, and the altar waits!"

"I think they will not take you to-night. The priests are weary from their labors, and they will sleep and rest; none will wish to guard the cave, and I think they will wait until to-morrow night—and we shall be gone."

"I am afraid! Could I not wait here till you return with ax and throwing-stick and darts?"

"The Fear That Walks the Night is abroad."

"I could sleep in the tree; there are many wide branches."

"The Devils of the Air are abroad; I have heard the flutter of their wings."

The girl shuddered and clung to her lover, "Oh!" she cried, "not that! Not that! Better the altar on the mountain-top and my body to the wild beasts. I will return to my father's cave. But—but—oh, Carver of Tusks, kiss me once again. And if I am not at the tree to-morrow at dusk—if I am guarded in the Cave of Purification; if my soul goes to the gods from the great altar—En-ro, you will not forget Va-m'rai?"

The young man kissed and soothed the frightened, trembling girl.

"Va-m'rai, by the Greatest One, Great Father of the tribe of the Ta-an, I swear no harm shall come nigh you," he said. "I will take you from the very altar, from the hands of the priests, if need by, and if I cannot—if I should fail—then by the Star-Marked One, the friend of lovers, I swear that my soul shall follow your in to the Long Dark!"

And he kissed her again, while she clung to him, weeping, like a child who wakes in the night.

"Now come," said En-ro at length. "We must return. Be at this spot when again the sun sinks behind the hills, and we will either make our way to the Land of the Dying Sun or else, perhaps, live by ourselves in the forest, as did Snorr, your father, when first he took A-ai from the Forest People."

So hand in hand the young man and the girl took their way down the path and through the ravine. Once they stopped while En-ro turned over the body of the negro he had crushed with the rock, to make sure that the man was dead, and they passed on, turning as they left the ravine and walking along the side of the hill toward the homes of the Ta-an, the Mountain Cave People. Presently they stepped from the forest to the open space about the caves, and as they did so a voice cried:

"Found! Found! Here is the victim!" and there came a rush of feet, and shouts arose:

"To the Cave! To the Cave of Purification! The victim to the Cave! Let her not escape!"

And the two were assailed on all sides by scores of tribesmen and priests, who tore Va-m'rai from her lover's grasp and hurried her away up the slope of the mountain, struggling with all her might, screaming, biting, striking—useless.

Again and again En-ro was flung back, fighting savagely, and the crowd swept over him; he was unarmed. Cut, stabbed, bruised, beaten with clubs, torn and breathless, he lay on the ground, and the crowd trampled him as he lay, and even as his senses left him the last thing he heard was Va-m'rai's despairing cry: "En-ro! Save me! Save—" Cut short by the splintering crash as the huge rock rolled into place, closing against all hope the mouth of the terrible, the fatal Cave of Purification.

2

FLIGHT AND PURSUIT

WHEN THE CARVER of Tusks came to himself again the big, round, yellow moon was setting, and he knew that the dawn was near. The chill of the night had stopped the flow of blood from his wounds, but he was stiff and sore and lame.

He tried to get to his feet, to stand up, but could not, and he lay quiet, listening to the far-off howl of the hunting wolves, Menzono, the Slayers, and he wondered, dully why they had not smelled him out and finished what the Ta-an had begun.

Slowly memory came back, and with it the thought of Va-m'rai in the Cave of Purification, and again he tried desperately to rise.

This time he got to his hands and knees, and crawled some fifty yards to a little spring of clear water that bubbled out from between two rocks, where he drank deeply once and again, then plunged his head and arms into the basin.

The sting of the cold water cleared his mind and braced his shaking limbs, and with the help of a stout stick he found lying by the spring he got to his feet and staggered off toward his cave, a mile or more away. He passed many of the caves of the tribesmen, and heard from within the grunts and snores of the sleepers, and far up the mountain he could make out, black in the moonlight, the form of the priest who guarded the cave where Va-m'rai was held prisoner.

At length En-ro got to his home, the cave where he lived alone—his mother had died years before, in the Great Famine, and his father had been killed a few months back, in a fight with En-mai-sun-so, the Beast That Wears a Horn on His Nose—and here, the Carver of Tusks dropped on his bed of leaves, drew his skin covers closely about him, and lay staring at the roof of the cave.

Through the long day he lay there, now burning with fever, now shivering with cold, but always thinking, thinking, turning over in his mind plan after plan to free the Swift Runner. He could hear the voices of the tribesmen as they passed to and fro, the calls of the women at their work, the cries of the children playing on the long, level bench of rock that lay below the caves; at times some one would pass the mouth of his cave and glance quickly in, but none entered to bring him aid, and En-ro knew well the reason—he had raised his hand against the priests, and was accursed.

He thought bitterly of Men-ko's promise that he should have great honor for moving the altar-stone, then brought his mind back to Va-m'rai and her danger, grateful for the law that would hold her seven days and seven nights in the Cave of Purification—before that time he would be well and strong!

Toward evening he rose, threw off his covers, went to the carcass of a sheep which lay on the stone shelf, cut off a chunk of meat, and, squatting at the mouth of the cave, tore the raw flesh in pieces with his strong teeth, gulping it down in great lumps and gobbets.

His hunger satisfied, he took his staff and went to the spring, where he drank deeply, returning again to his cave, the men and women—even the children, who generally crowded about him when he went abroad—drawing aside and staring silently at him as he passed. Back in his cave once more, he lay down, and, wrapping himself in his skins, was instantly asleep.

So passed the next day and the next, but on the fourth En-ro gathered together all his possessions, his ax and daggers of flint, his carving tools, his throwing-stick and darts, his skins—one lion's hide, three of the cave-leopard, and one of Menzono, the Slayer, all beasts that he himself had killed—and, not forgetting the ivory figure of the Star-Marked One, took his way with his load toward the forest.

Silently the tribesmen watched him go, none raising a hand to stop him, either in love or in anger, for he was outcast and accursed.

At the edge of the woods he stopped, turned, and looked back at the long row of caves, which, some higher, some lower, pierced the slope of the great mountain, at the level bench that lay below them, with forms of men and women and children passing back and forth along it, or gathered in groups for work or chat or play.

Above the caves rose the naked side of the mountain, and En-ro could make out the Cave of Purification, the priest guarding it, his arms folded, his skin gleaming yellow in the late afternoon sunlight.

The Carver of Tusks gazed sadly at the busy and happy scene—happy, but for one poor girl—and his heart was heavy as he thought that never again would he be part of it; never again would he clasp the hand of one of the Ta-an in friendship; his cave would be sealed up, his name forgotten, and he himself an exile in the Land of the Dying Sun, living his life out among the Little Hairy Men, whom he despised, or else drifting in the forest, alone but for his bride, living in danger of terrible, savage beasts by day, and by night dreading not only the hunting beasts, but also—and far more terrible than any beast—the spirits and fiends of the dark, the Blind White Wolf, larger than any three ordinary wolves, that moves silently on feet of air; the Faceless Man, who hides behind trees to leap on one's back; and, most frightful of all, the Invisible Thing, never seen, never heard, and known only when its claws fasten on one's shoulders and its long, sharp, curved teeth in one's throat.

So En-ro took his way into the deep forest, leaving behind the home and friends he had always known. He walked for three or four miles, then chose a large oak tree, with spreading limbs, dropped his pack beneath it, and climbed the trunk, cutting toe-holds in the bark with his ax as he climbed.

Reaching the thick branches, he pulled two together, twisting the ends to fasten them, then tore smaller branches and wove them in and out between the two till he had made a rude platform two or three feet wide and about eight feet long. He then clambered down and came back with his load, carrying it fastened to his shoulders by a twisted strand of a vine, and opened the pack, taking a skin to wrap himself in and a piece of sheep's flesh for food. After eating, he rolled in the skin, put the bundle under his head, his weapons at his side, and stretched out on his rude platform to sleep, uneasily and brokenly, dreaming much, and groaning and tossing as he dreamed.

In one of his dreams he thought Men-ko, the High Priest, had ordered him sacrificed on the Great Altar, and the priests were holding him down, one of them sitting on him to quiet his struggles; he tried to writhe away, but could not move; he tried to scream, but no sound came; Men-ko was drawing nearer, an evil grin on his face, and En-ro could see the gleaming knife of flint gripped in the priest's right hand.

Gasping, he woke—and lay still. On his body rested a huge venomous snake, its green and glistening body shining in a ray of moonlight that filtered through the trees, its villainous, lance-shaped head an arm's length or less from his face, its beady eyes blazing like dark stars into his own.

En-ro felt his scalp tingle and prickle as the hair rose like the hackles of Menzono's neck when he sees a foe, and the sweat started in little beads from the roots of his hair; the weight of the reptile's body, thick as a warrior's arm, and more than twice as long, was crushing the breath from his lungs, and the horror of its loathsome presence froze his blood—he could feel his hands and feet grow cold.

He knew his end had come; one move, one struggle, and those deadly fangs, freighted with poison, would sink in his flesh—a few minutes of agony, frightful beyond belief, and his swollen body, black and distorted, would lie rotting in the forest, shunned by bird and beast alike.

But, after all, it would be a relief to journey into the Long Dark; life held but little for an outcast from the tribe;

he would be spared much struggle, much suffering—the Long Dark.

Where had he last heard those words? Va-m'rai—he had promised—oh, Great Father! And En-ro gathered his forces; his brain grew clear. Could any man escape the Fanged Death, so close? Could any living man move more swiftly than that terrible head? No!

But he must try. Some slight movement of his body alarmed the snake, which raised its head and thrust out its forked, quick-darting tongue again and again, feeling for danger. Slowly, slowly, gently, cautiously, En-ro slid his hand down to his side and groped for his flint dagger, his eyes ever on those terrible, passionless eyes before him.

Slowly, slowly he drew it from his girdle; slowly, slowly he raised his arm, flexing the muscles gently, not to alarm the snake. Full five hundred breaths he drew while raising his hand, so slowly did he move, keeping the dagger-point ever toward the snake's head—the reptile would strike toward a moving object. But even this gentle motion roused the Fanged Death, which lifted its head and weaved it from side to side, searching for danger, seeking the threat.

Back and forth, in and out of the ray of moonlight went that evil, deadly head, the black tongue playing in and out like forked lightning, the little beady eyes glistening; back and forth, back and forth, till En-ro felt himself grow dizzy from watching, and braced himself against the sodden languor that overspread him.

At last his hand, clutching the dagger, was at his shoulder; he rested a moment, steadied himself and struck; the snake felt the motion of his body, the head darted forward, too swift for eye to see, the mouth was thrown open, the fangs, grazing En-ro's hand, clicked against the flint; the sharp point, driven by the double force of the snake and of the warrior's arm, pierced the reptile's head. En-ro twisted on his side and threw off the crushing weight, and the Fanged Death, slain by a human hand, writhing, twisting, thrashing, fell down, down, tearing leaves from the branches of the tree, till it landed on the ground, forty feet below.

En-ro, sick, dizzy, shaken, limbs, trembling, sweat starting from his body, lay, belly down, on the platform, his head over the edge, clutching the branches, vomiting again and again, and listening to the noise as the dying snake thrashed about among the underbrush. But after a time its struggles grew fainter and fainter, and at length ceased, the young warrior conquered the trembling of his limbs, and lay down to await the dawn.

The four days that followed were spent by En-ro in hunting. He lay in wait beside the trail that led to a waterhole, and with darts from his throwing-stick slew two wild sheep; with his flint hunting-knife he skinned and butchered them, taking only the very choicest pieces of the meat, for he dared not carry extra weight, and he made an attempt to sun-dry some of this, hanging portions by strands of vines from the limb of a tree, that it might be safe from beasts. After all, however, it was stolen by the birds, and he gave over the effort, storing the rest of his provisions under a pile of stones.

He also added to his stock of darts, cutting straight shafts from the trees of the forest, and binding to them, with thongs from the hides of the sheep, carefully shaped and polished heads that he had brought from his cave, though he knew that the green wood, as it dried out, would warp and twist.

Still, he counted on using these darts first, saving till afterward his ones of seasoned stuff. The new darts he placed in the sun, that the raw, untamed hide might shrink, and bind the heads firmly to the shafts.

He slew a young sheep, and made a water-bag of the skin, cutting off the head and hoofs, beating the carcass with a club till the bones were broken and the flesh loosened from the skin. Then, drawing out bones and flesh and entrails, and turning the hide inside out, that he might scrape it, afterward he tied the openings in the skin with other thongs of rawhide, except the one at the neck, which was nearly closed by sewing, using an over-and-over stitch; the skin would be water-tight when the thongs hardened.

He had no time to tan this hide, to keep it soft, so he filled the bag with small stones and let it harden, afterward shaking the stones out, the bag thus keeping its open shape.

On the morning of the ninth day that Va-m'rai had been in the Cave of Purification. En-ro, looking at the sky as soon as he woke, shortly after dawn, saw great banks of dark clouds gathering far down in the west. He climbed hurriedly down from his perch in the oak-tree, went to his store of meat, and hastily swallowed a few lumps of flesh. He knew instinctively, as any animal might, that with a hard day's work before him he was better off with but little in his stomach, so he rose from the ground with his hunger still only partly satisfied.

He then set about packing his few belongings, placing the new darts in his quiver, rolling the rest, except the water-bag and a small piece of meat, in the lion's skin he had brought with him to the forest; his ax and throwing-stick he, of course, carried in his hand, and his dagger in his girdle. The water-bag and meat he fastened to the outside of the pack, and then, hoisting the load to his shoulder, he set out through the forest.

He traveled hard and fast, not going directly back toward the caves of the Ta-an, but choosing his route so as to pass them, keeping farther down the mountain that he might not be discovered by some chance hunter and forced into a fight. Thus he made a wide circuit, climbing the mountain far to the west of the home of his tribe, and passing the homes of the Mountain Cave People a second time, but farther up the slope.

It was hard going at the higher levels, for the rocks were bare except for occasional patches of moss, and En-ro was obliged to go carefully, that he might not, by chance, be seen by some one from the tribe. He skulked along, taking advantage of every possible cover, crouching behind rocks, crawling from one to another, driven always by the need for haste.

And all the while the cloud-banks to the west were climbing, ever climbing, rolling in vast, dark-gray masses across the sky, and the sun was sliding down to meet them.

Often and often En-ro looked over his shoulder, and each time he hurried on faster and faster, for it was the custom of the Ta-an—indeed, it was the law—that the Sacrifice of the Great Hunt should take place during a thunder-storm, the first storm after the victim had spent seven days and seven nights in the Cave of Purification.

Once En-ro, peeping over a boulder, saw far below him the eleven lesser priests of the Ta-an grouped in a semicircle, the tall form of Men-ko between the horns, all tossing their arms wildly, their long hair flying, as, facing the west, they chanted the song of sacrifice. Behind them the tribesmen knelt.

The Carver of Tusks hastened on more rapidly than before, and presently came to the hiding-place he had in mind, dropping his load and flinging himself, panting, on the rocks to rest, just as the first peal of thunder sounded from the dark clouds that now spread over more than half the sky.

Presently En-ro raised himself and peered out from his place of concealment, whose rocks rose breast-high on him as he stood erect. A few yards to the east of him, and a little down the slope, stood the Altar of the Hunt, and En-ro measured the distance with his eye carefully and noted also the rocks that lay between; there must be no misstep later.

Far down the slope to the south he could see the tribesmen in a compact body, the priests leading, slowly climbing the mountain—the first peal of thunder was their signal to start—and in the front rank Va-m'rai. He could just recognize her, and could see that her hands were tied, of course! He knew they would be. He could see her stumble, and knew that she must be weak from starvation for the victim was given no food, but only water, while in the Cave of Purification.

En-ro crouched down again behind the rocks, made sure of his pack, laid ax and throwing-stick and darts, together with a piece of meat, on top of the pack—and waited.

It was growing dusk, for the sun had long since been hidden behind the heavy cloud masses that now covered the entire sky from horizon to horizon. Lightning blazed from the clouds, lighting up the scene, and as the procession, still chanting the Song of Sacrifice, swept up the mountain En-ro, peering through a crevice between the rocks of his hiding-place, could see Va-m'rai, her long brown hair flowing loose, her arms held by two young priests, looking anxiously from side to side for help or for some sign of relenting.

The thunder was now rolling continuously, it was growing darker and darker, and the lightning-bolts, flaming one after another, threw a weird, unnatural glare over the whole mountain; for an instant things were clearly seen, then shrouded in darkness that was doubly dark after the light.

Nearer and nearer climbed the sacrificial procession, till within a hundred yards of the altar the crowd halted—they might not come closer. The priests and the victim went on till they reached the altar, and En-ro could see then busied about it, the priests chanting the while. He could not hear the words of the chant—only at times, as the rolling of thunder was lighter, could he hear their voices rising and falling in the measured cadences of the prayer.

He crouched, tense, while Va-m'rai's hands were unbound and she was stretched on the altar. It was the law that none might go before the Great Father with hands or feet bound, but, that the victim might not escape, five great stones, the under sides flattened and hollows cut in them, were used to hold the struggler down, one being placed across the throat, one over each wrist, and one over each knee.

Va-m'rai was held by the priests, and the stones were placed, and now for the first time she struggled and fought, but to no end; the priests were too strong. And now in terror she shrieked and shrieked again: "En-ro! Help! Help! En-ro, save me!" and then again, despairingly: "En-ro!" And ever the lightning flared and the thunder rolled.

At these terrified screams En-ro trembled, gripping tight the haft of his throwing-stick—but he dared not move. And still Va-m'rai shrieked, turning away her face as the High Priest came forward, holding aloft the sharp flint knife that was to tear her heart from her bosom.

And now the priests retired, almost to the waiting crowd of tribesmen, for none might be near the High Priest at the supreme instant of sacrifice. Brighter and brighter flamed the lightning, nearer and nearer rolled the thunder, and now came the swish and rush and roar of the rain, as the clouds opened and poured their torrents over the mountain.

En-ro fitted a dart to the cup of his throwing-stick and rose to his feet as the priests, turning, knelt and lifted their hands to the sky. The High Priest drew near the victim, his knife raised, and En-ro saw that Va-m'rai, rolling her head from side to side, still struggled and fought against the weights that held her fast.

En-ro raised his throwing-stick and held it poised, and even as he started its forward sweep the whole heavens were rent apart, there came a terrific, blinding glare, a frightful shock, a stunning crash of thunder that shook the mountain beneath his feet, and the High Priest toppled forward, falling across the shrieking victim!

Instantly En-ro leaped forward, as the priests and tribesmen fell on their faces, ran to the altar, and with superhuman strength tore the stones from Va-m'rai's throat and arms and legs, lifted the girl in his arms, and ran once more to his hiding-place.

She clung to him, gasping and sobbing brokenly, and as he laid her down he felt that she trembled from head to foot, and held tight to his arm. He freed himself, caught up his pack, seized the girl's hand, and called:

"Come, Va-m'rai, Swift Runner! We must make haste! Come quickly!"

Va-m'rai rose to her feet, he helped her from the hiding-place, and, still holding hands, the two started back along the ridge of the mountain, in the direction from which En-ro had come.

The rain was falling less heavily now, and the thunder was passing away, rolling farther and farther off with each succeeding minute. From time to time En-ro stopped to listen anxiously, and at last, after such a pause, he grasped Va-m'rai's hand tighter and said:

"Hasten! Hasten! They have found him!" And he ran on faster than ever, half dragging, half carrying the girl.

"Found—whom?" she panted. "And why—do—the Ta-an—cry—the hunting call?"

"Men-ko!" he answered. "Hurry!" And they continued their flight, leaping and scrambling from rock to rock, splashing through pools left by the rain, bruising themselves in the darkness, slipping, falling, rising, ever hurrying, hurrying along the crest of the mountain, the thunder rolling farther and farther off, and the cries of the tribesmen growing fainter and fainter as they were left behind.

At last En-ro turned down the slope, and after another mile or so the fugitives plunged into the forest, and the going was easier. True, they were hampered by the underbrush, and from time to time one or the other ran violently against a tree, with a breath-taking shock, but En-ro had that morning blazed the trees with his ax as he passed, and they could follow the line of white marks that gleamed faintly in the dark woods.

At times some beast crashed through the brush, startled by the sound of human beings, but for the most part the only noises were those made by the man and girl, or the quiet drip—drip—drip of water from the leaves. All night long they traveled, far past the spot where En-ro had made his sleeping-place in the old oak tree—and the clear dawn found them, leg-weary, bruised, scratched by low-swinging branches, but many miles from the caves of the Ta-an.

While still on the mountain En-ro had given the girl a lump of meat, which she had carried in one hand, tearing pieces from it with her teeth and swallowing them as she ran, but now in the morning light they sat down beside a little stream and ate their fill, afterward lifting water from the brook in their hands to drink.

While they ate En-ro looked about him and saw that they were in a little glade, some fifty paces across, with long, rich grass covering the ground and bending over the edge of the stream. Rushes grew in the shallow places, and he could see many fish playing, or—the large ones—moving lazily about in the clear water, plainly visible against the gravelly bottom.

The character of the forest had changed, for there were more of the soft woods, and fewer, hardly any, pines or firs, and wild flowers made patches of bright color in the grass. One tall tamarack tree grew at the edge of the open space, towering above the maples and willows, and En-ro, finishing his piece of meat, climbed this and looked about over the forest.

Far to the north he could see the hills from which they had come, and far to the south another range, and he knew—as indeed he had realized during the night—that they had left the slopes, and were now on the floor of the broad valley across which he had so often looked from his home on the mountain. He knew, too, having heard it from the Little Hairy Men, that they must cross this valley, climb the farther mountain, then down a slope far longer than the one they had traveled, and then, turning west, make for the Land of the Dying Sun.

After many days' journey they would come in sight of the Great Blue Water, and, following along the shore, at length reach the new home they sought, where honor awaited an artist and craftsman.

For a long time he looked, choosing with practiced eye the easiest route, and fixing the direction in his mind, then climbed down, to find Va-m'rai, worn out with the journey and sodden with sleep, nodding beside the stream, her hands clasped about her knees, and her long hair, wet and dark and lustrous from the rain, matted about her shoulders.

He shook her gently by the arm and she raised her head and blinked at him, then smiled.

"Get up, Va-m'rai," he said. "We may not sleep here; it is no safe place."

"I can go no farther," she answered, rising stiffly. "Oh, Carver of Tusks, I can indeed go no farther!" And she tottered where she stood, from utter weariness, clutching her lover's arm to steady herself. En-ro looked at her doubtfully.

"Indeed, Swift Runner," he said, "I think you speak the truth! Well, we will rest here, but not on the ground." And he turned to a tree, climbed it, pulled two branches together, and wattled small branches and withes between them till he had made a platform. In the meantime Va-m'rai had spread out the skins, laying them on bushes to dry in the sun, which was warm and comforting, and had climbed the tree to help in making the resting-place.

When it was finished En-ro climbed down and got the skins and other things he had carried and returned. He spread a lion's skin on the platform, the two lay down in each other's arms, pulled the rest of the skins over them, and were instantly asleep.

The sun was setting when the Carver of Tusks awoke, waking instantly as does a healthy animal, and he shook Va-m'rai, who sat up and looked about for a moment, puzzled, then remembered where she was.

Her lover kissed her, and she responded, her arms about his neck, and he climbed to the ground, she following. They ate more of their store of meat, with berries pulled from the bushes, drank from the stream, and En-ro seated himself on the ground to watch while Va-m'rai combed her tangled hair with her fingers. After a time the girl spoke:

"Carver of Tusks, why did the Ta-an cry the hunting-call? Did they see you take me from the altar?"

"I do not know," he answered. "But I think they cried the hunting-call because they found the body of Men-ko, and knew or thought that I had slain him."

Va-m'rai left off combing her hair, sat up straight, and looked at her lover with wide eyes.

"They thought you slew him! But—but—was he not slain by the lightning?"

En-ro shook his head. Gradually an expression of horror came over Va-m'rai's face.

"You slew the High Priest?"

En-ro nodded.

"With a dart from my throwing-stick," he said, and the girl shrank away from him, looking at him with fear in her eyes.

"But—" she whispered, "but—that is sacrilege! To slay the High Priest at the altar! You will be accursed!"

En-ro shrugged his shoulders.

"Could I see you die?" he asked, and Va-m'rai turned away and looked in the water. Finally she turned to him again, and in her face admiration and love struggled with horror.

"You did that for me? You dared? Oh, En-ro, my love!" And she flung her arms about his neck and kissed him. "If you are accursed of the gods, so too am I, for I will share your lot, forever and ever!"

And she kissed him again and again, and laid her cheek against his, while he clasped her tight. After a time the Carver of Tusks rose and lifted the girl, and they climbed to their place of safety in the tree, wrapped themselves in the skins, and lay down once more, and once more they slept.

As the dawn was gilding the tree-tops, and while the deep shadows still shrouded the floor of the forest, En-ro woke, rose, stretched, and prepared to descend the tree, but suddenly he stopped—he had heard something coming through the forest. At first he took it for a wild beast, but as the noise came nearer and nearer he realized that it was made by men; he could even guess roughly that there were about ten or twelve.

He shook Va-m'rai awake and grasped his weapons, and together they listened to the rusting of the undergrowth. From time to time he could catch the sound of a voice, but could not make out the words. Tense and alert, the two peered down into the little clearing, and Va-m'rai whispered:

"Is it the Ta-an?"

"I cannot tell," answered the young warrior: "Wait!"

Soon the footsteps were at the edge of the glade, and dark forms came into view. En-ro counted them silently; one, two, three, up to eleven, and as they strode into the light, which was growing stronger, he ground his teeth and his hand tightened about the haft of his ax till the knuckles showed white—the leader of the negroes was Meng!

En-ro heard a gasp behind him, felt his arm clutched, and turned to see Va-m'rai staring down, mingled fear and loathing on her face. He laid a finger on her lips and she looked up at him, then nodded and pulled herself together.

The negroes spread over the little glade, speaking in subdued voices, which, however, carried to the listeners in the tree, and En-ro could make out the words, though they spoke in their own tongue, for he had some knowledge of their language. He whispered to Va-m'rai what they were saying, and it was clear that Meng, hearing of the rescue and flight, had got together a party of warriors and had set out to over-take the fugitives, to find and kill En-ro, and keep the girl.

The two crouched low on the little platform, hiding themselves as best they might. They knew they would be found, and that soon, but with the instinct of the hunted animal they put off the evil moment as long as they could; they would fight, but in the meantime something might happen—one never knows. The hunters might be scattered by a rhinoceros or by a herd of bison, they might get to fighting among themselves—one can never tell!

Lying on the platform and peering through the leaves, the artist and the girl saw Meng and his warriors, bending close to the ground, questing back and forth like hounds that have lost the scent, searching for the tale told by the prints in the long grass. They saw the negroes follow the tracks into the glade, find the place where the two had rested by the brook, pick up the trail there and follow it to the foot of the tree, and back again to the bank of the stream.

From time to time one or another of the hunters dropped on all fours and sniffed at the grass, and at last the band came to a halt under the tree, whence En-ro and Va-m'rai watched.

They spoke together for an instant, then Meng, thrusting the haft of his ax through his girdle and casting his spear on the ground, set himself to climb. En-ro picked up his throwing-stick, fitted a dart to the cup, and waited.

Higher and higher climbed the giant negro, nearer and nearer, and still En-ro waited, tense, his nostrils quivering. Soon Meng was on a level with the platform, and En-ro rose to his feet with a fierce, deep-throated roar. He swept the throwing-stick forward—the haft snapped in two—the dart flew far over Meng's head—a ferocious yell of exultation broke from the waiting negroes—and En-ro dropped flat on the platform barely in time to escape a storm of darts that whistled and snapped through the branches of the oak.

Meng climbed and slid to the ground, and spoke briefly to his men, and he evidently had changed his plan, for the negroes spread out and began to climb the oak and nearby trees, making a circle about the quarry.

Helpless, En-ro and Va-m'rai watched as the negroes climbed about them and closed in on all sides, and the Carver of Tusks knew that they meant to take him alive. Nearer and nearer came the hunters, crawling out on the limbs of the other trees, till at a cry from their leader they dropped together on the little platform, and En-ro, ax in his right hand and dagger in his left, leaped to his feet to meet the rush.

Then followed a desperate fight. En-ro with ax and dagger, Va-m'rai with skinning-knife, struggled, struck, bit, kicked, clawed, fought with hands and feet, with weapon and teeth and fist—but in silence, for the Ta-an uttered no sound in battle.

But the negroes! Yells and curses tore the silence of the little glade, screams and groans of agony, the crash and thud as falling bodies smashed through the branches to the ground, the panting of breathless men, the break as the boughs of the oak sagged and bent and sprang under the weight of the stamping, surging fighters.

En-ro struck but once with his ax before the attackers pressed too close for him to swing—but the negro plunged headlong to the earth, his chest crushed by the terrific blow. Va-m'rai stooped under an upraised arm and stabbed another in the belly, and he too fell, clutching one of his fellows and carrying him to death. En-ro jabbed his fist in Meng's face and the Bison staggered backward, tripped, and fell, whirling over and over till he hung, head on one side and feet on, the other, belly down, across a branch twenty feet below.

Again and again En-ro was borne down by weight of numbers, but ever he struggled to his feet and fought, blinded by the blood running into his eyes, half stunned by the blow that had laid open his scalp from front to back, till at last a negro, leaping on him from behind, clasped his legs around En-ro's body, pinning his arms to his sides and throwing him face down on the branches.

Instantly three others seized him and tied his hands and feet with rawhide thongs, and at the same moment Va-m'rai, stunned by a blow from a fist that landed full on the back of her neck, was seized and tied, and the fight was over.

The fugitives were quickly lowered from the tree, and their feet unbound, hobbles arranged so that they could walk with short steps, and Va-m'rai was revived by water thrown on her face.

While this was going on En-ro counted with satisfaction seven negroes stretched on the grass, dead or writhing in agony, but his satisfaction was short, for he and the girl were jerked roughly to their feet, turned in the direction from which they had come, and jabbed in the back with spears as a signal to march.

3

EN-RO MEETS THE RED GOD

HIS ANKLES HOBBLED with thongs of hide so that he could move only with short, tottering steps or in standing jumps, En-ro squatted on his haunches under a spreading pine and chipped flints into lanceheads and daggers, while his guard, a tall, muscular negro, watched from a few yards off, leaning against a tree and eying the captive white man as the Fear That Walks the Night eyes a fat buck on which he is about to spring.

Half-consciously, the Carver of Tusks felt contempt for the rude, poorly chipped ax the negro carried, so different from his own beautifully finished tools, but this was no more than a passing thought—his mind was too full of other matters.

Indeed, he was doing his forced labor with no more than half his ordinary attention—almost automatically—for his body ached and his brain whirled with rage and grief.

Hot fits of anger, when all grew red before him, alternated with cold fits of fear—not for himself; no warrior of the Ta-an feared to die! His skin was covered with half-healed wounds from the lances of the negroes who had prodded him along, and his muscles ached from the blows he had received in battle and in captivity, but worse than this, far worse than any mere bodily pain, was the thought of Va-m'rai, captive like himself, and destined to the arms of Meng, the Bison, while he, En-ro, her lover and betrothed, sat chipping flints, a slave to the negro chieftain.

About him the great forest closed in, its giant trees shutting off the view in all directions, while between the near-by trunks he could now and again catch sight of dark forms wandering idly about, and could hear the voices of the negroes as they chatted carelessly together.

From time to time one or another would come and stand watching him, exchanging a few words with his guard, who clearly felt his own importance; was he not there to see that the white warrior-artist kept at his work? And then the guard, to prove his power and consequence, would kick the white man, strike him with a stick, or spit upon him, while the others laughed.

So En-ro squatted, as he had done for the past five days, knowing that unless he could free Va-m'rai before Meng's wounds were healed they might give up all hope. Plan after plan, scheme after scheme he had turned over in his mind, watching always for the chance that did not come.

Among the flints that lay, unshaped, in a pile beside him, En-ro saw one that was almost a perfect dagger; that would need but little chipping—indeed, it might be used just as it was, and En-ro meant to take that one next, when he had finished the one he was working on. By now it was growing dusk, and soon the woman would be coming with his food.

En-ro looked up as a step sounded faintly near at hand, and his guard turned his head to see who was coming. Quick as a striking snake, the artist's hand shot out, caught the unshaped flint and flung it behind him, and as the guard turned back he saw the captive hard at work once more.

It was growing too dark to work, though, and as the woman came with the food En-ro gave over his labors, ate the raw flesh, and held out his hands for the bonds that were placed on him at night. The guard then tied him to the pine tree, and the two lay down to rest.

Almost at once the negro was asleep, but the Carver of Tusks lay staring upward into the darkness till long after all sounds had died out in the camp save only the grunts and snores of his guard. He heard the soft pad-pad of small beasts, the distant roar of Snorr-m'rai-no, and once the frightened squawk of agony as some bird of the night fastened beak and talon in his prey.

Through an opening in the tree-tops En-ro could see a bright star, and he said to himself that when the star reached the center of the open space he would act. So he forced himself to lie quiet while the star moved slowly across the sky, and at length, when the time had come, he rose gently, cautiously, to his feet, and took the rough flint he had seized from the pile that afternoon—he had taken care, without seeming to do so, to lie down on the rude dagger when his guard had tied him to the tree.

Carefully, noiselessly, with the flint in both hands, he cut the thongs that bound him to the tree, then those that held his feet. He then held the flint between his feet and sawed his handcuffs back and forth across it till he was free. He stepped across the soft earth to his sleeping guard, bent over the negro, who lay on his back with wide-flung arms, and with one fierce stroke—no lighter for the kicks and blows of the past week—he drove the dagger into the body of the unconscious man.

There followed a single, convulsive plunge of the dark form, one gasping sob, and the negro was dead, and En-ro, taking his ax and lance, slid like a ghost among the trees.

He had but a vague idea, caught from the chatter of his many visitors, of where he would find Va-m'rai, but he set out to look for her, treading silently on the carpet of dry pine-needles, and avoiding the dark bodies that lay stretched in sleep on the ground all about. He felt utter contempt as he saw how carelessly the negroes lay down wherever night found them.

"No wonder," he thought, "that Snorr-m'rai-no takes heavy toll of these fools! Why, even the beasts know better than to sleep unhidden on the ground!"

Presently, down a little forest aisle, he caught a glimpse of something white, and turned that way. It was Va-m'rai, sleeping under a tree, and now En-ro went even more cautiously than before, stooping-feet testing the ground before him that no cracking twig might sound an alarm, nostrils spread wide to catch any faintest scent, every muscle and nerve tense and ready to spring, eyes and ears alert.

The girl was bound and tethered as he had been, and was guarded by three negroes, and En-ro smiled scornfully as he saw that they too were asleep—"Fine guards!" he thought. "A warrior of the Ta-an who slept on guard would surely die!"

He stepped over them and cut Va-m'rai's bonds, the slight touch waking the girl, who sat up with a little cry.

"Quiet!" whispered En-ro, then helped her to her feet,

for she was stiff and lame from being tied. She clung to him, breathing fast with excitement and he kissed her, then hand in hand they stepped carefully over the sleeping guards and disappeared in the forest.

Dawn found them many miles from the negroes' camp. They had traveled hard, had waded for more than a mile up a running stream, and at last, climbing a low hill on whose rocky ledges they left no trail, had come to a small cave, hidden among trees. Here they gathered dry leaves for a bed and for covering, and lay down to sleep. When they woke the sun was sinking toward the edge of the world, and En-ro, rising, stretched himself and yawned.

"I must seek food," he said. "My belly cries out within me!" and Va-m'rai answered:

"I, too, will go."

"Nay, keep hidden and wait my return; there may be peril," said En-ro, but Va-m'rai put her arm about his shoulder and whispered:

"Let me go, my love! It is long that we have not been together, and what is peril to the daughter of a chieftain of the Ta-an?"

And En-ro laughed, whereby she knew her wish was granted. They went together to a game trail En-ro had marked, leading down to a place where the brook widened into a pool. Approaching silently and against the breeze, they hid behind a screen of brush and waited.

Presently they heard, far off, the sounds of beasts coming to drink, and soon three or four bison came into view. They tramped down to the water and drank, then stood in the pool for a time, stamping, shaking their heads, and splashing. Next came a herd of wild cattle, and hard on their heels a dozen or more wild sheep, all trooping to the water-hole together.

En-ro looked the sheep over carefully and was about to rise from where he squatted when he heard a stamping and thrashing up the trail, and a doe with a fawn appeared. The hunter's eyes gleamed and he crouched, tense and watchful. As the fawn drew opposite him he leaped to his feet and with a swift overhand motion hurled his lance.

The fawn dropped, the doe dashed forward, and instantly there was a wild stampede among the animals about the water-hole, bison, cattle, and sheep tearing madly off through the forest in blind terror.

En-ro threw the body of the fawn over his shoulder and he and Va-m'rai returned to their cave, where he skinned his kill and the two fed full on the tender flesh, then rolled stones against the mouth of the cave and lay down to sleep.

Next morning they fed, and En-ro squatted down before the cave to think, Va-m'rai sitting beside him. At length she could bear the silence no longer, and asked:

"Carver of Tusks, my love, do we start to-day for the Land of the Dying Sun?"

En-ro shook his head.

"The winter is coming on," he answered, "and we have no skins. We would die of cold. And I must make throwing-stick and darts, for Meng has mine. And no lance or ax or dagger have I, save only these foolish things I brought. And we must dry meat in the sun, to carry with us; we cannot be sure of finding game along the way."

"But you will not stop to carve your weapons with ornaments, will you? Can you not make the ones you have do till we are farther away? Let us get as far from Meng as we can!"

"I am not a fool! Time enough for carving when need does not press us so close. But weapons and tools and skins and food we must have for a long journey. And flints are plenty not far from here; I marked them as we came. Twice or three times seven days will we work, laying up stores, then start again on our journey. Meng will not find us here—we blinded our trail well."

Then for three weeks they labored hard, preparing for the long and arduous journey that lay before them, En-ro chipping flints and making darts, a dagger, knives, and a lance. From the thigh-bone of a sheep he fashioned a cup and bound it firmly to a shaft of wood as long as his arm, for a throwing-stick. It was the custom among the Ta-an to make the stick the length of the user's forearm from elbow to finger-tip, but so skilful was En-ro in the shaping of well-balanced darts that he could use a stick much longer than most, thus gaining force and distance, still keeping accuracy.

While the Carver of Tusks was making his weapons and tools Va-m'rai was dressing hides. En-ro had lain in wait by the water-trail and had killed a sheep—the one from which he took the cup of his throwing-stick and the thongs he needed-as well as two of the wild cattle that came to drink, and a leopard that disputed a kill with him.

These hides the Swift Runner spread, hair down, on the trunk of a fallen tree, scraping from the skin all particles of flesh and fat (she used a flint En-ro shaped for her) and rubbing fat from the beasts well into the skin, then hanging them up for a few days, after which she pressed out all the grease she could with a bone-scraper, and the hide was done.

While this was going on she also dried the flesh of the sheep and one of the cattle, cutting it into strips and hanging it in the sun, and made thongs from the sinews, for such are always useful, even, in a pinch, to bind lance and dart heads to the shafts, though for this purpose raw-hide is better.

One day En-ro was splitting a flint, using another flint as a wedge, driving it with a rude hammer-stone, when Va-m'rai called him:

"Oh, Carver of Tusks, here is a task well done! Come, look!"

She was a few yards away, working over the leopard-skin, and En-ro got up from where he squatted before the cave and went to the log astride of which she sat. She had finished pressing the grease from the skin, and showed him how thoroughly she had done her work.

"Feel!" she said. "Is it not soft and clean?" and she held it up to him. He took it, bent it this way and that, squeezed it in his hands, and grunted.

"Never have I seen a better!" he replied. "Indeed, Swift Runner, you, too, are a skilled craftsman in your work. No woman of the Ta-an, and but few of the men, can dress a skin as well. I could do no better myself!"

"Thanks, my lord and master!" said Va-m'rai, laughing, and she caught the skin from him, stood up and flung it around her, drawing it close, her shining eyes looking roguishly at him above the tawny, spotted hide. En-ro swept her into his arms and kissed her again and again, while she, closing her eyes, lay at rest in his arms. At length she pushed him away, saying:

"Back to your work, Carver of Tusks, and I to mine! Time enough for kisses when we reach the Land of the Dying Sun and all danger is past!" Reluctantly En-ro turned again to his shaping of flints.

When he rose he had dropped his hammer-stone in the grass and could not lay hands on it at once, so he picked up another that would serve. He struck a few blows with it, and from it there flew a shower of sparks. Amazed, he struck again, and again the sparks flew. He called Va-m'rai, who came, and she, too, was astonished, then suddenly pointed to a pile of dry leaves near at hand.

"Look, En-ro!" she cried. "What is that?" He looked, and a red glow was eating into the leaves, a little curl of something like mist, but darker, rising from it. More and more amazed, utterly dumbfounded, the two stared, and En-ro muttered:

"What can it be? Never have I seen such a thing!"

"Is it some new, some strange, wild beast, born of the stone?"

"I do not know, Va-m'rai. Look, it is devouring the leaves! It must be some strange beast!"

And indeed the leaves were changing; from being yellow and brown they were now gray and black, shrunken and shriveled, a faint yellow glow still lurking among them. En-ro laid his fingers cautiously on the blackened leaves and jerked his hand back with a cry.

"The beast has bitten me!" he howled. And he looked at his fingers, where blisters were rising. Va-m'rai, shivering with terror, caught his hand and looked also.

"Strange!" she whispered. "It is not like the bite of any beast! Then suddenly: "The skins! The meat! The beast will devour them!" For all the while the red glow was spreading toward the tree where these things were hung, and yellow tongues of light were licking higher and higher, and the strange, dark-gray mist was leaping and billowing upward among the trees. Shaking with fright, the two ran wide around the new beast and caught the skins and the meat from the tree, carrying them back to the cave, where they thrust them in and crouched in terror before the opening, clasped in each other's arms, En-ro clutching tight his ax, determined to sell his life dearly should the beast turn on them.

But the strange new beast went his way down the mountain, growing stronger and bigger all the while, leaping ever higher and higher among the trees, destroying and devouring everything in his path, sending his many red and yellow tongues far above the tree-tops and lighting the dusking forest with a weird light.

A harsh, acrid smell came to the nostrils of the two, and they flinched and braced themselves as from time to time curling wisps of the dark mist drifted toward them, swirling around them and wrapping them in its folds.

So they crouched all night long, listening to the roar of the strange beast and to the crash of trees crying out in agony as the beast devoured them, watching the glow in the sky and the repeated glow on the ground where the beast lagged to finish destroying tree or bush, wondering if the beast would return for them, and waiting anxiously for the dawn. Once En-ro spoke:

"When the beast does not bite he is warm and comfortable, warmer than skins, warmer even than yourself, Va-m'rai." But Va-m'rai did not answer; she only shuddered and drew closer to her lover, and stared out into the forest.

When morning came the beast had disappeared save only where he lurked near the ground, finishing his meal, and En-ro and Va-m'rai, with the growing light, stepped out to see what they could learn. A hundred yards or so down the slope lay a wide brook, and here the beast had stopped; beyond it the forest stood fresh and green. And an equal distance to their right this same brook, turning, had halted his march.

To the left, and above them as well, the beast had not gone, and here, too, the forest was unharmed. But in the space between! Not a tree was left standing save as a blackened stump, not a bush was to be seen, not a leaf nor a plant of any sort; all was black desolation, with here and there a red glow in the trunk of a tree, where the beast had not quite finished his terrible work.

Long and silently En-ro looked out over the ruin, then shook his head and whispered:

"Va-m'rai, this is no beast. Look! Do-m'rai himself, the Hill That Walks, could not have wrought such destruction. See where stood that great pine! Could any beast have destroyed it so utterly? He has devoured everything! No, this is no beast; it is—" and his voice fell lower still as, awestruck and reverent, he whispered: "it is a god!"

Va-m'rai, her left arm about his shoulder, her right hand clasping his, her eyes following his pointing finger, whispered in a shaking voice:

"The Red God!"

All the rest of the day En-ro sat thoughtful before the

cave, and would not speak. When Va-m'rai asked questions he only grunted impatiently, till at last she feared that he had sickened from the bite of the strange god, and queried:

"En-ro, are you sick? Do you feel pain?" But he only shook his head.

"What is it, my love? Have I angered you?" And she knelt beside him, but he shook his head again and snapped:

"Be quiet! I wish to think." And when night came he lay down to rest, still wrapped in his unaccustomed silence.

Early the next morning he rose and, going to the mouth of the cave, looked about till he found the hammer-stone he had been using when the Red God was born. Va-m'rai watched him curiously, but said nothing, and by and by he turned to her and spoke:

"I am going to try if I can bring the Red God to life again," he said. The girl looked at him in horror; she was sure his mind was gone—probably the terrible experience had turned his brain and he would be like Ken-so-man of the Ta-an, whom all feared and shunned. But she hid the sick fear that filled her heart and spoke gently:

"Bring the Red God to life again?" And she managed a twisted smile. "Have you not seen Him enough? Look about you!"

"Do you remember that He was warm, when not too near? And that He lives on wood and leaves, but does not eat the rocks? I am going to try to make Him my slave!"

And now Va-m'rai was sure her lover was insane, and she sank down in despair on the ground and drew the leopard-skin over her head and wept.

En-ro took the hammer-stone and a flint and turned away through the woods, skirting around the burned part till he came to the stream that had stopped the Red God. He climbed up on a great flat rock and in fear and trembling struck the flint with the hammer-stone, a shower of sparks following the blow. A dozen times he did this, then sat and thought a while, summoning his courage for the next step.

Laying aside the stones, he climbed down and gathered a handful of dry leaves, spread them on the rocks, and again struck sparks. The fourth time a red glow appeared on one of the leaves, and a little curl of smoke drifted and swirled upward.

En-ro shrank back, but watched eagerly as the Red God devoured the leaves, and once more he tried. This time he dared hold out his hand toward the pile, and found it warm; he laid the ends of his fingers on the leaves and jerked his arm back with a yell—the Red God had bitten him again; and Va-m'rai Heard the yell and shuddered where she crouched.

He found a stick, held the tip among the burning leaves, and a yellow tongue licked up from it. Again and again he tried, lighting a small heap of leaves, feeding the Red God with fresh leaves, twigs, branches of the trees, laying stones on it, blowing on it, spitting on it, carrying water from the brook to pour on it, relighting it, scattering earth on it; trying every possible food, and trying everything he could think of to slay the god.

He climbed down from the rock, cleared a space on the earth, and brought the Red God to life there.

All day long he labored; beasts peeped at him through the leaves and from behind bushes, but he paid them no heed; the sun rose high in the heavens and sank again in the west, but still he strove and thought and studied and experimented, till as dusk drew its shadows through the forest he returned again to the cave, where Va-m'rai still crouched, the skin still drawn over her head.

He did not speak to her, but took a piece of meat, squatted with it before the cave, and ate it, still sunk in thought, his mantle of abstraction still wrapped about him.

Presently he slept, but with the first gray of dawn he was on foot, hurrying back to the rock dike, carrying flint and hammer-stone. All that day and all the next he toiled and studied, paying no heed to Va-m'rai, who went about her duties listlessly—what was the use of preparing for a journey if En-ro was mad?—and returning to the cave only to sleep.

But about the middle of the afternoon of the third day he was satisfied, he had learned what he wished to know, he threw water on the heap of brush before him, and rose to his feet, flung out his arms, and in a deep, full-throated roar that carried to the ears of Va-m'rai where she toiled over her dressing of hides he shouted:

"Victory! Victory! The Red God is slave to En-ro of the tribe of Ta-an!"

Taking flint and hammer-stone he returned to the cave, flung his arms about Va-m'rai, and hugged her tight, kissing and caressing her, she returning his kisses, joyful that his reason had come back.

"Va-m'rai," he said, "En-ro, the Carver of Tusks, has found a new tool and a new weapon; he has made the Red God his slave, to work for him, to warm him in winter, through the long cold days when the snow lies deep on the hills and the tribesmen shiver in their caves, drawing their garments of skins closer about them, and, to protect him from the beasts of forest and cave. Come now and see!"

"Oh, En-ro, my love," begged Va-m'rai piteously. "Is the madness not yet gone? I beg you, let the Red God sleep; do not wake Him! Who knows what harm He may bring you: I am afraid—I fear Him! For my sake, En-ro, for the sake of Va-m'rai, who loves you and is outcast from her tribe, who is alone in all the world but for you, do not wake the Red God!"

En-ro laughed.

"Have no fear, Va-m'rai! The Red God is my slave; he obeys my will, even as my ax and lance and darts. Come, see!"

He drew the girl, still begging and protesting, to the cave, where he cleared away the brush and twigs and leaves from a space the height of a man in width, scraping clear down to the brown earth. He gathered dry leaves and twigs and sticks, making a little pile, then squatting down, he struck sparks till a little glow appeared among the leaves, Va-m'rai watching fearfully the while.

He blew gently on the glowing leaves till a flame appeared, then carefully laid small sticks on them, building up and building up, till the Red God leaped and roared from the pile. He turned to the girl and waved his hand proudly, but she asked:

"I see, but what will the Red God do for you?"

"Draw near," he answered, and Va-m'rai slowly and hesitatingly came closer.

"Hold out your hands toward the Red God," he said, and she did so. "Do you feel the warmth?" Va-m'rai nodded.

"The Red God will keep us warm through the long cold, but more than that. Look now!"

Taking the brand from the fire, he led the girl a hundred paces or so into the forest, to where he had caught a wolf in a snare. Going close to the snarling beast, En-ro thrust the brand in its face as it leaped toward him, and the wolf recoiled, howling. Again and again he beat the cowering animal with a blazing stick, till the wolf crouched on the ground, singed, whimpering, terrified. En-ro turned to Va-m'rai.

"See!" he cried. "If Menzono the Slayer dares not face the Red God, what other beast will dare?"

"But, Carver of Tusks," asked the girl, doubtfully, "will not the Red God turn on you, His master? And His wrath is terrible! Remember what He did to the forest, that night!"

"No, Swift Runner," answered the warrior. "It is but when the Red God is strong and large that we need fear Him. When small and weak He is easily slain. Tem, the water, will slay Him, and he can be beaten to death with green branches. Va, the wind, helps him grow, but he grows only if we feed him much food. By giving him small branches we can keep him small and weak.

"No, Va-m'rai, have no fear; the Red God is my slave, to do my bidding, now and forever, to bring us warmth and comfort and safety; he is stronger than lance or dart or ax, and it may be that we shall find other things He can do for us—I have not tried more than to find how I may command and rule Him; the rest is for the future."

The words were no more than out of his mouth when there came a rush of feet through the forest, and Meng, leading a band of negroes, broke into the open space where En-ro and Va-m'rai stood, and the two were seized. En-ro caught without his weapons, laid about him fiercely with a flaming stick, and shrieks and cries of pain rose from the burned attackers, but the negroes were no cowards and they came again and again to the fight, despite the strange new weapon the artist wielded.

Va-m'rai fought like a wildcat, desperately, with tooth and fist and claw—the Bison himself received a long and bloody gouge from a thumb-nail that barely missed his eye—but it was of no avail, and shortly the fugitives from the Ta-an were bound hand and foot and carried back to their cave, where they were roughly flung on the ground while the negroes seized the store of meat and gorged themselves, all but Meng lying down to sleep.

Meng, full-fed, walked over to where the captives lay, and looked down at them, an evil smile on his thick lips. In pure venom, he jabbed En-ro with his lance, and the blood started from the wound.

"You thought to escape me!" snarled the Bison in his own tongue. "You shall not do so again. Day and night shall you be watched, and daily shall you be beaten with rods till you die! And you shall chip no more flints; no weapon shall reach your hand for the few more days you have to live. And Va-m'rai shall see you die, she shall see you beaten daily, and when you are dead she shall be my woman, and, at your dying moment, you shall see her in my arms!"

And once more he drove his spear into En-ro's thigh.

"Beast!" answered the Carver of Tusks. "Foul beast! Child of a hyena! Misbegotten son of the Devils of the Air! Black of skin and blacker of soul, do you think to frighten a warrior of the Ta-an? Fool, even yet shall you die at my hand! And Va-m'rai shall never be yours; a girl of the Ta-an would die rather than be your woman—know you what the maidens of the tribe call you? 'Ape-man'! Ho, ho! Ape-man!"

Bristling and foaming at the insult, Meng raised his lance to slay, but En-ro only laughed. Slowly, reluctantly, the Bison lowered the weapon, saying:

"It will be more pleasant to see you die through days than to end you quickly. What is this strange new weapon you have found? It was the clouds rising from the mountain and the gleam of the weapon that guided us to you."

"What is it? It is your death! Find out for yourself what it is—Ape-man! You shall know it soon enough!"

Snarling, Meng raised his lance again, but lowered it and turned to the cave, where he prodded one of his men awake with the butt of his spear, gave a few orders, and lay down. The negro, yawning and stretching, took ax and lance and went to watch En-ro and Va-m'rai, not taking his eyes from them during the long night.

In the morning the negroes awoke, ate, unbound the feet of the captives, and jerked them upright, then prodded them with lances, and the procession started for Meng's camp, Va-m'rai ahead with a negro on each side and one behind; then, guarded in the same manner, En-ro, and the other negroes closing up the rear.

En-ro still carried in his girdle the flint and the hammerstone.

4

THE RED GOD BITES

FOR THREE DAYS En-ro, bound to a tree and guarded by four negroes, was beaten. Twenty-five strokes each day were laid on, from a lash of rhinoceros hide in the hands of a stalwart warrior—twenty-five and no more, for Meng did not wish him to die quickly, as would have happened had the beatings been too heavy.

And in agony Va-m'rai watched, bound to another tree ten paces distant. She tried to turn her head away, but it was forced around and held; she tried to close her eyes, but what she imagined was worse than the sight.

And when each beating was over En-ro's back was rubbed with salt and with sap from a pine, that the bleeding might be stopped and the victim ready for the following day.

But never a sound did the white warrior make; never a sign did he give of the pain he endured. In silence and unflinching he bore the torture, and when the twenty-five lashes were laid on he turned to Va-m'rai and smiled, giving no glance toward Meng or any other. This utter contempt stirred up in the Bison a rage beside which his former anger was trifling.

On the morning of the fourth day Meng and his warriors

went to hunt, though indeed the Bison's own wounds were not yet fully healed, and he lacked much of his ordinary vigor. But before leaving the camp he went to taunt En-ro and to enjoy the sight of the white man's back, raw and swollen from the lashings.

Every bitter word, every foul taunt, every insult the Bison could command was hurled at the Carver of Tusks, but the artist of the Ta-an did not even turn his head; steadily and in silence he gazed past the negro as though he were not there, and more than once Meng's lance was raised to kill, but lowered again as the giant thought of the days to come. At length he departed, leaving the four negroes on guard, saying to them:

"Keep this man with your lives; wily and strong is he, a great warrior, as you should know, and will trick you if chance offers, or overcome you by his great strength. Go not too nigh him."

"Yes, Master," answered the negroes, bowing, and one spoke, timorously:

"But, Master, should he by strength or wile win loose, what then?"

Meng glared at him fiercely, his lips curling back from his teeth in an evil grin as he replied:

"Then wait not my return, but run on your spears, for if he be gone and you alive, be sure that, bound hand and foot, you will lie on the home of the Little Red Ants, whose teeth are like poisoned needles!"

The negroes shuddered; to be eaten alive by swarming millions of ants!

So Meng and his followers left for a day's hunting, and En-ro sat on the ground beneath his tree, the four men watching him. All day long he sat there, shifting from time to time, and eating from the lump of flesh thrown down beside him, or drinking from the gourd of water that one of the guards carried from a nearby stream; Meng wished him to be strong to bear the torture, and En-ro also wished to keep his strength—though for another reason!

Va-m'rai he could not see; she was taken away to some hiding-place after each day's beating was done.

And so the weary day dragged on, the sun climbing over the tree-tops and sinking again in the western sky, while the patches of light on the ground, sifting through the trees, grew shorter and rounder, then lengthened out again as the sun declined, growing more and more yellow toward evening. The guards chatted among themselves, and once or twice spoke to En-ro, asking some question or other, of which he took no notice.

At times they jeered at him, made fun of him, taunted him, for they were proud to be, guarding a white man, a warrior of the Ta-an; they promised him a harder beating on the morrow, they jested and boasted that the white man would cry for mercy, they mimicked the writhings and the screams that would be his, and once or twice flung clods of earth at him, but he gave no sign that he had seen or heard.

The dusk was falling, and the shadows were growing deeper and heavier under the trees, though the tops still glowed in the clear golden light, when one of the guards rose, stretched, and walked over, lazily, to where En-ro sat.

He examined the white man's bonds with care, then loosened those on his wrists. Another negro came forward, carrying a lump of meat, some berries, and a few nuts, which he laid down by En-ro, the two then drawing back three or four steps, still keeping their eyes on the prisoner.

The Carver of Tusks began to eat, when his eye was caught by a faint movement in the forest, behind the backs of his four guards. He watched intently, and soon made out a huge, tawny head with gleaming eyes, that he knew for a lion's.

"Snorr-m'rai-no!" he breathed, and even as the negroes whirled about the lion sprang. His great paws struck the nearest man to the earth, the warrior's arms flinging out wildly and his ax whirling through the air to En-ro's feet.

The lion stood with his paws on his prey, looking about, his head thrown back, and in that instant another of the guards rushed in and struck the beast with his lance.

The lion turned to meet the attack, and a furious battle followed, the three unhurt negroes assailing him on all sides, dashing in to strike and dashing away as the great cat whirled, while the guard whom he had struck down crawled away to safety.

En-ro seized the ax that lay beside him, with two blows cut the rawhide thongs that bound him, snatched flint and hammer-stone from his girdle, and frantically struck and struck again, showers of sparks falling on the dry, wind-blown leaves that lay all about, till a glow appeared among them.

One eye on the fight, En-ro blew this to flame, then leaping upward with all his might he caught and tore from the pine a half-dead, resinous branch, and thrust it into the fire.

The Red God bit into the dry wood, and in a few seconds it was blazing. Meanwhile, the fight had gone against the negroes; the Fear That Walks the Night was too strong for them, and two lay dead, one torn half in two from side to side by a single sweep of the razor-sharp claws, the other crumbled in a grotesque heap, his spine broken and his chest crushed by a blow of a giant paw that had caught him as he turned to run.

And the third! Blind, a frightful welter of blood, he rolled on the ground, moaning and slobbering in agony, for a downward sweep of the lion's paw had caught him on the forehead and had ripped and torn the skin and flesh and muscles from brow to knee, laying bare the bones and tearing his jaw from the socket. Him Snorr-m'rai-no seized, sinking his teeth in the wretch's shoulder and flinging the doomed man over his back, to carry him off.

At that moment En-ro, ax in his right hand and flaming branch in his left, leaped before the lion and with one sure, swift stroke drove the brand over the huge beast's eye.

Roaring with pain, the lion dropped the negro and turned to meet this new attack. He crouched for an instant, every muscle tense, then sprang at En-ro, who met the leap, drove the still blazing branch far down the lion's throat, and leaped aside. The lion, furious with rage and torture, dropped to the ground and placed one paw on the branch to tear it from his throat, and En-ro seized that instant.

Whirling the great stone ax aloft with both hands, he leaped forward and brought it down with all his might full on the lion's head. Driven by the strongest man in all the tribe of the Ta-an, the sharp flint edge shore through flesh and bone—and the fight was over.

En-ro turned to where the Red God was devouring the dry leaves and branches, tore a green limb from a near-by oak, and set himself to beat the Red God to death, even as he had slain Snorr-m'rai-no. The Red God had grown fast during the fight, and En-ro worked furiously, beating out the little licking tongues that flickered and grew and spread, but at last it was done and the forest was safe.

En-ro wiped the sweat from his face with his forearm and stood panting heavily, looking over the burned space to where lay Snorr-m'rai-no, dead among the dead negroes. The wounded negro whom the lion had first struck down lay groaning among the bushes a little distance off, and En-ro, stepping over to him, slew him with a blow of the ax that had killed the lion. As he turned away, he saw another negro coming toward him, carrying an ax, and the Carver of Tusks sprang toward him, his weapon raised.

But the negro, a little, wizen, gray-haired man, fell on his knees and held the haft of the ax toward En-ro in token of surrender, and En-ro stayed the blow.

"Oh, Carver of Tusks, mighty warrior, great artist, master of the Strange God, spare me!" said the negro. "Nu-kzen am I, Molder of Clay, and because I have long worshiped your great skill in carving the tooth of the Hill that Walks, I bought this your ax from the warrior that took it from you after the great fight in the tree. And because you are a mighty warrior and have slain the Fear That Walks the Night, and because you are master of the Strange God and can bring Him to life or slay Him at will, therefore I now bring this ax to you, praying that you will accept it and show your favor to me who am your slave."

En-ro took the ax, his own ax, and balanced it thoughtfully in his hand, joyful to feel it again, for it had been fitted to his grasp through many days of labor, fitted in grip, in length, in weight, and in balance, and he had decorated it with loving care, carving figures along the haft, and a knob for the end. His heart leaped within him, and, looking down at the negro, who still knelt before him, head bowed, he said:

"Nu-kzen, I accept your gift. You shall go with me, but not as my slave. Because you, too, are an artist you shall go as my friend, friend to En-ro the Carver of Tusks, warrior of the tribe of Ta-an, and master of the Red God! And I will teach you to carve the tooth of Do-m'rai, the Hill that Walks, and to command the Red God. But first you must help me get Va-m'rai, the Swift Runner and to escape from the hands of Meng."

Nu-kzen looked up at him with worship in his dark eyes, the look of adoration one sees in a faithful dog, and answered:

"Indeed, my master, I will help you escape, but why wait for the Swift Runner? Why not let the Bison have that? There are many women, and such a one as you need not lack!"

En-ro scowled blackly, and Nu-kzen, shivering, crouched lower as the Carver of Tusks replied:

"Nu-kzen," he said, "speak not thus! Such as you cannot understand, but for a warrior of the Ta-an there is but one woman while that one lives, and he is bound to fight for her, even to death. Rise now, and help me set her free!"

Obediently Nu-kzen rose, and the two set out to find Va-m'rai and free her, that they might make their escape, but before they had gone twenty paces from the spot where they stood there came the sound of the hunters returning. Far off, the two artists heard many voices chanting the hunting song, then they could make out the rustling and crackling of the underbrush as the laden troup marched along, and soon the leaders came into view, Meng first, six of his chosen warriors following on his heels—then a dozen or more young men who had not yet risen to the dignity of warriors, but for a year or two longer served as bearers—then the remainder of the lighting men of the Bison's tribe.

On long poles across their shoulders the bearers carried the game, several sheep, two of the wild cattle of the lowlands, and a deer, the feet of the beasts being tied together and a pole thrust between them, that a man might lift each end.

Staggering and sweating under their loads, the porters came forward, but halted in confusion, dropping their loads to the ground as Meng, catching sight of En-ro unbound, stopped in anger.

He glanced around, saw the dead guards on the ground and Nu-kzen standing at the white warrior's side and thought that he, the negro artist, had traitorously set En-ro free.

He scowled fiercely, and with a bellow like that of the beast from which he took his name, raised his lance, rushing at Nu-kzen, who fell on his knees, hands lifted, and cried aloud for mercy.

En-ro stepped quickly between the two and turned the lance aside with a swift movement of his ax, and Meng's rage shifted to the Carver of Tusks, who confronted him fearlessly. The Bison drew back, poised his spear, the point an arm's length from En-ro's breast—and stood rigid, for En-ro did not move; arms at his sides, the ax swinging lightly in his right hand, he stood glaring into Meng's eyes, and his own were narrowed to little slits, in the depths of which glinted sparks of light. His head thrown forward, his jaw out-thrust, his mouth drawn to a straight, hard line, his muscles relaxed but ready, every line of the white warrior's body cried aloud "Danger!"

So for the space of thirty breaths this duel of eyes lasted, the two men staring, unflinching, each at the other, silent, while the band of negroes looked from one to the other, from the white man, tall and straight and handsome as a god to the black chieftain, scarred and ugly and evil, his lance-point at the other's breast.

Not a word was spoken, not a sound was heard save the rasping of branches and the rustling of leaves, and once, far off, the harsh scream of a hyena, till one of the younger men, unable to bear the strain, moved his feet, and Meng's eyes wavered, shifted, dropped, and with a deep growl he drew back a pace and lowered his spear.

The tension broken, the negroes spread over the place, soon finding the dead lion and chattering excitedly over the discovery; Meng came and looked, and asked Nu-kzen what had happened, and the little artist, wizened and gray, tiny beside the huge bulk of the Bison, told of the fight, with many gestures, pointing often toward En-ro, who stood apart, looking contemptuously at the chattering, swarming negroes—"not so different from the apes!" he told himself.

Presently Meng came toward En-ro, to question him, and the white warrior noted that, for all his efforts, the Bison could not keep a note of respect from his voice.

"You slew Snorr-m'rai-no with a new weapon?"

asked Meng, and En-ro looked the negro chieftain over contemptuously, replying:

"By the aid of the Red God, who is my slave, I slew him."

"And the Red God obeys your commands?"

"In truth."

"Show!"

En-ro gazed thoughtfully at the Bison for a few moments, then stooped and with his ax cleared a space on the ground; gathered some dry leaves, and crouched over them, the negroes pressing close. He rose to his feet and motioned them back, for he was not minded to let them see too much.

"Stand farther off!" he cried. "Back! Back! The Red God bites hard!"

They fell back twenty paces or more, and he turned his back to them, crouched over the leaves again, and struck sparks, blowing the leaves to a flame, then took a dry branch and laid it in the flames till it was burning well, and swung around toward the watchers, whirling the brand in the air, sparks flying from it in all directions—and the negroes, all but Meng—and even he was impressed—fell to their knees with cries of fear and reverence.

The Bison stood upright, but shrank back as En-ro approached, and asked, his voice quavering despite his struggle to control it:

"Does the Red God indeed bite hard?"

En-ro did not answer, but glanced with a smile toward the carcass of the lion, and Meng's eyes followed his.

"Will He bite a man?"

"Try!" said En-ro, thrusting the branch toward the Bison, but Meng was of no mind to be bitten; instead, he looked toward the crowd, singled out a young man, and, pointing to him, cried:

"Bind him and lay him here!" Instantly a dozen others seized the victim, tied him hand and foot, and carried him to where the two stood, laying him on the ground and hurrying fearfully back to the crowd once more.

"Prove the Red God's teeth on him!" said Meng, and the Carver of Tusks laid the blazing stick on the victim's chest. The tortured man writhed and groaned and the stench of burning flesh rose in the air, till Meng said:

"Enough!" and En-ro lifted the brand, while the Bison stooped and examined the frightful burn, then straightened up, saying:

"You shall be tortured till you teach me to command the Red God!" and turning to his warriors, cried: "Seize him and bind him!"

En-ro leaped to the pile of blazing leaves, stamped them swiftly out, and stood, swinging the flaming brand, and not a man of the negroes stepped forward—none rose from his knees! A rustle, a whisper, ran through the crowd, but not one moved, and Meng glared about, his anger rising; his breath came hard, his chest heaved, he looked from one to another of his men, then, lifting his spear, rushed across the open space and plunged the weapon full into the breast of the nearest man.

The warrior swayed, toppled sidewise, and fell dead, but still none rose to his feet. Instead there ran a gasp through the ranks, and one said humbly, fearfully:

"Spare us, Lord! We dare not! This man commands the gods!"

Meng looked irresolutely about him for a moment, then

rushed away into the forest—this was beyond any experience he had ever known!

Thereafter En-ro was not molested as, Nu-kzen at his heels like a faithful dog, he wandered about the camp; indeed, the negroes, timidly at first, then more boldly, made friendly advances, bringing him food and small gifts, which he accepted, graciously, whereat the givers were delighted—pleased to be noticed in friendly manner by one who, single-handed, had slain a lion, flattered and grateful for the kindness of one who could command the gods.

Meng, however, did not appear, nor did his sons; all seven remained hidden in the forest, together with the three priests of the tribe, and En-ro was uneasily conscious that they might be planning an attack on him. Still, he could not leave without Va-m'rai, and though he questioned one offer another of the negroes, none could tell him where she was concealed.

The camp lay in the form of a rough circle perhaps three hundred paces across, in the deep forest, there being numbers of little paths, just wide enough for one man, going out from the central space, though one could not see more than a few steps along any one of them, for they twisted and turned confusingly.

Did one follow one of the paths to the end, however, he found an open space like the central one, but smaller, with possibly half a dozen or a dozen rude shelters made of two sticks thrust slanting into the ground with brush laid across them, or, more likely, simply a few spots where, having cleared away the underbrush, the negroes lay on the ground to sleep, for each of these little clearings was the home of a family.

Elsewhere the brush grew thick and dense, so that in most places a man could hardly make his way through it except by cutting a passage before him as he went.

En-ro explored one after another of these clearings in the hope of finding the girl he loved, but, though the families invariably received him with reverence, prostrating themselves on the ground, while the head of the family reverently lifted En-ro's foot and placed it on his own head, they could tell him nothing; Va-m'rai seemed to have disappeared utterly.

He dared not seek out Meng and provoke or challenge him to a duel; he felt confident that he could overcome the Bison in fight, and he knew that the main body of the negro tribe feared and worshiped him far more than they did their chief; but he feared that at the first hint of such an attempt one of Meng's sons or one of the priests would slay Va-m'rai.

Plan after plan to discover the girl's whereabouts he turned over in his mind, but could find no satisfactory one, and he was beginning to grow discouraged; he was almost ready to attack the Bison and run the risk of Va-m'rai's death. On the other hand, he knew that Meng dared make no attempt on the girl beyond holding her hidden; such an act would be carried to En-ro's ears, and would bring about what Meng most feared—an assault from the Red God.

Late in the afternoon En-ro and Nu-kzen were squatting under a tree, the former looking steadily into the forest, thinking, the latter gazing adoringly at the white man, the master whom he worshiped. At length En-ro turned toward the little negro and smiled at his evident admiration, whereat the latter, encouraged by the sign of favor, spoke:

"Master," he said, "do you desire your weapons, your dagger, your lance, your throwing-stick, and darts?"

En-ro's eyes blazed.

"If I desire them!" he said. "There are but two things I desire more; the Star-Marked One, taken from me after the fight in the tree, and Va-m'rai!"

"It is known to me who has the weapons; perhaps we can get them. As for the others, that is still to learn."

"Speak!"

"Sen, who lives down that path"—Nu-kzen pointed—"has them. We will go quietly along the path, and you will hide yourself in the bushes, leaping on him as he passes. Then you may take again your weapons, which the Bison gave him as a mark of favor after they were taken from you."

"But why should he pass? Must we lie in wait till he is moved to go elsewhere?"

Nu-kzen chuckled.

"I will go to him," he answered, "and tell him that Ba-kai, whom he loves, awaits him here. She scorns him, and for many moons has he pursued her; he is besotted with love, and will come. Oh, yes, he will come—to meet her!"

En-ro leaped to his feet and shook himself, and the two stepped across the open space to the path Nu-kzen had pointed out. Soundlessly they followed its windings, till at last the murmur of a voice came to their ears, and, rounding the last turn, they peeped cautiously into the open space where Sen lived.

Nu-kzen, peered under the white man's arm, lifted to hold back a leafy branch. En-ro could see, lying about on the ground, several dark forms, Sen's wives, and across the clearing he could make out, in the dusk, the shape of Sen himself, kneeling before a bush, his back to the path.

The Carver of Tusks gasped and could hardly restrain himself from dashing forward, for, propped in a forked limb of the bush, he could see the gleaming figure of the bride of O-Ma-Ken, the form of the Star-Marked One! But he drew back and hid himself in the brush a dozen paces down the path, while Nu-kzen went forward and touched Sen on the shoulder as he prayed; then as the man turned, gave the false message. Sen rose to his feet, his face working with delight.

"I go!" he said. "I go! Indeed, there is great magic in this figure! It was but now I prayed to the Star-Marked One for the favor of Ba-kai, and behold, you come with a message from her!"

"But take your weapons!" cried Nu-kzen, as Sen started away. "Be not utterly a fool! Who knows what beasts may be abroad? It is the hunting hour."

"Thanks, my friend!" said Sen, as he lifted the weapons—En-ro's weapons—from the ground. "Love has so filled my heart, and joy, that I am forgetful!"

Nu-kzen grinned sardonically as the other hurried down the path, then stepped to the little figure, carved from the tooth of Do-m'rai, took it reverently from the bush, placed it in his girdle, and followed Sen, grunting:

"He has four wives; he will have no need for this—five is too many!"

Meanwhile, En-ro crouched in the bushes, waiting, and

as Sen hastened by, forgetful of all else than Ba-kai, the white man rose to his full height and sprang out. Sen, his inner mind warned by some rustle of the leaves, whirled in his tracks and raised his dagger, but before he could strike En-ro closed with him, caught both the negroes wrists in his strong hands, and so, arms spread, breast to breast, they tugged and strained, Sen striving to free himself, En-ro struggling to throw him.

For a dozen breaths they strove, and Sen opened his mouth to yell, but in that instant En-ro's knee, driven fiercely up, struck the negro below the breast bone, and he went limp. Mouth open, head lolling back, gasping for breath, paralyzed by the terrible blow, the negro slumped like an empty skin; En-ro twisted him round, passed his left arm under Sen's left, gripped the skin of the negro's right breast, and held him up.

He placed his right hand on Sen's forehead and swung the helpless man sharply back and down, striking the back of Sen's neck with his knee as the victim fell.

There was a sharp snap, and En-ro let fall the lifeless body, stopped, and took his weapons, then raised the body and hurled it into the brush, Nu-kzen, who had followed, watching with a smile.

"That was a fortunate thought," said Nu-kzen, and, stepping forward, laid the figure of the Star-Marked One in En-ro's hand. The Carver of Tusks, trembling with joy and excitement, pressed the little figure to his bosom, then placed it in his girdle and laid his hand on the negro's head.

"Nu-kzen," said he, solemnly, "you have served me well; in reward you shall learn to command the Red God. Come!"

Oh, Master!" exclaimed Nu-kzen, overwhelmed at this great honor, and again, "Oh, Master—" but he could get no further; he could not command his voice.

Together the two went back once more to the central clearing, and there En-ro, gathering leaves, striking sparks and making a fire, instructed Nu-kzen, repeating for the little negro all the knowledge he had gained of the Red God and his ways. Then Nu-kzen, repeating after his master all that had been said, repeating it again and again till it was firmly fixed in his mind, took the flint and hammer-stone, and in turn, trembling with excitement and fear at the great power he was summoning, struck sparks and blew the glowing leaves into a flame, then fell at En-ro's feet, clasping them in his arms and abasing his head. But the Carver of Tusks raised him, saying:

"Rise, Nu-kzen! This is not seemly for one who commands the Red God! Hereafter you will bow to no man save me alone; before all others you will carry your head upright and not even to me will you kneel. But tell no one of this knowledge I have bestowed on you; in the hands of one ignorant or careless or evil the Red God might work much harm, even to destroying the entire forest, with all living things therein."

And Nu-kzen swore to keep the secret, and En-ro lay down to sleep, the little negro sitting at his head to keep watch, his wizened body and kinky gray curls seeming almost those of a great gray ape as he squatted with gleaming, watchful eyes to guard the warrior-artist of the Ta-an, the master whom he adored, to whom he had sworn fidelity even unto the last, as long as breath lived in his body and his limbs had power to move.

5

NU-KZEN'S REPORT

SOME TIME DURING the night En-ro awoke. He looked at the stars, and saw that it was long past the hour when he had told Nu-kzen to waken him for his watch, and he wondered that he had not roused himself, for he could, for the most part, awake after any time he wished. Then he remembered the day before, the weariness with which he had lain down, and understood.

But why had Nu-kzen not called him?

He looked about in sudden fear—Nu-kzeh was gone! The Carver of Tusks leaped to his feet and searched with his eyes the clearing, but the moonlight showed no human form, only the strange, ghostly clump of birches opposite the place where he stood, the dark mass of the oaks and maples, and the tall shaft of the great pine that he knew so well, with the thick underbrush forming a barrier beneath the trees.

En-ro's first thought was that the little negro had been overpowered and carried away by the Bison's orders, but there was no sign of struggle, and in any case he himself, sleeping lightly as any beast of the forest, could not have failed to awaken.

No, Nu-kzen must have gone of his own free will—but

why? Treachery? En-ro shook his head; the oath of fealty which the Molder of Clay had sworn was not to be broken by any man—one breaking such a vow would be hunted of men, outlawed, slain on sight, and would go astray on his voyage through the Long Dark; the gods would bewilder him, and he would emerge from the Long Dark to eternal torture-hunted forever by the Faceless Man, the Invisible Thing that makes no sound, and all the fearful spirits that people the Place of Evil.

En-ro shook his head again, looked about for tracks, realized that he could follow no trail by the cold light of the moon, and sat down to wait for the day.

At length a faint gray light crept into the sky, the stars paled, and one by one winked out, the light grew stronger, and the forest woke. A pearly mist hung like a veil among the trees; above, in the branches, birds chirped faintly, first one, then another, and presently, as the, light grew, one burst into song, to be followed by others and yet others, till the full chorus was ringing through the woods, and bird after bird, his song of greeting sung, at length went flashing and darting among the branches in search of insects.

Small animals scampered about the forest floor, their rustlings and squeakings sounding loud through the brush, overhead a squirrel chattered and scolded, and a great green snake, like that the Carver of Tusks had slain when he woke to find it coiled on his breast, slid past, the artist watching, making note of its sinuous, graceful body, and evil, triangular head, and thinking to himself that some day he would carve such a one, coiled about the haft of a war-ax.

And now the sun, rising higher, sent shafts of light

streaming down through the mist, warming it, so that it began to tumble and roll in billows, rolling upward, and at last shredding thinly out, the gleaming, sparkling grass and the ghostly trees showing clearer and clearer, more and more distant, till presently the mist had altogether disappeared and the clearing stood warm and bright under the full light of day.

En-ro was beginning to be worried; it was strange that Nu-kzen should be gone so long, and the Carver of Tusks had about made up his mind to go in search of the little negro when that one came stepping into the clearing, a smile on his face and the carcass of a fawn balanced on his shoulders, his arms clasped about its legs. He marched across to where En-ro stood, dropped the fawn, and said, his smile growing broader:

"Great news, Master! But eat first."

"Where were you?" asked En-ro, and Nu-kzen grinned from ear to ear as he replied:

"Spying, Master. Spying on Meng."

En-ro leaned forward and gripped the other's arm, thrusting his face close to Nu-kzen's.

"And you learned—?"

"Much, Master!" And Nu-kzen, still grinning, scratched his side with his long nails, repeating: "Much, Master. But eat; my news will keep, and a full stomach is good in the early morning."

And he fell to butchering the fawn, stripping the hide from the flesh with speed and skill, carving out a piece of the tender meat, and giving it to En-ro, then cutting a piece of meat for himself.

The two squatted on their haunches and ate, tearing the

still warm flesh with their strong teeth and wiping their hands from time to time on the grass.

Various negroes drifted into the clearing and looked at the pair, each and every one bowing and saluting respectfully the white man and his companion (for they honored Nu-kzen as the friend of one who could command the gods) then wandered out again about their own affairs.

By and by Nu-kzen rose and went to the carcass, stripped the meat from one of the marrow-bones, and, asking permission with a look, took En-ro's ax and split the bone skillfully and neatly, offering it, laid open, to the Carver of Tusks, who took one part and motioned the negro to take the other.

"Thanks, Master," said Nu-kzen, and the two men scraped out and ate the sweet marrow, smacking their lips with pleasure.

Their stomachs full, they gave their hands a final cleansing, then stretched out on the grass, and En-ro said:

"And now the news."

"During the night," began Nu-kzen, while still you slept, one came by, treading softly. I watched, but could not see his face—for he kept to the shadows—till he trod on a stone or a root, which, turning beneath his foot, threw him heavily, so that he rolled into a patch of moonlight. Swiftly he caught himself and was back again in the dark, but I had seen-it was Ken-zan, who is oldest son of the Bison's fourth wife, and closest to Meng of all his children. He is a young warrior—it was but last summer that his ears were slit and his teeth chipped to points by the priest—and he greatly desires honor. By the law of our tribe, as perchance you know, he can buy no wife till he has done some great deed—"

"The Ta-an have the same law."

Nu-kzen bowed, and went on:

"So now he seeks honor. I rose and followed. Ken-zan could not know"—and Nu-kzen chuckled—"no man among the tribe can see or hear the Molder of Clay when he follows a trail. I followed, and he led me to Meng. I hid in the brush and listened, and there it was that I heard the news. Master, the Bison desires your life." En-ro laughed.

"That is no news!" said he.

"True, Master, but he means to have it. Speaking, the Bison said: 'Ken-zan, my son, you have seen this warrior from the Ta-an command the Red God; you know that did he raise his hand the tribesmen would slay me, and you, and all my sons; you know that he stays his hand but because he fears for Va-m'rai, and can he find where she is hidden it is death to me and to all who are faithful to me.

" 'I greatly desire this woman, but more do I desire to slay this man and devour his heart, that his courage may come to me and that I, the Bison, may be the bravest man in all the world, as now is En-ro. You saw how he shamed me before my warriors; how I dared not thrust him through with my lance. Therefore do I desire to eat his heart, that such great courage may be mine.

" 'But the Ta-an do not thus; to them a fallen warrior is but a fallen warrior, and they do not devour him, believing not that his courage can enter into them with his heart. But the priests of the Ta-an will greatly desire to know the secret he holds of how to command the Red God—and he is outlawed by them.

" 'Go you, therefore, to the priests of the Ta-an, tell them of what you have seen him do, and say to them: Behold, if Meng, the Bison, may keep Va-m'rai to wife, and may have the heart of En-ro, he and his sons will fall on the same En-ro, bind him, and deliver him to you, that you may torture him till he reveals to you the secret of his mastery over the Red God.'"

"Ken-zan then rose and answered: 'I go, my father,' took his weapons, and set out for the homes of the Mountain Cave People."

During Nu-kzen's story En-ro's face had grown darker and darker, and when the little negro had finished he burst out:

"By all the gods, I swear to give Meng to the beasts!" and leaped to his feet, but Nu-kzen placed a hand on his master's arm.

"And Va-m'rai?" he asked, and En-ro stopped short, thought a moment, and seated himself again, his head in his hands. Long he thought, then lifted his head and said:

"Nu-kzen, you have done well! Will you help further?"

"To the death, Master!"

"Good! Go now to the Ta-an, find Snorr, the chieftain, and tell him that I can command the Red God. Tell him what you have seen me do; that by the aid of the Red God I slew Snorr-m'rai-no; that the Red God will fight for me; that he will warm us in cold, when Co-sa, the ice, has locked the streams and built bridges over the pools; take flint and half the hammer-stone, and bring the Red God to life, that Snorr may see and know that you speak truth.

"Bid him then lay the matter before the council of the Ta-an, asking them whether this gift may lift the ban of outlawry that lies upon me and upon Va-m'rai. Snorr has no love for the priests, and it may be that he can sway the council to spare me; it may be that he cannot make head against the priests, but it is our only hope.

"Go now, return swiftly, and bring me word. In the space of your journey I will endeavor to find where Va-m'rai is hidden. Go now!"

Nu-kzen rose, bowed, took his weapons, cut a piece of flesh from the fawn, and slipped into the forest as silent as the fleeting shadow of a cloud. En-ro bent his head once more in his hands and thought.

The sun crept slowly down toward the horizon, and presently a cloud drew across it, so that the air grew chill. En-ro shivered and looked up, and he saw that the whole sky was covered with dark gray clouds; a drop of rain fell on his hand and he shook it off impatiently. He gazed at the sky, then at the trees about him, noting the brown of the oaks, the red of the maples, and the yellow of the birch. A birch sapling, no larger than a man's arm, grew near by, and En-ro saw how its leaves flamed against the dark, green of the pine that stood behind it.

"It is the autumn rain," he thought, "that takes the leaves from the trees. Three days will it rain!" And he was disgusted and annoyed at the prospect of the discomfort that awaited him. He rose, shook himself, and stretched, for he was cramped from squatting so long, then took his way to the shelter of the great pine, whose branches grew low to the ground. By now the rain was falling steadily, with a pattering sound, and the sky was dark; it was growing dusk in the forest. Stronger and stronger fell the rain, and En-ro wrapped himself in a skin and lay down under the tree, resolved to be comfortable as long as he might—until the rain should penetrate the fronds of his shelter and bring the inevitable drenching.

All that night it rained, not in torrents, not with lightning and thunder, but in a steady, relentless, swishing downpour that penetrated and drenched and saturated everything, so that En-ro awoke chilled and shivering.

As he squatted, tearing a piece of the fawn for his breakfast, one of Meng's warriors passed through the open space, and En-ro could see that he was miserable, chilled to the bone, his garment of skin sodden and clammy. By some association of ideas a vague thought flashed into his mind, to be instantly seized and developed. Somewhat after this fashion ran his reasoning:

"Tem, the water, makes us cold and wet; the Red God makes us warm. Tem fights the Red God, and when the Red God is weak Tem slays Him; may it not be that the Red God, strong and vigorous, will fight and conquer Tem, making us not only warm, but also dry?"

At once he set to work, scraped a clear place on the earth, hunted about till he found, in the hollow of a log, some dry leaves that a squirrel had stored there for a bed, took slivers of bark from the pine, and knelt over his little heap, striking sparks with flint and the half of the hammer-stone he had kept.

After much labor he succeeded in getting a little glow among the powdered leaves—he had rubbed them to dust between his hands; they caught the sparks better so—and, feeding more leaves and little splinters of pine, blowing gently the while, he soon saw the tongues of the Red God licking upward from the little heap. He added more twigs, then resinous sticks and branches, and soon the Red God leaped and roared.

En-ro stood by the fire, turning around, warming himself, drying the water from his own skin and from the leopard skin he wore, and soon he was quite warm and dry and comfortable once more. He thought to himself that the Red God, though an evil master, was a good servant, and he was pleased at the idea of such a friend through the long winter months; no longer would he huddle in skins in his cave, not daring to go out.

With a friend like the Red God warmth and comfort were his wherever he might be. And, too, the Red God would fight for him; had He not done so against the Fear That Walks the Night?

Idly he wondered, toasting himself, what would happen when the Red God met Sa, the snow; would they fight, as did Tem and the Red God, with hissing and smoke and anger, or would the Red God devour Sa, even as He devoured branches and leaves? He decided that they would fight, for Sa was brother to Tem, changing, indeed, into Tem at times, by force of magic.

Thus he squatted by the fire, warming himself, meditating, and listening to the roar and crackle of the flames and the steady patter of the rain-drops on the leaves. Presently he looked up and saw one of Meng's warriors standing some paces off, watching the fire intently, and leaning on his spear. En-ro fixed his eyes on the negro, who, drawn by the psychic power of the steady concentration of mind, soon became restless, then turned toward the white man. En-ro smiled encouragingly, waved his hand to the fire, and said:

"Draw near and be warm; I will not let the Red God harm you; only go not too close, for He bites even me if I go too near.

The negro, a slow step at a time, approached till he felt the comfortable warmth, then stood still, watching again. At length he turned to En-ro with a question: "The Red God will bite even you?"

"If I go too near."

"Are you not His master, and He your slave?"

"In very truth."

"Why, then, will He harm you?" asked the negro, puzzled.

En-ro laughed, and in turn asked:

"Ka-tem of the Ta-an, is he known to you?"

"The tamer of beasts? Yes."

"You know that he has tamed and keeps for a friend, Menzono, the Slayer?"

"In truth."

"What, now, would happen should Ka-tem, the master, take his food from Menzono, the slave?"

"The wolf would bit Ka-tem."

"Bite Ka-tem, his master?"

"In very truth!"

"There is your answer; as Menzono would bite Ka-tem, even so would the Red God, fiercer and more powerful than a thousand Menzono, bite me, His master."

The negro nodded in acknowledgment of the explanation and its reasonableness, warmed himself more, then saying:

"Thanks, Ba-non!" strode away into the forest, leaving En-ro more than a little pleased, for by the title of Ba-non, signifying "Lord," or "Master," the black warrior had formally admitted the white man's superiority; it was a word of utmost respect—one almost altogether reserved for divinity.

So passed three days of the rains, crowds of negroes coming at times to warm themselves at En-ro's fire, bringing gifts, chiefly of food, and maintaining always; a demeanor of the greatest respect; there was no pushing, no crowding, and always the Carver of Tusks saw his power growing among the black men of the Bison's tribe.

Once Meng came and looked on from a distance, evidently enraged, but not daring to protest; he watched for a time, turned, and disappeared in the forest, and presently came back with three of his sons, striding up toward the fire where En-ro sat, surrounded by a dozen or more warriors.

En-ro leaped to his feet, seized his ax and a flaming brand, and advanced to meet the four, but a low growl ran through the group of negroes and lances were lifted—the negroes ranged themselves behind En-ro, and Meng, turning, plunged again among the trees—and En-ro knew that his life was safe from open attack; Meng's power was broken!

But after all, the Bison had still a dozen adherents; his own sons would do his bidding—and worst of all, he still held Va-m'rai; her life and honor were in no wise safe—and there were the priests of the Ta-an to reckon with!

On the fourth day the rain ceased though the woods, save in the little space about the fire, were still wet, and En-ro sat by the flames, thinking, planning how to recover his loved one. Suddenly he heard behind him a voice, hardly more than a whisper:

"White warrior!"

Instantly he seized his great stone ax, and, quick as a striking snake, rolled out of the circle of firelight. From the underbrush there came a strange, cackling laugh, and a figure stepped into the light, saying:

"Does the white warrior fear me? Behold, I have no fear of him! Indeed, life is not so sweet that I fear to die!"

En-ro saw now that it was a woman, and drew near, ax ready, for he feared a trap.

"Who are you?" he asked, and the woman, cackling a horrible laugh from her toothless gums, answered with a question:

"Would you wish to see Va-m'rai as I am?" and En-ro, looking closely, shuddered. About her waist the negress wore a girdle of leaves, but except for that was entirely naked. Below the girdle her skinny legs seemed scarce able to bear her weight; above it her breasts hung flabby and pendulous on her gaunt ribs. From her bent and stooping shoulders swung scrawny arms that ended in veined and knotted hands, twisted and drawn like the talons of some bird of prey, and on those shoulders, bowed with heavy toil, her head, with hollow cheeks and sunken eyes, quivered and shook with palsy. En-ro stared in horror at this frightful apparition, the woman repeating in a husky voice:

"Would you see Va-m'rai such as I?"

"Great Father!" breathed En-ro. Then: "Who are you?"

The negress cackled again, lowered herself shakily to the ground, and when seated replied:

"Meng's wife! One of his wives; the first."

"Meng's wife!" repeated En-ro, amazed and puzzled, and she nodded.

"His first. Looking at me now, would it come in your mind that I was once young and beautiful? Nay, answer not! I have read the answer in your face!" And she cackled again, then went on: "I was once young and strong and beautiful; beautiful, perchance, as Va-m'rai, for all my skin is black and you would not think to compare me with her. But on an evil day my father sold me to the Bison for wife; sold me for three bear-skins, a necklace of bear's claws, and the carcasses of ten wild sheep—a good price, was it not? Great feasting was there that day! And twice ten and two children have I borne the Bison, and hard have I labored, carrying water, curing skins, doing the work of two women; not that I loved labor (though I am not more lazy than another), but driven by blows and kicks and beatings."

She paused, and En-ro noticed that her body was marked by the scars of beatings, the scars left by the terrible, stinging, cutting lash of rhinoceros hide.

"And when my beauty faded," she went on, wheezing for breath, "Meng ceased to love me and made me slave to his younger wives, and beatings from them also did I take. And as each of them fades he takes another, even as he wishes now to take Va-m'rai for his sixth—but dares not while you are in life. And now, would you not see Va-m'rai such as I, take her from the hands of the Bison; take her far off, where he cannot reach you?"

And there was a certain dignity about the wretched woman as she gave her warning.

"Great Father!" whispered En-ro, then aloud: "But how can I? It is not even known to me where the Swift Runner is hidden!"

"The 'how' is in your hands; that I cannot tell you. But

go you down that path"—she rose to her feet and pointed with a shaking hand—"follow its twists and turns, and at the end you will come upon a clearing. Fronting the path is a great oak, its heart rotted with age, and in the hollow is Va-m'rai. Oh, fear not for her yet. She is well fed, well cared for—Meng would not harm her beauty!—and not till you are gone will he take her to himself."

"But why do you, Meng's wife, tell me this? Is it for love? For jealousy?"

"What am I, to be jealous? And I do not love you or Va-m'rai—what cause have I for love?"

"Why, then?"

The negress looked steadily at the white warrior, her breast heaved, her skinny form shook, and leaning nearer she hissed:

"For hate!" and was gone, swallowed up in the forest.

En-ro stared after her for a time, then turned and gave more food to the Red God, and as the flames leaped up again he sat down by the fire to think, to plan, to find some way of freeing the girl he loved. And as he watched the leaping flames he sighed, for he had little hope that the Ta-an would come to his aid; he knew the power of the priests, and it did not seem to him that Snorr could sway the tribe against them; no, he was doomed to be a wanderer, an outcast all his days, or else take up his home among the Little Hairy Men whom he despised.

But it would be sweet to be received again among his own tribe—resolutely he put the thought away and bent all the force of his powerful mind to planning the rescue of Va-m'rai.

Of a sudden he heard a light step behind him and whirled instantly, grasping his ax.

"Ba-non!" said some one, and he saw that it was Nu-kzen.

"Welcome, Nu-kzen!" cried En-ro, as the little negro drew near, grinning his inevitable cheerful grin. "What news?"

"Evil news, Master!" said Nu-kzen, sitting down by the fire. "Evil news—and good, together. But let me rest awhile; then we must make haste."

"I have found where Va-m'rai is hidden."

"Good!" answered Nu-kzen. "Now listen, Master. Reaching the Ta-an, Ken-zan sought out the chief priest and told him of the Bison's offer. It was accepted; Meng is to have Va-m'rai, you are to be tortured till you tell the secret of the Red God—"

"That will be never!"

Nu-kzen shrugged his shoulders and went on:

"And then you are to be slain on the altar, for that you slew Men-ko; your heart is to be given to the Bison, and your carcass to the beast. That for the evil news. Now for the good.

"I had speech with Snorr, and a council was called, but I could not hear what was said, for I was guarded in Snorr's cave. A fine cave, Master! I was taken before the council, and showed them how to bring the Red God to life, showing them also what He will do. Snorr spoke, Ko spoke, and others, but I was taken away again and could not hear. In the end, the council split, the priests ranging themselves on one side, the warriors on the other.

"That night the twelve priests of the Mountain Cave People set out to find the Bison and receive you, bound.

Next morning, learning of this, fifty warriors, led by Snorr, set out in pursuit. Escaping from my guards, I fled to warn you, passing the priests in the night, for"—with a touch of pride—"none can travel the forest as can Nu-kzen! But the priests are hard on my heels, no more than half a day's march behind. Oh, Master, leave this woman and save yourself! There are many women!"

"Leave her? Never!" And En-ro, cursing furiously, seized his weapons. "Nu-kzen, you have done well, but speak not to me of leaving her! A warrior of the Ta-an leaves not his chosen one while breath lives in his body! Is the forest wet throughout?"

"Here in the lowlands, yes, but in the hills the rain is over and the wind has swept the trees. Why do you ask?"

"Because"—and En-ro ground his teeth as he answered fiercely—"if need be, I will loose the Red God to sweep it, and you and I and Va-m'rai and Meng and his warriors, and the tribesmen of the Ta-an shall die before his wrath, sooner than the Bison shall have Va-m'rai! Come now; the sky is lightening to the dawn—we go to find my woman!"

He felt his girdle to make sure that be still carried the Star-Marked One; he looked to his weapons, ax, and throwing-stick he took in his left hand, lance in his right, dagger in his girdle, darts in the leopard-skin quiver over his shoulder; he cast a glance at the fire to be sure it would not spread, and took his way, Nu-kzen following doglike at his heels, toward the little path to which the Bison's wife had pointed the night before.

6

THE SON OF THE RED GOD

THE SKY WAS growing light, but under the trees it was still dark, with the dense, enfolding blackness of the forest night, a blackness that wraps one like a thick, furred skin about the head, pressing down and about on all sides, a stifling, smothering blackness, that yet holds vague gleams of light, half seen, half guessed—not light, indeed, but rather spaces less densely black than the deepest dark.

Behind them, as they turned their heads from time to time, En-ro and Nu-kzen could see, guiding them on their desperate errand, the glow of the dying fire, leaping occasionally into small dancing flames as some stick, burning through, fell with a crackle, throwing a shower of tiny sparks into the air.

Above them the tall trees spread a domed ceiling of arching boughs, through the openings of which, vaguely outlined in ragged forms against the blue of the sky, shone and winked the stars, and once En-ro, turning and lifting his eyes, caught a glimpse of Ku-no-en-m'rai-ten-no, the Guiding Light of the Night That Does Not Move, the star that does not rise or set, the star by which the warriors of the Ta-an were taught to steer their way through the trackless forest.

The clear, fresh, sweet scent of dawn came pleasantly cool to their nostrils, and insects buzzed and hummed through the air; sleeping birds chirped in their dreams, and the Devils of the Air fluttered through the little glade, one even swooping so close to En-ro's head that its wing-tip brushed his ear and he stopped for an instant in fear and horror; then, gathering his strength and courage, pressed on.

Once a roosting bird lost his balance and fell from the tree where he slept, catching himself in mid air—with a squawk and a flutter, and the two men stopped in their tracks, listening to see if any of Meng's warriors had been roused by the noise, but no one stirred, and presently they went on treading lightly and testing the ground before them for betraying twigs and leaves before resting a foot firmly.

From a distance there came to their ears the fierce hunting roar of Snorr-m'rai-no, followed by the agonized scream of a wild horse as the great beast of prey dragged it down, and Nu-kzen poked his master in the back, as though to remind him of what waited for them, once they had left the negroes' camp.

Presently they came to the hither end of the path the Bison's wife had pointed out to the Carver of Tusks, and Nu-kzen, drawing close, caught En-ro's arm. Placing his lips close to his master's ear, the little negro whispered—hardly more than breathed a few words, En-ro listening, half guessing at the message.

"Ba-non," said Nu-kzen, "is it in the hollow oak that your woman is hidden?"

"Yes," spoke En-ro softly, nodding.

"I am a fool, Master! I should have known! But see, we can reach the oak without following the path. Here the brush grows thin, and by crawling belly-down on the earth, as does Sen-zo, the Poisoned Slayer, we can avoid the guards Meng will have placed on the path. Let me go search!"

En-ro nodded again, and Nu-kzen, laying aside his single garment and taking only a flint dagger in his hand, flung himself on the ground and was instantly out of sight. En-ro lay down to wait. Time passed, the Carver of Tusks listening with all his ears, attention at utmost strain, fearing the sound of a struggle that would announce discovery.

The tension grew more and more painful, for as the light grew and he could catch glimpses of vague forms about him, these forms took shape in his mind. The twilight was peopled with enemies creeping, creeping, surrounding him, warriors, beasts, devils, strange, nameless Things, forms he could recognize, forms he could not make out; they swam and shifted and danced before his eyes, till En-ro was ready to leap to his feet and rush upon them, to die fighting.

Then he shifted his eyes, closing them for an instant, and opening them, saw that the forms had changed and were still, and he knew them for creatures of his brain.

So he lay, his faculties tense, his nerves strained, his attention concentrated—and suddenly a hand was laid on his arm! Barely could he keep from screaming, but he held himself firm, though all his strength could not keep back a shudder. Slowly he turned his head, and as he did so a voice breathed in his ear: "Master!"

It was Nu-kzen.

"You found?" asked the white warrior.

"We can pass the guards who are on the path. One watched at the hollow tree."

"And we can pass him?"

Nu-kzen chuckled faintly, and En-ro could see in his mind's eye the inevitable flashing, white-toothed grin.

"He will not trouble us," answered the little negro, laying the blade of his dagger on En-ro's arm, and En-ro felt that it was wet.

"Come, Ba-non," said Nu-kzen. "On your belly, and let not your weapons clink."

En-ro stripped off his leopard-skin and wrapped his weapons in it, all but his dagger, taking care that a thickness of the hide lay between each two weapons, and Nu-kzen did likewise. Then, each taking his dagger in his teeth, the two flung themselves on the ground, the negro leading, and crawled, dragging themselves along by elbows and toes, into the underbrush.

If it had been dark in the open forest, here under the bushes it was doubly, trebly dark, for all the coming dawn. Here not the faintest ray of light penetrated, the stars were hidden, close over their backs the brush joined, and time and again En-ro would have lost his guide but for one hand resting on the negro's heel and leg.

And now En-ro was glad of the rain, for, the ground still wet, the leaves and twigs did not rustle as when dry and crisp. The wet ground was cold and clammy, and in places there were patches of mud and sodden leaf-mold, but discomfort was naught beside safety.

So the two crawled on, and soon En-ro had lost all sense of direction; trained to follow the stars, he was not so keen an animal as the little negro, who could orient himself without other guide than that strange sense whereby the beasts find their way, wherever placed.

Suddenly Nu-kzen halted, a sickening odor of musk came to En-ro's nostrils, and he heard the warning hiss of a deadly viper. Nu-kzen picked three or four leaves from the ground, chewed them vigorously for a moment, and spat violently in the direction of the sound.

En-ro was conscious of a pungent, penetrating smell, not unpleasant, and he heard the serpent rustling away through the bushes.

Nu-kzen resumed his slow crawl, En-ro following close behind. On and on they crept, till by and by the bushes drew farther apart, thinned out, and En-ro could make out through the gloom a vague light ahead.

A dozen paces more, and they were in a clearing larger than most of those that lay about the central space; roughly, a circle some fifty or sixty paces across, with a great oak directly opposite the two, and on their right the path from the central clearing.

In the face of the oak toward them was an opening nearly as high as a man's head, and before it lay a dark body—the guard—huddled grotesquely where he had fallen from the blow of Nu-kzen's dagger. On his face he lay, one leg extended full length, the other drawn up with bent knee, under his body, his left arm flung out, his right resting on the back of his neck.

As they drew near En-ro could see a dark stream that had trickled from under the body, to sink into the ground an arm's length away.

"He knew not his death," whispered Nu-kzen. "I came

on him from behind, reached across his body, and struck upward."

En-ro grunted approvingly and passed into the hollow tree, where Va-m'rai, ankles tied, lay on her side, her legs drawn up, for there was not room within to stretch out. The Carver of Tusks broke a fragment of wood from the tree and dropped it gently on the sleeping girl's bosom.

Instantly she was awake and looked up with frightened eyes; then, seeing who stood before her, leaped to her feet, her mouth opening for a cry; swiftly En-ro laid a hand on his mouth, and she was silent, but hobbled to him as he stepped to meet her, flinging her arms about his neck and clasping him tight.

His arms were about her, her head pressed against his bosom, and he could feel her body shaking with her sobs. Gently he raised her head and looked in her eyes, tears of joy and happiness streaming from them, and their lips met in a long kiss. Leaning back against his circling arms, the girl whispered:

"My love! My love!" and could say no more.

"Quiet, Va-m'rai!" warned En-ro. "Quiet and swift! We must go!"

Stooping, he cut the thongs that bound her ankles, and they passed out from the hollow tree. Even as they stepped outside Nu-kzen raised his voice:

"Swiftly, Master! They come!" And En-ro, looking about, saw—for by now it was light in the clearing—a dark warrior stride from the path on the left.

"Ken-zan!" cried the little negro, and the approaching warrior raised his head. Behind him came another, then another, and after them the huge form of the Bison;

followed by others and still others, pushing and crowding—white men, clad in skins, horns of deer and wild cattle on their heads—the priests of Ta-an!

"This is the end!" cried En-ro. Turning, he laid his dagger in the girl's hand. "Va-m'rai, be not taken alive!" And her grip closed over the sharp flint as she answered:

"Daughter am I to a chieftain of the Ta-an! Fear not for me!"

Stooping, En-ro seized his leopard-skin from the ground, and with a twist unrolled it, the weapons falling from the folds; he grasped his ax, even as Meng, seeing his enemy before him, and the girl free, rushed with the bellow of rage at the Carver of Tusks.

But before En-ro could move to meet him, Nu-kzen, armed but with a dagger, leaped to defend the master whom he loved, and fronted the Bison. Roaring, Meng thrust fiercely at the little negro with his ax, and Nu-kzen reeled backward; the great ax whirled in the air and fell—the blow took Nu-kzen on the shoulder, and he fell, asprawl, his arms flung wildly abroad; the ax had turned in the Bison's hands, but the terrific blow, even striking flatwise of the blade, had crushed the little negro's shoulder, smashing collar-bone and ribs, and driving the shattered bones into the lung. Blood gushed from Nu-kzen's mouth as he lay, and Meng rushed on.

"Alive! Alive! Slay not!" shouted the priests, but Meng, blind with rage, cared for naught but to come to grips with the man he hated and feared, the man who had shamed him before his own warriors, the man who had defied him, who had taken his honor from him, and, heedless of the shouts, he dashed across to where stood the Carver of Tusks, waiting, quiet and self-contained, only his gleaming eyes showing the lust of battle that filled his bosom.

Above, among the trees, the birds chattered and sang as though peace ruled through all the world; in the clearing the mists of dawn rolled and billowed, rising from the ground, sweeping about the forms of the two enemies, half hiding them from the sight of the warriors and priests who pressed closer to see the fight; a dozen paces away, Nu-kzen, conscious once more, raised himself to sweep from his eyes the fog of death that was spreading over them, that he, too, might watch the duel; vaguely, in the tense silence, En-ro heard a shout, far off, ring through the forest; fiercely the Carver of Tusks glared at the Bison, and not less fiercely, foam dribbling from his lips, the Bison glared back from where he had halted three paces away.

"Ape-man!" taunted En-ro. "Ape-man! Coward! Torturer of women! Woman! You shall carry water for me and cure skins before my cave!"

Shaking the foam from his chin, screaming with anger, the Bison whirled up his ax and leaped toward his foe. Warily. En-ro watched, and as the ax swept down he leaped back—in again—and Meng, bleeding from a gash on the thigh, fell back a pace, as En-ro followed, his own ax raised.

But the Bison was no new-fledged fighter; as En-ro's ax fell the blow was turned and Meng's weapon jabbed at En-ro's face—the Carver of Tusks jerked his head aside—and the sharp blade tore his ear.

So back and forth they fought, feinting, dodging, striking, advancing, retreating, ever seeking an opening, ever striving to land a deadly blow, till both were weary and blown. Both were bleeding from a score of cuts, little cuts that none the less drained their strength away, and both were panting; blood and sweat mingled and ran down their bodies, the salt taste of the sweat was in their mouths—still back and forth they fought.

Closer and closer pressed the watchers, and Va-m'rai still crouched against the oak, her hands, gripping the dagger, held tight to her bosom. The sharp edge of the flint had scratched her skin, and a trickle of blood flowed down her breast—she did not know it, so intently did she watch the fight!

Suddenly her stifled cry came to En-ro's ear—dodging, he had caught his heel in a projecting root—he flung out his arms to catch his balance—the ax flew from his hand—he fell! The Bison, a grin stretching his thick-lipped mouth, sprang forward, lifting his ax for the blow that should end the fight—En-ro rolled swiftly over and over—seized his ax, and leaped to his feet—the Bison's ax swept down, struck the ground—he tugged to free it—saw death coming on him—flung up his arm, screaming—and En-ro's ax, driven with all the strength of his powerful arms, driven with hate behind it, struck full and square between the Bison's shoulders!

The Bison pitched forward on his face, coughed, grunted, and lay dead at En-ro's feet. En-ro freed his ax, leaned heavily on it, panting, and looked about him at the ring of faces, mingled white and black, that surrounded him.

For a time—for perhaps ten breaths—no one moved or spoke; the only sounds to be heard were the songs of the birds, the labored breathing of the victor, and the choking coughs of Nu-kzen, as he lay where he had dropped from the Bison's blow. Then the chief priest, Ja-men-ka, elected after En-ro's dart had slain Men-ko, stepped forward and raised his hand.

"Take him!" he cried, but before any could move another voice spoke, behind the ring of priests and blacks, exclaiming:

"Stop!" and through the crowd came the form of Snorr, Great Chieftain of the Ta-an, thrusting aside those who stood before him, even as a swimmer throws aside the water, and the crowd parted to let him pass, as the water parts before the swimmer's breast. Ranging himself beside En-ro, he faced the priests and warriors, crying:

"Look about you!"

Negroes and white men, priests and warriors, they turned as one man, to see filing from the debouching path the fifty plumed warriors of the Ta-an, their oiled bodies glistening, the polished flint of their lances sparkling in the morning light that flooded the clearing. Silent but for the martial stamp of their feet on the ground and the click and clink of their anklets of shells and claws, these encircled the group, and at a word from Snorr each man brought his lance to level, the points directed inward to form a wall, breast-high, of sharpened flint.

Then, and only then, did Snorr turn to En-ro.

"Carver of Tusks," he said, "your messenger, who now lies there, brought word to us that you can command a strange new god, till now unknown to men; that this god serves you, that he will warm you in the Long Cold, and that he will fight for you; and your messenger told us also that it is your will that the Ta-an shall know of this god, and that he shall warm and aid the People of the Mountain Caves. Did he speak truth?"

En-ro, still breathing heavily, bowed.

"Warriors of the Ta-an!" cried Snort, turning again to the crowd, "an ancient prophecy, known to but few among us, proclaims that there shall one day rise among us a warrior who shall command the gods; the prophecy bids us serve him, obey him, and worship him, making him Great Chieftain of the Ta-an. I, who am your chieftain, obey the words of the Great Father. See now!" And he turned once more to En-ro, laying at his feet the carved wand of the tooth of Do-m'rai, the Hill That Walks, the baton of ceremony, the badge of chieftainship.

"Great Chieftain of the Ta-an," said Snorr, "I bow to you and entreat your favor." And kneeling, he lifted En-ro's foot and placed it upon his own head. "Give your commands; shall we, your servants, slay these men or let them live?"

En-ro stooped and took the baton, looked about him proudly, albeit a bit dazedly, and answered:

"Slay not; let them depart and come no more among the People of the Mountain Caves."

Instantly the ring of warriors parted on the other side, the lances pressed in toward the opening, and negroes and priests together were driven toward the path. Returning, the warriors knelt before En-ro, who gazed upon them, seeking words. Va-m'rai rose from where she crouched and drew to his side, laying her hand timidly upon his arm; his arm went about her waist and he drew her close; with his free hand he raised Snorr from where he knelt, and spoke aloud:

"Warriors of the Ta-an!" he cried, "I accept the high office; in war and in peace I will lead you, and we shall make the name of the Ta-an known and feared far and wide, far as the words of men are carried, even to the Land of the Dying Sun, the home of the Little Hairy Men! Your honor is mine; my honor is yours, and while breath lives in my body never shall I cease to labor and to fight for my people."

Snorr raised his arm:

"Men of the Ta-an, greet now your chief!" and a cry rang through the forest as the warriors tossed their lances high into the air:

"Long life to En-ro, Great Chieftain of the Ta-an!" But Snorr raised his hand once more.

"No longer En-ro, Carver of Tusks," he spoke, "but henceforth and forever Na-t'san, the Son of the Red God." And once again the forest heard a shout, deep, full-throated, from the Warriors:

"Long life to thee and thy bride! Long life and honor and happiness to Na-t'san, our leader, Great Chieftain of the tribe of Ta-an, the Son of the Red God!"

A MONTH HAD passed; the Long Cold had closed in, and the days were growing shorter; Co-sa, the Ice, had locked the streams and built his bridges, cold and hard and glittering, over the pools; Sa, the Snow, had come in flurries, drifting among the rocks, heaped by the wind in piles that shone white in crannies and crevices; long since the squirrels had stored their winter's food, and Mo, the bear, had hidden himself for his long sleep; the Long Cold was upon the People of the Mountain Caves.

The sun was sinking toward the western hills when the Great Chief of the Ta-an, the Son of the Red God, climbed the mountain toward the altar whence—ages ago, it seemed—he had rescued Va-m'rai. He wished to be alone; to think and plan, and, reaching the altar, he seated himself upon a stone, his elbows on his knees, his chin supported in his hands, gazing abroad over the fair valley that lay below him, stretching far and wide on either hand, rolling down, then rising once more with gentle sweep to the distant hills that, a far blue wall, stood outlined against the deeper blue of the sky.

But the chieftain, seated, did not bend his mind to labor; a mood of reverie took him, and, sitting there, he drifted back over the happenings of the past few months, busy months, filled with struggle and effort, with danger, trial, battle, and, in the end, triumph.

He smiled proudly as he thought of the shouts of the tribesmen, the triumphal journey homeward, the finding of his cave, whence the sealing rocks had been rolled away.

And then he thought of Meng, and his muscles tightened and his eyes flashed as he remembered the great fight, and the blow that had brought him victory, and from the Bison his mind drifted to Nu-kzen, faithful, as he had sworn, even to death, and something rose in his throat and choked him as he remembered how the little negro had pressed the hand of his kneeling master and had smiled even as the bloody foam rushed to his lips and his brave spirit started on its journey into the Long Dark.

By now the sun had set, and it was growing dark, and below him, dotting the slope of the mountain, the chieftain could see the twinkling fires of the tribesmen, for each man had got him a flint and hammer-stone and had learned the secret of calling the Red God to life; it was no part of the chieftain's plan to keep this knowledge to himself; he felt within him the power of invention, the power to lead and to command, and he meant to give this and all other knowledge freely to his people, that they might grow in strength and wisdom.

And now the mood of reverie left him and the spirit of prophecy came upon him, so that he saw visions; the valley and the fires drew back and faded before his eyes as though a veil were drawn across, and through this veil the chieftain saw dimly vague forms, crowding, thronging, fighting great battles, doing great works, armed with strange weapons, using strange tools; a pressing, mighty nation, spreading to the uttermost limits of the world, rich and powerful, strong and great.

He thrilled, his bosom heaved, his breath came hard, and he rose to his feet; erect he stood, raising his arms to the heavens.

"Oh, Great Father," he prayed aloud, "let Thy spirit descend upon me; grant me strength and patience, wisdom and might, that I may in very truth be deserving of this great honor that is mine; that well and truly may I serve my people to the end of life!" And as if in answer to his prayer the wind was stilled, and in the silence, the utter silence of the lonely mountain, the chieftain felt a great peace descend and wrap him about, enfolding him, filling his bosom and flooding through his veins.

And slowly the vision faded, and slowly, with bent head, humbly yet proudly, Na-t'san the Son of the Red God, guided by the gleaming, twinkling fires of his people, took his way down the mountain to the cave where Va-m'rai, the tender, the brave, the true, awaited his coming.

THE LORD OF THE WINGED DEATH

1

THE GRANDSON OF EN-RO

THE SUN WAS sinking behind the western hills and the peaks of the mountains glowed warm and rosy while the wooded valley was wrapped in shadow as Ken-o-san, the Hunter of Beasts, climbed the slope to the level bench of rock, fifty paces in width and two thousand in length, on which fronted the caves of the Ta-an, open to the south, but sheltered by the mountain, rising high above, from the fierce blasts that in winter swept down from the northern ice-fields.

Directly opposite the young warrior, as he topped the slope midway between the ends of the row of caves, an old white-haired man, seated on a lion's hide spread on the rocks, basked in the late rays of the sun, and toward him Ken-o-san made his way, stopping a few paces from the elder, and bending to draw with his finger the three interlocking circles that marked the respect due a chieftain of the tribe. The old man, waving his hand, said:

"Sit, Ken-o-san, son of my son. You would speak with me?"

The young man bowed and squatted on his haunches, but did not answer at once; he seemed to find trouble in choosing words, and the old man watched him gravely and in silence.

There was a marked contrast, aside from that of age, in the two men. The younger, hardly more than twenty or twenty-two years old, was small of stature and slight of build, but wiry and muscular, lithe and active, and his quick movements bespoke a store of nervous energy beyond that of most men—indeed, for all his small size, he was known as one of the strongest men and most deadly fighters in all the tribe.

The older man, on the other hand, was broad of shoulder and long of arm, and in spite of the fourscore years that had whitened his hair, there still dwelt in his mighty frame a power that was the envy of all the young men of the Ta-an; not more than a month before he had heaved to his shoulders and carried away the carcass of a bear that no three men in the tribe could lift.

But for all the difference, the two men were strangely alike. Each had the same oval face, the same broad, high forehead, the same high-arched nose, though the eyes that looked out beside it were in the elder brown, and in the younger—unusual among the Ta-an—a cold blue-gray. And on each face was the same look of pride and strength, as of one born to be a leader of men. At length Ken-o-san found words for his desire, and spoke:

"Oh, Na-t'san, Son of the Red God," he said, "Great Chieftain of the Ta-an, father of my father, I come to ask your aid. It is known to you that I love Nan-ai, the Poplar, fairest of all the maidens of the Ta-an." He stopped, looked inquiringly at the chieftain, who bowed gravely; the young man went on:

The Lord of the Winged Death
by Paul L. Anderson

"But Ban-ku, her uncle, who since the death of her father and mother keeps the maiden in his care, will have none of me. He looks with disfavor on me, nor will he hear aught that I may say to him."

"And is Ban-ku to blame," asked the chieftain sadly, "that he looks with disfavor on you?" The young man flushed hotly and looked down, saying nothing.

"And what is it that you would have me do? Command Ban-ku to give the maiden to you? By the law of the tribe I may not do so, nor, in very truth, would I were it permitted. Listen, Ken-o-san! Son of my son are you, blood of my blood, and to you should I give the staff of ceremony, the carven tooth of Do-m'rai, the Hill that Walks, when it falls from my hand, your father being dead. To you should fall the leadership of the Ta-an, in war and in peace, even as it fell to me from Snorr, Great Chieftain, in my young years. But are you worthy?"

Ken-o-san raised his head and opened his mouth to speak, but the chieftain lifted his hand and the younger was silent. The chieftain went on:

"Small of stature and slight of build are you, but despite that a fighter second to none, as you have shown in battle with the beasts of forest and mountain, and—sorrow and grief that it should be said!—in private feud. But what has ever been done by you for the welfare of the tribe? Aught? One thing? Speak! Nothing! No older than you was your father when he taught the tribesmen to burn their food in the fire that it might be pleasant to the taste; no older was I when I taught them to bring to life the Red God that he might warm them in the Long Cold and might war with them against their foes; no older was Snorr when he taught them to range themselves in ranks in battle and to aid one the other in the fight.

"But you! Fighter that you are, skilled in the use of weapons, swift of hand and foot and eye, born to command, it is your pride and your pleasure to be leader of a score of young men who at your word attack tribes with whom the Ta-an are at peace, who lie in wait for those wandering in the forest to beat and rob them, and—greatest shame of all—beat and wound and rob and slay your own tribesmen!"

The young man had been drooping lower and lower as the chieftain went on, but now he raised his head and burst out:

"Never have we slain a man of the Ta-an! Who says so speaks falsely!"

Na-t'san did not reply; he leaned forward where he sat, bent his shaggy brows together, and stared at the young man. For the space of ten breaths the younger endured this deadly stare, then his own eyes wavered and fell. The chieftain drew a long breath and relaxed, then said, coldly and impressively:

"Forget not, Ken-o-san, that the law of the tribe gives

me power of life and death over all the tribesmen; should I strike you dead where you sit, there is none to question. Set, therefore, a guard on your tongue when you speak with me! True it is, you did not slay Sar-no-men; he lives yet—but are thanks therefore due you? Was it not your endeavor to slay him? Did you not leave him for dead in the forest? And did you not rob him, taking from him even his very garments?

"And is not this a disgrace for a warrior of the Ta-an, one whose smallest finger has been cut off in token that he is full member of the warrior clan; one who is son and grandson to chieftains? Indeed, Ken-o-san, long have I been in two minds whether it were not well to do as Ja-ko, the chief priest, advises, and slay you lest you do grievous harm to the Ta-an!"

The young warrior leaped to his feet, and his gray eyes flashed.

"Did Ja-ko so counsel?" he asked.

"I have said!" replied Na-t'san.

For a moment Ken-o-san stood, shaking with rage, his eyes narrowed to slits, his mouth opening and closing convulsively as he strove to speak, then whirling on his heel, omitting all farewell to the chieftain, omitting the signs of respect to which the tribesmen were commanded by law, he strode across the level space and plunged down the slope toward the forest, in which he was presently lost to view.

For an hour or more he tramped through the darkening forest, crashing through the underbrush, striking against low-hanging branches, cursing and foaming with rage, heedless of the blows he received, heedless of what hunting beasts might be abroad, heedless even of the leather-winged devils of the air that fluttered and swooped about his head. At length, weary, but with unabated anger, he turned his steps once more toward his cave on the mountain.

For a moment he stood, hesitating, for in his blind rage he had not noted where his steps were leading, and as he looked about he caught sight of two gleaming eyes staring at him from a thicket. Green, shining like stars in the dusk, they glared, unwinking, toward the young man, who stood stock-still and glared back, striving to pierce the screen of leaves and make out what beast it might be that barred his way.

Well he knew the eyes for those of some beast of prey that had followed his trail in search of a chance to spring; some hungry beast that would fight to the death—but what? Snorr-m'rai-no, the lion? Su, the leopard? Menzono, the wolf?

Unmoving as though carved from stone, the young warrior kept his place; slowly, slowly, the beast crept from the thicket—it was Su, the leopard! Nearer and nearer, slinking along, belly to the earth, the tip of its tail twitching, the great beast, a giant of its kind, crept, and still the warrior did not move—one might have thought him frozen with terror.

Closer and closer, its evil head thrown forward, its green eyes glowing now like coals, its powerful muscles rippling under the sleek hide, drew the great beast—it stopped an instant—gathered itself together, and with a mighty snarl, sprang on its prey!

But in that instant Ken-o-san, watchful, swift as light,

swifter than the Poisoned Slayer when it strikes, shifted his lance, planted the butt on the ground, and held the point, unwavering, toward the leopard.

The sharp, flint lance-head struck the beast full in the throat and pierced through and through skin and flesh to the spine—impaled by the force of its own leap, the leopard fell—the stout shaft snapped under the weight—and with a crash the great beast dropped at the hunter's feet, one mighty claw grazing the warrior's knee!

Ken-o-san drew back a step and raised his ax, but the leopard was dead, and with a smile of satisfaction the warrior drew his skinning-knife of sharpened flint to take the hide.

It was no light task to strip the hide from a full-grown leopard, but Ken-o-san worked fast and skilfully, aided by the light of the moon which had risen, and now shone, round and yellow, through an opening in the forest.

At length he had finished, and rolling the hide in a ball, he placed it on his head, picked up the blade of his lance—he had had no little trouble to free it from the leopard's spine—and taking his other weapons, ax and throwing-stick and darts, dagger and skinning-knife, he started for home, orienting himself by the moon and stars.

As he marched, Ken-o-san crooned to himself a little song, one that he made up as he walked, telling of his fight with the beast, for Ken-o-san was not only a warrior, not only the leader of a band of young roisterers; he was also a famous singer, known to all the tribe, sought after for his songs of battle and victory, of love and life and death, of feasting and joy, and for his dirges over the warriors slain in battle.

> Hidden to all seeming,
>   By his eyes I knew him,
> Through the branches gleaming;
>   With my lance I slew him—
>   Pierced him through and through.

Here the singer broke off and glanced down at the blade of his lance, a gift to him from his grandfather, Na-t'san, given when the young man knelt before the altar to have his finger stricken off in token of his acceptance into the warrior clan.

In his young days Na-t'san had been a famous shaper of tools and weapons, chipping them from the flint and polishing them with skill, and he had been also a noted carver of ivory—indeed, his youthful name, En-ro, meant "Carver of Tusks"—nor had his hand lost its skill with the passage of years.

And this lance, its broad blade perfectly shaped, its stout oak shaft ornamented with a carving of the Poisoned Slayer coiled about it, had been the chieftain's gift to his grandson when the latter came to warrior's years. It was the young man's most treasured possession, and he felt regret that the weight of Su had broken the shaft. Still, another could be fitted—his train of thought shifted, and his forehead was drawn with anger, and he ground his teeth as he remembered what Na-t'san had said.

And now, breaking from the forest, Ken-o-san saw above him the fires of the Ta-an, as men and women and children warmed themselves before their caves. It was growing late, for many of the tribesmen had already gone to rest, but some were still about, and Ken-o-san remembered what his grandfather had told him of his own young days, before the coming of the Red God; how as darkness fell the tribesmen drew into their caves and rolled great stones before them for protection against wild beasts; but now, since the Red God, thanks to the chieftain, obeyed the Ta-an, none feared—the beasts dared not approach the fires.

Climbing the slope, Ken-o-san was making his way toward his own cave, when he saw something that caused him to turn toward one of the fires twenty or thirty paces away.

A group of tribesmen were squatting about the fire while one of their number, standing, was haranguing them, tossing his arms wildly, his voice rising and falling with excitement. Drawing closer, Ken-o-san recognized Ja-ko, the chief priest, and listened. He heard the priest say.

"And shall the Ta-an bear with this? What though he is child to Na-t'san, the great chief? Shall he therefore rob and beat and slay the tribesmen? Were it not better that he should be slain than that the Ta-an should go in fear of their lives? And his band of ruffians—" here Ken-o-san, throwing down the leopard-skin and striding within the circle of firelight, touched the speaker on the shoulder.

Ja-ko turned, stared, and fell back a step, shuddering, for indeed the young man was a fearsome sight. Spattered and splashed with blood from the leopard, naked save for a single garment of lion's hide, his light brown hair tousled and matted, his breast heaving as his breath came hard with anger, his gray eyes shining green in the firelight—small wonder the priest shrank from him!

But Ja-ko was no coward; after that first start of surprise

he faced Ken-o-san firmly enough, trusting, indeed, in the dignity of his priestly office to overawe the young warrior. And so the two stood looking at each other, while men rose hastily from around the fire and, eager to miss no word or act of the scene, closed in a ring about them, the light, blazing up from fresh sticks, casting a weird, dancing glow upon the fierce faces and half-naked bodies. Presently Ken-o-san, controlling his rage, spoke:

"Ja-ko," said he, "you have asked my life of the chieftain; failing there, it has been your endeavor to rouse against me the Ta-an. Shall you not therefore die? Is it not the law that whoso plots against the life of a tribesman is guilty of murder; guilty even though the plot fail? Is not your life then forfeit to me? Speak!"

Ja-ko scorned to answer the specious charge; he drew himself up proudly and replied:

"You dare not lay hands on the chief priest of the Ta-an! Even you, robber, layer of ambushes, your hands red with blood of innocent men, dare not do this thing!"

Ken-o-san laughed, then raising his head he shouted loud:

"L'vu! Kan-to! Sar-no-m'rai!" Instantly three young men jumped up from where they sat by a distant fire and came running, followed closely by a number of tribesmen who, scenting trouble, came to watch. Two of the three were ordinary enough, save for a certain swiftness and decision about their actions which distinguished them among men none of whom lacked in these qualities, but the third, L'vu, Ken-o-san's closest friend and trusted lieutenant, was a huge, burly hulk of a man, to all seeming a mere gross body of fat, slow and lazy, his round moon-face shining with good-nature.

But woe to him who relied on this aspect! Under great layers of fat lurked powerful muscles, so that L'vu was one of the strongest men in the tribe, yielding only to Ken-o-san and to Na-t'san, the chieftain; for all his great bulk, L'vu could move swiftly enough when need arose—indeed, it was astonishing to see so gross a man move like the Poisoned Slayer! And though he was kindly and pleasant enough at most times, so that the children of the tribe ran after him as he walked abroad, rage could so transform L'vu's face that in battle men ran from him before a blow was struck.

But he adored Ken-o-san; he worshiped the man who, small and slight beside his own huge bulk, could yet outdo him in all manly sports; could send a dart farther and surer than he could speed it; could out-fight him with the stone ax, and could throw him wrestling.

These three men pushed through the crowd, and, L'vu on the right, the others on the left, ranged themselves beside their leader, eager and expectant, waiting his orders, and still other tribesmen, coming up, joined the circle that, three deep, enclosed the angry men.

"L'vu, Kan-to, Sar-no-m'rai," said Ken-o-san, "this priest, this eater of food that others have slain, this slayer of bound victims—he has asked my life of Na-t'san, the Great Chieftain; failing, he has sought to rouse the wrath of the tribesmen against me. Shall he live? Bind him and carry him to the great altar! We ourselves will hold a sacrifice!"

At these blasphemous words a growl ran through the crowd, and weapons were grasped; men pressed forward as though to fall on the sacrilegious wretch who would slay the high priest. Ken-o-san, running his eye over the crowd that hemmed him in, spoke quietly:

"To me, men! A circle!" At once some twenty young warriors, men of his own age, leaped forward from the crowd, and, evidently executing a well-planned maneuver, placed themselves shoulder to shoulder in a circle about the five men, their lances lowered, the points directed outward. Before this trained front the tribesmen fell back, still growling and handling their weapons, and for a moment it seemed as though civil war was about to break. But a well-formed, handsome man of middle age stepped forward, crying:

"Ken-o-san! Let me have speech with you!" Ken-o-san looked, hesitated, then said:

"Let him pass!" and the circle of lances opened to admit the speaker, closing again behind him as he stepped to Ken-o-san's side. He grasped Ken-o-san by the arm, speaking eagerly yet evidently with restraint:

"Ken-o-san! Ban-tu-v'rai am I, Ban-tu-v'rai, whose daughter you did save when her baby feet, slipping, let her fall into the mountain stream. At risk of your own life you saved her; by that life which you saved I conjure you, cast not your own away! It is death to lay hands on the high priest!"

Ken-o-san looked about the circle of lances, and smiled, and Ban-tu-v'rai, following the glance, read the young man's thought.

"What can twenty men do against two hundred? Every warrior of the Ta-an will be on your track, to hunt you down, outlawed, and slay you! Even should you force out through the crowd, your life will be forfeit!"

Still Ken-o-san hesitated, muttering:

"He sought my life!" and Ban-tu-v'rai clutched his arm the tighter.

"Ken-o-san!" he cried, "if not for your own sake, if not for the sake of me, Ban-tu-v'rai, who loves you, then for the sake of A-ta, my daughter, spare him! Even now her baby fingers grasp for yours, and in her sleep she whispers: 'Ken-o-san!' Let her not know you, when she comes to woman's age, for an outlaw, slain for sacrilege!"

Ken-o-san's breast heaved, his eyes fell, and he stood silent, while the crowd watched eagerly, tensely. Presently he looked up, waved his hand, saying:

"At my back!" and the ring of lances, melting, re-formed in a compact and orderly group behind him. L'vu, Kan-to, and Sar-no-m'rai released their hold on Ja-ko's arms and stepped to their places by their leader. Ken-o-san and Ja-ko faced each other, three paces apart, and the watchers could see by the light of the leaping flames that the priest was trembling; whatever might happen to Ken-o-san, death had cast the shadow of his wings over the high priest that night! At length Ken-o-san spoke:

"Ja-ko, give thanks to Ban-tu-v'rai and to A-ta, his daughter! As I live, as O-Ala-Ken, the Great Father, sees me, this night a child has saved your life! Cross not my path again!"

Turning on his heel, he uttered a word of command; his lances parted to let him pass, closed, swung about, and the party marched with measured step along the bench of rock to the great cave of Ken-o-san. The group about the fire separated, each man going to his own cave; the fires died down, and night, its silence broken only by the hunting roar of Snorr-m'rai-no, the Fear That Walks the Night, by the bark of hyenas, and by the flutter of the devils of the air, settled over the homes of the Ta-an, the People of the Mountain Caves.

But Ken-o-san did not sleep. Squatting on his haunches before his cave, L'vu beside him, he thought long and hard. L'vu at times spoke, and his leader grunted in reply; at times Ken-o-san offered a word or two, and L'vu, listening eagerly, assented or shook his head, as the suggestion pleased him or seemed to him impossible.

All night the two sat thus, while the full round moon traveled slowly up the wide, blue arch of the sky and slid down into the west, the black shadows of the men growing shorter and then again lengthening out.

Before them lay the bench of rock, its edge falling steeply away to the forest-covered valley that stretched for miles, greenish-black in the moonlight, turning gradually to blue where the far southern hills rose against the sky; as the moon sank toward the western hills the contours of the forest changed, the forms altered, and at last, the moon having set, the eastern sky began to pale, the stars winked out, the first glow of dawn grew clearer and clearer, and then, and not till then, the two rose stiffly, yawned, stretched, and entered the cave, picking their ray among the sleepers till they reached their own places, where, wrapping themselves in skins, they lay down to sleep, their planning done.

2

THE GREAT SICKNESS

"**THE MORNING FOLLOWING** his talk with Ken-o-san, when he had vainly administered such stinging reproof, Na-t'san, Great Chieftain of the Ta-an, sat before his cave, gazing out over the familiar valley which lay spread below him, the same densely wooded valley across which, nearly sixty years before, he had fled from the wrath of the tribesmen, taking with him Va-m'rai, his betrothed.

His mind roved back over the years that had followed; over the struggles, the labor, the joys and sorrows; the birth of his son, father to Ken-o-san, and his death in battle with the Gra, a neighboring tribe.

The chieftain's eyes turned to where Va-m'rai, the morning meal done, was carrying the small bones of a bear to the refuse heap below the cave, and his face lit with tenderness; a true and faithful wife had she been through many years. And then he grew sad and thoughtful, for it behooved him to choose one who should follow him as leader of the Ta-an, nor could he think of any worthy; Ken-o-san, to whom the honor should fall, was not to be trusted—his hot young blood brooked no restraint; not for him to labor for his fellows!

As the chieftain mused thus, turning over in his mind

the names of a score of tribesmen, he was conscious of a shadow falling on the ground before him, and looked up, to see Nan-ai, loved one of his grandson, standing respectfully a little distance away. She stooped and drew on the ground with her finger, and the chieftain waved his hand.

"Sit, Nan-ai," said he gently and pleasantly, for he was fond of the girl, as indeed were all the Ta-an, not only for her beauty, which was like that of the slim and graceful poplar from which she took her name, but even more for her gentleness, her cheerful manner, and her unfailing kindness.

"Sit, Nan-ai," repeated Na-t'san, as the girl hesitated, and with the words she sank cross-legged on the ground, buried her face in her hands, and broke into a tempest of tears. Na-t'san waited, considering thoughtfully; Ken-o-san was a fool, he told himself, to risk losing the love of such a one through evil courses. Her fair white shoulders and limbs, revealed by the single garment of leopard-skin she wore, and her long, thick, wavy brown hair reminded the chieftain of what Va-m'rai had been in her young days, before the passage of years brought her a matronly fulness, and he admitted to himself that Nan-ai might well bear comparison with his own woman; less fire and strength, perhaps, than were Va-m'rai's, but on the other hand a greater tenderness. In very truth, a good mate for a warrior of the Ta-an! Presently he spoke once more, kindly:

"Nan-ai, dry your tears; not till you tell your trouble does it lie in my power to aid," and the girl's sobbing grew less; she sat up, flung back her hair over her shoulders, and clasped her hands on her bosom.

"Oh, Na-t'san, Great Chieftain, it is said that you can

command the gods; sway them now, I pray, to change the heart of Ken-o-san; it is but last night that he threatened the life of Ja-ko, the high priest, for what he had said, and would have slain him had not Ban-tu-v'rai persuaded him."

"You love Ken-o-san?"

The girl bent her head, and tears sprang to her eyes.

"Indeed, Na-t'san, more than life itself do I love him! And should he be slain for sacrilege I would surely die. But"—and she gripped her hands tight together—"gladly would I die could my death turn Ken-o-san from his evil ways! Oh, great chief, command the gods, that Ken-o-san may turn again and have honor among the Ta-an!"

Na-t'san shook his head.

"Nan-ai," said he sadly, "in some things can I command the gods, but not here: it lies with Ken-o-san himself, and will be not turned for honor and for you, I can do naught. Indeed, Nan-ai, his evil ways are a greater grief to me than to you; blood of my blood is he, and my love for him is greater than your own. Yes, in very truth," he went on, as the girl smiled incredulously, "not till you have held in your arms a child of your own blood can you know my love for Ken-o-san. But I can do naught; he must choose his road."

The girl rose and bowed in silence, then burst once more into tears and turned away. The chieftain fell again into deep thought.

The sun had climbed to its full height and was casting its shortest shadow when Ja-ko came hastening along the bench of rock toward the chieftain's cave, and it was evident that he was greatly disturbed; his garment of wolf-skin was awry, so that the tail of the beast hung at the wearer's side instead of behind, and the hood, formed from the hollowed-out skull, was pushed back from Ja-ko's head. He hurriedly drew the propitiatory circles, and seated himself, panting, even before Na-t'san had given permission.

"Great chieftain," he burst out, "five days since a warrior of the tribe sickened and died; next day three were sick, of whom one recovered, and to-day seven, of whom three are already dead. A pestilence is upon us!"

"In what manner died they?" asked Na-t'san, quietly.

"With purging and vomiting does the sickness begin, with pain in the belly and with thirst; pains in the body and legs follow swiftly, and the one possessed grows cold, the skin drying and turning blue; the eyes sink within the head, and death follows quickly, at times, within an hour from the first stroke."*

As the priest's description proceeded, a look of horror overspread Na-t'san's face, and at the end he whispered:

"The Great Sickness!"

Ja-ko looked puzzled for a moment; then comprehension woke in his eyes, and he, too, shared the chieftain's horror and dread.

"To me it is known but from tales," said the priest, and Na-t'san nodded.

"Fifty summers ago—no, fifty-three—it smote the Ta-an, so that full half the tribe fell before it, and once in the time of Snorr, though then not so heavily."

"Can aught be done?"

Na-t'san shook his head.

"Can you not intercede with O-Ma-Ken, the Great Father?"

---

* This description of the symptoms appears to identify the great sickness as Asiatic cholera.—AUTHOR.

"The tribe is in his hands! But I can ask; it may be that he will hear my prayer."

"Is it"—the priest hesitated—"is it a curse? Perchance the Great Father is angry with us that we—that we—"

"That we— Speak!" said Na-t'san sternly.

"That we—permit—Ken-o-san—"

The chieftain's eyes blazed as he burst out:

"The gods vent not their wrath on a tribe for the evil deeds of one man! Let not your enmity toward Ken-o-san grow too great, Ja-ko; forget not that the Great Chieftain has power of life and death over the priests as well as the warriors!"

Ja-ko cowered before the anger that flamed from the eyes of the Son of the Red God, and Na-t'san went on, more quietly;

"I will fast and pray; it may be that O-Ma-Ken will vouchsafe a sign." He waved his hand, and the priest, rising, bowed and took his way to his own cave.

For some time after Ja-ko was out of sight Na-t'san sat in meditation, then rose and turned into his cave, seeking Va-m'rai, who, at the sound of his step, came forward from the darkness at the rear, where she had been busy over some household affairs. The chieftain's eyes rested on her with affection and with pleasure, for Va-m'rai, unlike most of the women of the Ta-an, had not grown fat and gross with the passage of years; the lines of her form were fuller and rounder, it is true, than in youth, but the play of her muscles was not masked by deep layers of tissue, and for all her age—within a year or two of Na-t'san's—she still, like her husband, carried herself proudly erect, her years showing only in the wrinkles graven about her eyes and mouth, and in the strands of gray that lay among her brown hair.

"Swift Runner," said the chieftain, "the Great Sickness has come again upon the Ta-an; six are dead, though the first was smitten but five days since. Ja-ko, the chief priest, has come to me for aid, and I go to fast and pray on the mountain, that O-Ma-Ken may perchance show his mercy and take from us this pestilence."

Va-m'rai bowed in assent.

"When do you return?" she asked. "I shall be lonely."

Na-t'san shrugged his shoulders.

"Who knows the mind of the Great Father, or who can read his thoughts? I return when I return. It is for the Ta-an!"

Va-m'rai bowed once more, and pressed his hand caressingly; he stooped and kissed her cheek, then turned and walked slowly from the cave.

The Great Chieftain passed eastward along the bench of rock for perhaps five hundred paces, then turned north up the side of the mountain, following a path which led to the great altar hundreds of feet above; reaching the place of sacrifice, he turned east once more, passing along the ridge of the mountain far beyond the last of the caves of the Ta-an, to where a spring bubbled in a rock basin the height of a tall man across and half that in depth.

The water of the spring had traveled far, for north of where it broke from the earth no hills rose higher than this in the space of a long day's journey; icy cold it was, and clear as air, the bottom showing perfectly, as though no water lay above it.

This was the Water of Prayer, the spring from which

drank chieftain or priest when fasting on the mountain, and it was forbidden to all others; the spring from which the young men drank during the seven days' fast that preceded their acceptance into the various clans—warrior, artist, or priestly—lay below and to the west—Na-t'san had passed it on his way up to the place of fasting.

Halting by the Water of Prayer, the Great Chieftain looked about him; to the south lay the valley he knew so well, rolling in gentle waves to the Blue Hills, beyond which lay the Great Blue Water; east and west, far as he could see, stretched the bleak, naked rocks of the mountain; to the north lay rugged, almost impassable cañons, and beyond them, rising rank after rank to the sky, ranges of hills, the more distant ones towering above the nearer, growing fainter and fainter as they receded, till the last, dim and indistinct, could hardly be told from the blue background of the great, over-arching dome above.

Down the slope and to the west the chieftain could make out the hazy smoke from the fires of the People of the Mountain Caves, though the figures of the men and women were too small for even his keen eye to distinguish; his mind flew back to the former visitation of the Great Sickness, when he was still a young man, and his very soul grew faint within him at the thought of another such pestilence.

Stooping, he drank deeply of the water, then, stripping the garment of lion's hide from his body—his weapons he had left in his cave—he plunged into the basin of the spring.

The icy water sent a shiver through his limbs, and he gasped from the shock, but resolutely he immersed himself so that not the smallest portion of his body might remain unpurified; he rubbed himself all over with his hands, dipped under again, and leaped out, standing stock-still in the sun till every drop of water had dried from his skin.

He repeated the ceremony of purification a second time and a third, then, leaving his garment lying by the spring, he passed on two or three hundred paces along the ridge, till the sound of the water overflowing the basin and dashing down the side of the mountain was lost to his ears.

Here he halted, turned his face to the sky, and, standing erect with his arms spread, prayed aloud to the god of his worship.

"Oh, Great Father O-Ma-Ken, who seest all things, I, Na-t'san, Son of the Red God, Great Chieftain of the Ta-an, cry aloud to Thee for mercy! Look down upon Thy stricken people, on whom is fallen the Great Sickness; hear their prayers; let the pestilence depart from them; and grant me, I pray Thee, a sign whereby Thy favor may be known."

He ceased, bowed reverently, and with slow steps took his way to where, a little distance apart, a weather-worn rock shaped like a rude armchair offered a natural seat; here he sat down, leaning back, and began his fast.

For thrice seven days the Great Chieftain sat on the mountaintop, and during that time no morsel of food passed his lips; twice each day, at dawn and at sunset, he went to the spring and drank of the Water of Prayer, each time praying aloud to the Great Father, using as nearly as he might the words of his first supplication, and returning straightway to his seat, where he spent the long hours from dawn to sunset and from sunset to dawn, naked as when he came from the water.

And during all that time there came no answer to his prayer; no vision, no sign from O-Ma-Ken, till Na-t'san began to despair. Once a hyena, ranging over the hills, passed near where he sat, and, drawn by the scent of flesh, came and sniffed inquiringly at the chieftain's feet and knees and hands; Na-t'san did not move; he was under the protection of O-Ma-Ken, and the beast, recognizing by the body-scent that the man had no fear, snarled and passed on; he dared not attack one who, unfearing, sat so still.

At length, during the night that followed the twenty-first day of the fast, visions began to come to the chieftain, hallucinations born in his over-wrought brain, visions generated by starvation, the earliest sign of their coming being when the rocks that lay all about under the light of the waning moon commenced to waver and dance, their outlines shifting and quivering and melting in the half light to strange forms, changing as the chieftain watched to scattered ranks of dead and dying tribesmen, who, stricken with the Great Sickness, tossed and turned and writhed in the agonies of the disease, lifting wasted arms to the silent sky, turning their sunken eyes upward and sending their groans and cries to the unheeding air.

The heart sickened within the chieftain as he watched, and at length, unable to bear the terrible sight, he closed his eyes, but still he could hear, through the sighing of the wind, the groans of the dying. He opened his eyes once more, and the vision had passed; the rocks had taken on their true form, and lay still under the moon.

Presently Na-t'san's eyes were caught and held by a little

patch of light far down the slope of the mountain. "Some flowering bush," he thought, but as he watched the spot of light it began to grow, to change in outline, to draw nearer; closer and closer it came, moving slowly but steadily up the hill, and at length he saw the form of a human being approaching.

Nearer and nearer it drew, and now the chieftain could make out the figure of a woman as the spot took definite form. On she came, halting but a few paces from Na-t'san, and he felt that this was no vision, but a real woman of flesh and blood. The wasted forms of the dying tribesmen had been but half real; there had been an undercurrent of thought in his mind that they might be part of a dream, but this figure, this woman—she was real, sentient, alive!

Tall she was, and beautifully formed, her light-brown hair, unbound, lifting and waving in the slight breeze that blew always on the mountain; clad in the skin of a white leopard from the Country of the Snows, the garment reaching down to the middle of her thighs and looped up over her left shoulder, leaving bare the arms and shoulder and the right breast; beautiful of feature as of form, carrying her head proudly and moving with exquisite grace and dignity, she was indeed fit bride for O-Ma-Ken, the Great Father.

By the star blazing on her forehead, Na-t'san knew her, and breathed to himself reverently: "The Star-Marked One!" With difficulty he restrained himself from falling at her feet—he must remain seated till the Great Father himself spoke! Smiling gently, the Star-Marked One addressed Na-t'san:

"Na-t'san, Great Chieftain of the Ta-an," said she, "the

Great Father is pleased with you. He sends me and bids me say to you that the Ta-an are doomed; take, therefore, Va-m'rai your wife, gather your belongings, and flee to the Land of the Dying Sun, leaving the tribesmen to their fate; save them you cannot, but save yourself you may. This from the Great Father, through me, His bride."

The chieftain was puzzled; the figure was that of the Star-Marked One, but the words were the words of evil—a chieftain of the Ta-an desert his people? Na-t'san shook his head—a spasm of wrath passed over the face of the woman—and the chieftain knew! He smiled—the figure of the woman was distorted and her face twisted with rage—suddenly she shot up to twice her former height—wavered—vanished like a puff of smoke—and once more Na-t'san was alone on the mountain.

And now the moon was sinking toward the western horizon, a blood-red moon, huge, bulbous, false in outline; even as Na-t'san watched it split into three moons, that whirled wildly about in mad circles, shooting off at times far up toward the zenith, and falling back once more to their place low down in the sky. Great clouds were drawing athwart the heavens, and as the chieftain turned his eyes again down the slope the rocks began for the second time to move, taking different forms.

But this time they were not the forms of men; fiends, devils, horrible things grew and danced and swam before the chieftain, now drawing nearer, now receding. The Faceless Man, grotesque in outline, twisted and writhing, a white, misty blur where his face should be; the Great White Wolf, that moves on silent feet—close to Na-t'san he rushed, his green eyes blazing, his red mouth wide open, slavering, his white teeth splotched with red, then, whirling, joined again the mad devils' dance that spun and swam and reeled about the chieftain's chair of rocks; one of the devils of the air, leather-winged, but huge as an eagle, swooped at Na-t'san, but he sat firm, and the giant beast swerved quickly, the tip of his wing brushing the chieftain's ear, and the rush of air, clammy and ghastly as that of a tomb, sending a chill through his veins.

And now, more terrible than all, Na-t'san could vaguely see, drifting like a silent mist, transparent, the rocks showing through its wavering outlines, that most dread of all the spirits of the Place of Evil, loosed for this night to carry freezing fear to his soul.

Even the chieftain's eyes, sharpened and made keen by prayer and fasting, could hardly make out the vague, intangible form; none other could have caught the faintest glimpse of it—it was the frightful, the dreaded Invisible Thing, formless, inchoate, unseen of men, that springs silent and deadly on one in the forest, tearing the soul from the body and carrying it to the Place of Evil.

Sick terror flooded the chieftain's soul, his blood grew cold, and his bones turned to water within him—instantly a great triumphant sound swelled from the fiends that rode the air—halting in their dance, they turned to where the chieftain sat—rose high above him—in vast, horrible, ghastly flood poured down upon him—rigid he sat, commanding his shaking limbs by the force of his mighty will—he closed his eyes—he breathed a prayer; "Great Father, save me!"—he opened his eyes—the evil ones had vanished, and once more the mountaincrest lay empty and silent under the moon.

Then the clouds that covered the sky, through the breaks of which the moon peered, began to swirl and take form; slowly at first, then faster and faster they drew together into one mighty mass, and the whirling ceased. The great gray mass drooped lower, touched the mountain, and slowly, slowly, with stately, measured movement, came toward Na-t'san, and as it came it grew lighter and lighter, filled with an unearthly radiance that, piercing through the cloud, grew momently more intense.

Within fifty paces of the chieftain it halted, and he, blinded by the light, dropped his eyes, but could yet feel the glow beating on the lids. Then from the cloud issued a voice, mighty as the rushing of the storm with the power behind the words, but restrained and gentle, soothing beyond belief, and at the sound Na-t'san sprang from his seat and fell upon his knees, bending his forehead to the earth.

"Na-t'san, Great Chieftain, well hast thou borne the trial, and I am pleased with thee. For thy sake will I spare the Ta-an, and this My word shalt thou carry to thy tribe. The pool from which the tribesmen drink is accursed, and they are therefore poisoned; gather them then together, warrior and artist and priest, man and woman, child and suckling; gather weapons and garments and tools, and make thy way, leading them, to the Land of the Dying Sun, where you shall find a home. My hand is over thee and them on the way and in the new home. And drink no more from the pool, but of springs. I have spoken."

Na-t'san remained on his knees till the light had faded utterly, then rose and made his way to the Water of Prayer, where he drank deeply, resumed his garment of lion's hide, and took his way down the mountain, stumbling and falling often in the dim light, for the moon had sunk, and he was weak from fasting.

Just at dawn, haggard and drawn, he reached his cave, and Va-m'rai, who had been on the watch for him, brought him hot food, pieces cut from a new-slain bison and roasted over the fire. Having eaten, the chieftain flung himself on his couch of skins and rested for a time, then called his wife.

"Go fetch Ja-ko," he said, but Va-m'rai did not stir.

"Ja-ko is dead," she replied. "The day following that on which you went to seek a sign, Ja-ko, the chief priest, was found in his cave, his soul having fled into the Long Dark."

"The Great Sickness?" asked Na-t'san, but Va-m'rai shook her head, tears springing to her eyes.

"Nay, the Great Sickness was not upon him; he died from a dagger-thrust."

The chieftain sat upright, fear dawning in his eyes.

"Ken-o-san?" he asked, and Va-m'rai dropped her head lower.

"The slayer is not known; none saw Ja-ko die. But—but—Ken-o-san's own dagger lay beside the body, and Ken-o-san, gathering his warriors to him, has fled into the forest!"

A spasm of agony crossed the chieftain's face, quickly controlled, and his mouth set in a firm, hard line, his white brows drawing together. He rose to his feet, strode out from the cave, and seated himself by the fire, saying:

"Fetch Sar-men-ko, second of the priests, and Ka-tem, son of Ka-tem, tamer of beasts."

Va-m'rai hurried on the errand, and Na-t'san sat by the fire, his face buried in his hands. Presently the chieftain's wife returned, the two men hurrying after, and at the sound of their steps Na-t'san looked up. But for the misery in his sunken eyes none could have guessed what he suffered, and he spoke firmly.

"Sar-men-ko," he said, "Ja-ko, the-chief priest being dead, his soul journeying into the Long Dark, you are henceforth chief priest. Gather together the tribesmen, with their women and children; let each take his possessions; let those too sick to travel be carried on litters. How many have died of the Great Sickness?"

"Two tens and seven, Great Chieftain. And twice that number lie sick."

"Let the sick be carried on litters. We go to the Land of the Dying Sun; it is the word of O-Ma-Ken, Great Father of the Ta-an. And let none drink from the pool, but from springs; when the sun rises tomorrow we go. Make haste!"

Sar-men-ko bowed and departed on his errand, and soon there rose a wailing from the women of the tribe; but the men labored in silence, preparing for the long journey.

In the mean time, Na-t'san addressed Ka-tem:

"Ka-tem, Trainer of Beasts," he said, "you have said that Menzono the wolf, taught by you and kept in your cave, can follow a trail through the forest."

Ka-tem bowed.

"An old trail?"

Ka-tem shrugged his shoulders.

"At times," he replied. "At others, not."

"Take then Menzono, holding him in leash; take fifty warriors of the Ta-an, and seek Ken-o-san in the forest. Bring him to me alive if it may be, but if not, then dead.

Bringing him, follow us to the Land of the Dying Sun, overtaking us as soon as may be."

"Have you aught of Ken-o-san's, that Menzono, smelling it, may know what trail to follow?"

Na-t'san rose, stepped into the cave, and returned with a worn, discarded garment of fawn skin, tanned soft in the smoke of the fire. Suffering written in every line of his haggard face, he handed this silently to Ka-tem, who took it, bowed, and departed.

Within an hour Ka-tem, holding Menzono in leash, and at the head of fifty warriors, each full armed with lance and throwing-stick and darts, with ax and dagger of flint, was on the trail of Ken-o-san and his men. Behind, the People of the Mountain Caves made hurried preparation for the long journey to the Land of the Dying Sun.

Possessions were gathered and wrapped in skins for carrying, tools and weapons, garments, flint, and fire-stone; meat was hastily dried over the fires, roots and berries collected; from cave to cave went men and women, taking a last farewell of the homes where they had been born, where they had lived so long, where parents and friends had lived and died; and everywhere rose the sound of wailing and sorrow at leaving their homes on the slope of the great mountain.

Last of all, litters were made for the sick, saplings being cut from the forest, crosspieces tied to them with thongs, and skins fastened to the oblong frames thus made; four men would carry each litter.

All through the night the work went on, each man, each woman, lying down to sleep as his or her share was completed, and all through the night the sound of lamentation swelled along the bench of rock where blazed and flamed, leaped and sank, the fires of the Ta-an. And when the dawn broke, first gray then red, and the great sun rose in majesty above the eastern hills, the People of the Mountain Caves, Na-t'san at their head, took one last farewell of the home of their forefathers since time began, and resolutely set their faces to the south for the first stage of the long, long journey to the Land of the Dying Sun.

3

THE GREAT DISCOVERY

FIVE DAYS' JOURNEY to the south of the homes of the People of the Mountain Caves, deep in the heart of the forest, Ken-o-san and his men had made their camp. It was the leader's plan to make this a permanent home, buying or stealing women from neighboring tribes, letting a village grow up, and so perhaps establishing a new tribe.

Therefore, Ken-o-san and his followers had first built a stockade for protection against wild beasts and against wandering tribes or small bands of foes. The trees had been cleared from an oval space some fifty paces broad and seventy or eighty in length, the place being chosen because but a few small trees grew there at the time the outlaws came.

Straight, sound trees, of the bigness of a man's leg were hewn down, trimmed of their branches, and the smaller ends sharpened to a point, the butts being sunk deep in the ground, two handbreadths apart; the stakes, when placed, were fastened together near the top with twisted strands of creeping vines, and thus a fence was made, twice the height of a tall man, the posts being slanted outward at the top so that it would be almost impossible to scale the barrier, which neither man nor beast could overleap.

A gateway, just wide enough for one man to pass, was left, and a heavy gate of thorn-bushes was hung to this by thongs of rawhide, a stout stake, butt to the door and sharp end thrust into the ground, serving to hold it against outside pressure, but being easily removed to allow of opening the passage.

A score of warriors could easily defend such a stronghold against ten times their number—if the attackers were not armed with fire. But Ken-o-san had foreseen this also; a little brook, running through the center of the stockade, furnished drink for the holders, and at the same time made possible defence even against the Red God, and the entrance and exit of the stream were protected by heaps of the same thorn-bushes from which the gate was made.

Altogether, it was a well-planned, well-constructed—though rude—fortification, and Ken-o-san surveyed it with no little pride when the work was complete. Inside, a dozen small huts, of poles thrust slanting into the ground with branches wattled across and broad leaves laid over them, gave shelter from storms, and these, ranged in a semicircle, fronted toward the gateway, the cooking-fire being built between them and the gate.

"It is well done," said L'vu, as he and Ken-o-san examined the finished work, and the leader agreed.

For some days Ken-o-san and his men lived here in quiet, making weapons, replenishing their stock of darts, eating, sleeping, hunting, or resting, and the leader was beginning to think of a raiding expedition, when a strange thing occurred, which took the whole of his attention for a time, and indirectly changed the entire current of his life.

Sar-no-m'rai had been hunting, and it happened that

the thong of his throwing-stick, fastening the cup-shaped head to the long and flexible shaft, had come loose and was dragging. To prevent the thong from catching in the brush, he had tied the free end about the handhold of the shaft, and, returning, had laid the stick and his quiver of darts down by the fire, that he might skin and butcher the fawn he had slain.

Ken-o-san, watching, had picked up the throwing-stick, and sat idly twanging the taut thong, as one might pluck the string of a harp. Still idly and unthinking, he laid a dart across the stick, drawing back the string, the butt of the dart resting against it, and released it.

To his amazement, the dart sped, whirring, across the enclosure, above the stockade, and disappeared in the forest, and Ken-o-san realized, as he watched its flight, that with but little effort he had sent the dart from the bent bow with far greater force than he could have thrown it from a stick.

Interested, he tried again, pulling back the string till the head of the dart lay flush with the shaft of the throwing-stick, and once more the dart sped, this time burying the flint head deep in one of the posts of the fence. Again and again he tried, and at last, returning the throwing-stick to Sar-no-m'rai, who had watched in astonishment, he went to where there lay a pile of sticks, seasoned, waiting to be made into shafts for lances, and chose one with care.

Through the rest of that day and all the next he labored, shaping the wood to his liking, then tied a thong of deer-hide along it, and bent his bow.

The thong slipped, and after some thought, Ken-o-san cut a notch in each end with his hunting-knife of flint, and found, bending the bow once more, that the string now held. He then selected one of his own darts and tried its flight.

Straight and true it soared, far more distant than he could have thrown it, but he felt that he could have sent it farther had he been able to draw the bow more deeply, and he straightway set to work to make longer darts and a larger bow, and after a week of labor he had a bow that overtopped his head as he stood erect, by more than two handbreadths, with a stock of darts full half the length of the bow.

With these he experimented, learning to shoot with the new weapon, and finding, among other things, that the dart could be kept from slipping off the string by cutting a shallow nick in the butt. With this new weapon he practised, telling none but L'vu what he was doing, and L'vu it was who suggested an improvement which Ken-o-san adopted.

The leader had found that for all his care in selecting straight, smooth, well-balanced pieces of wood for his arrows, they did not always fly true; they went farther than a thrown dart, and for much of their flight went true, but, the force waning slightly, they wabbled and went astray.

L'vu had once seen a bird who had lost his tail in combat trying to fly, and the wabbling flight of the arrow reminded him of the ridiculous spectacle; he suggested to Ken-o-san the addition of a tail of feathers, and it proved a success. True, the feathers could not be attached behind the shaft, but a few tightly bound about the shaft slightly forward of the nock steadied the flight of the arrow.

The new weapon perfected to his satisfaction, Ken-o-san practised with it for a few days, then invited the band to watch; to see what he had done. Going to an open space in the forest, on a rocky ridge, he asked L'vu to speed a shaft from his throwing-stick, sending it as far as his strength would permit.

L'vu stepped forward from the group, chose his dart with care, grasped his throwing-stick, tested it with a swing or two, dried his hand on his wolf-skin garment, and laid the dart along the stick, butt resting in the cup carved from the thigh-bone of a sheep, his three outer fingers grasping the haft of the stick, his thumb and forefinger steadying the dart; throwing his left foot well forward, he bent backward, swinging the throwing-stick far out behind, the cup nearly touching the ground, then with a mighty sweep he brought his arm forward and up, over and down, his giant body swinging with the swing of his long arm, the dart flying from the stick at its highest pitch.

Far down the clearing it sped, and a murmur of approval rose from the warriors as they watched its flight.

"Run, Sen-va, and fetch it, counting the paces of the throw," said Ken-o-san, and a young man leaped from the group.

"Set up a branch where it fell," shouted Ken-o-san, and Sen-va waved his hand in token that he had heard. As the warriors watched, the messenger obeyed, and, returning, gave the dart to Ken-o-san.

"Twenty tens and seven paces, master," cried Sen-va, panting, and the warriors nodded; two hundred and seven paces was a good throw.

"Can any better it?" asked Ken-o-san, looking about the group, but none offered; some smiled, eying one another, and some shook their heads, but none stepped forward.

"Lend me your throwing-stick, L'vu," said Ken-o-san. "It may be that I can speed a dart to a more distant rest."

Taking the dart and throwing-stick L'vu had used, Ken-o-san prepared carefully, and hurled from where L'vu had stood; all could see that the dart fell beyond the branch, and Sen-va, running, returned with the message:

"Ten paces and two past L'vu's flight, master." This was indeed a mighty throw, one worthy of a chieftain, and the warriors buzzed their admiration.

"Look now; watch well!" said Ken-o-san, and he lifted his bow from where it lay in the grass, the warriors craning their necks to see; they knew their leader had been working at some strange new weapon, and were eager for a sight of it.

Carefully Ken-o-san tested the bow, plucking the string gently, so that it hummed like a hive of bees; carefully he selected his best arrow and fitted the nock to the string. Bracing himself, he threw out his left arm, the arrow resting on the thumb of his hand, clenched about the middle of the bow; the fore and middle fingers of his right hand were hooked about the string, the butt of the arrow nestling between them; he lifted his left arm, rigid as stone, till the arrow pointed half-way between horizon and zenith, then pulling back his powerful right arm—the muscles rippling under the shining skin like those of Su, the leopard—till his fingers touched his ear, he stood an instant, a magnificent statue, still as though carved from ivory.

He opened his two fingers—the great bow twanged with a deep hum—and swift as a flash of light the arrow flew.

Far, far beyond the upright branch it sped, a fleeting streak against the green of leaf and tree, and at the farther end of the glade it buried itself in the forest, lost to sight of the watching men.

A gasp of astonishment, a murmur, and then a swelling shout from the throats of all as the meaning of this strange thing dawned upon them, and Sen-va, for the third time, ran, presently he returned and knelt at the feet of Ken-o-san.

"Master," he said, "forty tens and nine of paces from here the forest closes in; your dart has gone beyond that distance and is lost among the trees!"

Four hundred and nine paces and more! And L'vu's throw was two hundred and seven! Silence fell on the group of warriors; they gazed from one to another, and at length L'vu, stepping forward, without, a word fell on his knees and raised Ken-o-san's hand to his own bowed head. Rising, he stepped aside, and Kan-to followed, then Sar-no-m'rai, and after them each and every one of the band knelt in reverence before their leader. Their homage paid, they stood back, and Ken-o-san, his eyes shining with pride, spoke:

"To-morrow, and in the days to come, shall each among you learn to make and use the new weapon. Each one shall be armed therewith—and you shall say who can stand against us in battle!"

Talking, eagerly questioning their leader, the band returned to the stockade, where each man examined the new weapon, noting length and weight and balance, in preparation for the one he would make for himself when the next day's sun should dawn.

For some time after the stockade was the scene of busy labor. Raids and women alike forgotten, each of Ken-o-san's band set to work to make him a bow and a store of arrows and to learn to use them, to shoot swift and straight with the new weapon, and there was great laughter over the first efforts of the learners—the arrows did not always find the mark!

The rawhide thongs used for bow-strings did not work well; wet, they grew soft and stretched, and, drying out, were hard and stiff, so Ken-o-san experimented constantly, trying one thing after another in the search for better strings, but to no avail.

Indeed, it was not till more than a year later, when many stirring events had passed, that he found the answer in the intestines of a sheep, strips, of which, twisted and dried, proved the perfect string, not only for this purpose, but for many other uses as well. But in the mean time the rawhide thongs were renewed often, and, this done, they served their turn.

Ken-o-san's men were gradually arming themselves, and some had grown so expert that they used the new weapon in hunting, discarding entirely the, old throwing-stick, and darts; the bow not only sent an arrow farther than a man could throw it, but it likewise sped it straighter and with greater force.

One day Kan-to, Sar-no-m'rai, and ten others returned from a hunt, bringing startling news. Three days had they been gone, and they came in with much food. Two wild cattle, slain by Kan-to, both, were carried on poles. The feet of the beasts were tied, the poles thrust through, and four men, two at each end, hoisted the poles to their shoulders and staggered through the forest.

Two other men bore each a burden, fastened in the skins

of fawns, one load being edible roots—tubers—the other acorns, and these loads were dropped within the stockade, where the band set to work to prepare food, some skinning and butchering the cattle, others washing the tubers for roasting in the fire, while still others hulled and crushed the acorns, washing the pounded meats over and over to take out the bitter taste; this done, they would dry and grind the meats to powder, mix this powder to a paste with water, and bake a rude, unleavened bread.

Kan-to and Sar-no-m'rai, however, hurried straight to Ken-o-san, bowing before him. Kan-to, the elder, spoke:

"Chieftain," he said, "we bring news."

"Speak!" replied Ken-o-san.

"Ka-tem, with fifty warriors, seeks us, we being outlawed."

Ken-o-san thought a moment; then with a swift flash of intuition, cried:

"Menzono!" and Kan-to bowed.

"Can he find us?" inquired Ken-o-san, and Kan-to, smiling, shook his head.

"Nay, chieftain," he answered. "Stealing close, Sar-no-m'rai, with an arrow, slew Menzono. Our trail we blinded well, and but by chance may Ka-tem now find our camp. But listening to their words as they spoke at evening round their fire, we learned other news of import.

"The Great Sickness has smitten the Ta-an, and they go, men and women and children, from Na-t'san, the Great Chieftain, to the very lowest, to seek a new home among the Little Hairy People. Even now are they on the march, having passed us half a day's journey to westward, as Sar-no-m'rai and I, overhearing the words of Ka-tem's men, have proven; we searched and found their trail, not more than seven days old—a very path through the forest, the whole tribe having moved along it, tramping down the grass as does Do-m'rai, the Hill that Walks."

Ken-o-san sat for a time in thought, his chin cupped in his hand, elbow resting on knee, while the two messengers stood respectfully, waiting. At last he spoke:

"To-morrow at dawn we move. Pass the word among the warriors, letting each man take weapons and food for a journey. We go to follow the Ta-an, not seeking battle, but waiting a chance to take what we most desire, women for the tribe we seek to found. It may be that the Great Father will send His favor upon us, and I shall seize Nan-ai, whom I greatly wish for wife. If not, another, perchance, and a wife for each of us. But say to the men that we seek not to slay; by craft and not by force must we gain our desire. Outlaws though we be, yet are we not fallen so low as to slay our own tribesmen. I have said!"

Kan-to and Sar-no-m'rai bowed and withdrew, but still the young leader sat leaning on his hand and gazing toward the busy group about the fire. Little did he see of what passed; his thoughts were far away, and ever there rose before him the tender face and slim, graceful form of Nan-ai, whom he loved so well.

It was with no little regret that he reviewed his life of violence—violence that had made him a wanderer, an outlaw, the hands of his own tribesmen turned against him; violence that begat violence, for now he was on his way to take the woman he desired, since she might not give herself to him with honor; to take her by might, even as the tribe of the Gra took their women, and as did the black men who lived in the forest.

And even greater outrage might arise, for should he meet with one of the Ta-an his life was forfeit, his hands must keep his head, and on him might fall the dishonor of slaying one of his own tribe.

He wondered how Nan-ai would come to him; willingly, or must he drag her by force of arms? He could not tell, but ardently he wished that he had chosen another path, that he had followed the wise words of Na-t'san, his grandfather, preparing himself for the chieftaincy that should be his. Presently L'vu, bringing food: roast meat, and berries, and hard, unleavened bread of acorn flour, came and sat beside him, and the young leader roused himself from his reverie to eat, then saying:

"L'vu, at earliest dawn we take the trail," went to his hut, and rolled himself in his skins to sleep. Presently all the camp save only the sentinel slept, one man remaining on guard, to keep up the fire and watch and listen for danger. Twice during the night, as the stars swung overhead in their course, the guard was changed, and when the first faint gray of dawn appeared to pale the stars, the guard, first heaping, up the fire, roused the sleeping men, stirring the ribs of each with the butt of his spear till the sleeper woke and got to his feet.

Ken-o-san slept last; not till the morning meal was prepared and the burdens ready did L'vu, going to the leader's hut, rap gently against the ground beside Ken-o-san's head with his lance. Ken-o-san, opening his eyes, lay still for an instant, then leaped to his feet and went out, L'vu following, marveling as ever at the way the leader woke, not like a man, but like a wild beast.

Others of the tribesmen, roused by a noise, sat up and looked about, then seeing that all was well, got to their feet slowly, with much grunting and stretching, but Ken-o-san, waking, lay still; eyes open, not a muscle moved, till he knew the source of the sound or the touch that woke him; then, satisfied of its origin, whether for good or for evil, he was instantly afoot, wide-awake.

This habit, with his trick of sleeping lightly and waking easily, made him a dangerous man; it was difficult to steal upon him unawares, and more than one enemy, trusting to the moments of half-asleep that hamper the acts of most men, had died ere he knew whence came the blow that struck him down.

This trick held good with Na-t'san, and old men of the tribe had said that Snorr, chieftain before Na-t'san, had owned it too, and L'vu, following his leader from the hut, wondered dimly if it was the mark of all chieftains; did it betoken some strange quality of mind that set them above common men? He could not tell, and now was no time to consider it—the band was about to march.

When the sun stood over the tops of the trees, Ken-o-san and his men came upon the track left by the Ta-an, and the leader, looking, said to Kan-to:

"Indeed, you spoke truth! It is even as the track of Do-m'rai! And now we follow, keeping hidden."

So for twice seven days they marched, Ken-o-san and his band, keeping always in the track save when hunting. Five days after they first turned into the track, Ken-o-san caught sight, one afternoon, of a worn-out quiver of fawn-skin, cast aside along the trail, and, something about it seeming familiar, he examined it closely, then turned to Sar-no-m'rai.

"Sar-no-m'rai," said he, "know you this?"

Sar-no-m'rai nodded, not speaking, for he was a man little given to speech, never making use of two words when one would do.

"Ka-tem's?" asked Ken-o-san, falling into his follower's trick, and Sar-no-m'rai nodded again.

"Ka-tem and his band have then joined the Ta-an? They have given over the search for us?" Once more Sar-no-m'rai nodded.

"How far back?" went on Ken-o-san.

"Five days."

"And how long has this been known to you?"

"Five days."

"You read the trails where they joined?" A nod from Sar-no-m'rai.

"Why, then, did you not speak?"

"Chieftain," answered Sar-no-m'rai, "the trail was plain; in truth it seemed to me that you yourself would see it."

"Plain to you, perchance!" said Ken-o-san, then turning to L'vu and Kan-to: "was it plain to your eyes as well?"

"No, chieftain," they chorused, "it was not known to us."

Ken-o-san turned once more to Sar-no-m'rai, admiration in his face.

"Sar-no-m'rai," he said, "well are you named the Eyes That Walk By Night! Skilled am I in reading signs, but not such sight as yours can I boast! Have you perchance seen aught else; is aught known to you that I have not seen?"

Sar-no-m'rai meditated, then replied:

"We are in the country of the Gra, of whom Su, the Leopard, is chieftain."

"Do they follow us?"

Sar-no-m'rai shrugged his shoulders.

"Can I know?" he asked. "But soon or late they will find this track."

"And they will attack the Ta-an? There will be a battle? That is your thought?"

Sar-no-m'rai nodded once more, and Ken-o-san fell into thought, standing with arms folded and head bent, while about him his men waited in silence under the high-arching trees. At length he lifted his head and spoke:

"Good!" he said. "Follow on! It may be that in the rush and confusion of war we may find what we seek!" And once again the band moved on.

On the fifteenth day of the pursuit Ken-o-san and his men topped a little rise and halted to look over the country before plunging into the valley that lay spread out before them. The leader, searching the valley, caught sight of a slight smoke a day's journey or more ahead to the south, and, pointing to it, asked of Sar-no-m'rai:

"The Ta-an?"

Sar-no-m'rai nodded, and pointed far to the east. Ken-o-san looked long, but could see nothing, and he asked:

"What?"

"Smoke."

"I cannot see it; the Gra?"

Sar-no-m'rai nodded, then pointing to the low range of hills which closed the valley to the south, said:

"Beyond those mountains lies the Great Blue Water. Once have I been here; while hunting."

"Can the Great Blue Water be seen from the hills?"

Sar-no-m'rai nodded again.

"A day's journey beyond. Once over those hills the Ta-an will turn toward the Dying Sun. The Gra have word, brought by their hunters, of the People of the Mountain Caves, and they follow for battle."

Ken-o-san looked at Sar-no-m'rai in amazement, then turned to L'vu and Kan-to, shaking his head, and back again.

"How know you that?" he asked. "Are you not romancing?"

Sar-no-m'rai pointed to a spot north of that where he had indicated the fires of the Gra. "Other fires," he answered. "The women and children follow slowly, while the warriors press on to overtake the Ta-an."

Ken-o-san gazed all about, at the broad and fertile valley, grown with trees and brush and grass, that lay at his feet, east and west along the valley he looked, then back over the forest through which he had come, thinking deeply the while. Presently he said:

"This night we make camp here; tomorrow we follow on, but leave the track, striking off there." He pointed to the southwest. "We will pass the hills between the Ta-an and the Dying Sun, lying in wait for them to come. So shall we spare ourselves many weary strides, yet be near when the Gra attack. A fireless camp tonight."

So the men, supping on flesh dried in the smoke of their earlier fires, wrapped themselves in their hides of lion and leopard, of wolf and bear, and lay down to rest under the stars, thinking with eager anticipation of the great battle they should see ere many days had passed.

4

PRISONER TO THE GRA

KEN-O-SAN, OUTLAWED AND driven from the tribe, pursued by armed men seeking to avenge the death of the chief priest, another suitor offered himself for the hand of Nan-ai. This was Mat-kai-no, son to Ban-ku, and therefore cousin to Nan-ai herself, and, living close to her, both in the mountain caves and on the long journey, he had much chance to press his suit.

Often was he with the girl, and many gifts he brought her, saving for her the hearts and marrow-bones from the beasts slain by him while hunting food for the tribe; from bushes he plucked the daintiest berries for her use, and ever he was at hand to aid her did she grow weary on the march.

But Nan-ai would not listen to his words of love; her heart was with Ken-o-san, a wanderer, nor could Mat-kai-no or his father, Ban-ku, move her to look with favor on the young man, though he was fit to mate with any maiden of the Ta-an, being tall and strong and handsome, forward in hunting—albeit it was whispered among the warriors that he was not so forward in battle—and rich in worldly goods. Even when Ban-ku reminded the girl that she could never wed Ken-o-san, she did not yield, vowing that she would have none other.

"Bethink you, Nan-ai," said Ban-ku one evening, "Ken-o-san is outlaw, his life forfeit, and were it not so, were he among us once more, you could not marry him. It is disgrace to a woman of the Ta-an to mate with a murderer, and when to his crime he has added that of sacrilege, in that he has slain the chosen one of the Great Father— This being so, why will you not choose my son? Rich is he, honored among the Ta-an, and not unhandsome. Can you not yield? He loves you well, and tenderly will he care for you!"

But Nan-ai burst into tears, and when Ban-ku pressed her to answer she leaped to her feet, her eyes flashing, and stamping her little foot, she cried:

"Never! Never! If I cannot be bride to Ken-o-san a maiden will I live! Never will I wed, with Mat-kai-no or another! Never!"

And so Ban-ku returned to his son, saying:

"Her heart is still with the outcast. Let be; time brings many changes! Do you cease to speak to her of love, but be patient and watchful of her comfort. So shall you at length wear down her patience!" And with this Mat-kai-no was forced to be content for the time.

But Ban-ku was wrong; even had Ken-o-san been dead, and had Nan-ai given over all thought of him, still would she not have wedded Mat-kai-no, for she hated and feared him, not showing her thoughts, for she loved his father well.

Once in the forest she had come on Mat-kai-no torturing a wolf he had caught in a trap; he had bound the beast's jaws that it might neither bite nor howl, he had bound its limbs to four trees, and was slowly flaying the hide from the living flesh, delighting in the wretched beast's frantic and futile struggles.

Tenderness with beasts was no part of a warrior of the Ta-an, nor of a woman of the tribe, but wanton cruelty was not in their character, and the girl, horrified at such brutality, stepped in, and ere the young man could prevent, she seized his ax and with one merciful blow freed the tortured animal from its agony. And though for the sake of her uncle, who had cherished her as might a father, she had said no word of Mat-kai-no's cruelty, from that day she could not see the young man or hear his voice or have him near her without an inward shudder.

About the time that the Ta-an reached the last valley, before climbing the hills that sloped down to the Great Blue Water, a number of warriors were sent out to hunt, to get food for the tribesmen, the Ta-an remaining camped on the northern slope of the hills, for it was summer, and there were no cold storms to fear.

Among these warriors was Mat-kai-no, for he was skilled in the hunt, never returning with empty hands, and so for three or four days he traveled eastward, toward the Land of the Rising Sun, following along the base of the hills, resting each night where darkness overtook him.

He would begin to look about, as dusk was drawing toward, for a level spot near water, and here, gathering sticks to keep his fire through the night, he would cook meat, wrap himself in skins, and lie down.

He could, it is true, have found game nearer where the Ta-an were camped—indeed, he did make several kills on the way—but part of his task, equally important with the other, was to search for a pass through the hills, which, although low, rose steep and rugged by the encampment, almost impassable to women and children, though the warriors alone could have scaled them.

Others had gone to the westward on a like search, but Mat-kai-no, ever drawn on by the changing contour of the hills, pressed forward, till on the fifth day he found himself in a dense jungle, through which he could hardly make his way, the ground beneath the trees being blocked by thick undergrowth.

Mat-kai-no had about determined to retrace his journey and report that he could find no path when suddenly he broke through the screen of underbrush into a well-worn, trampled trail, one of the many game trails that threaded the jungle, leading toward some watering-place or other. It was well-beaten and distinct, wide enough for two men to walk abreast, a veritable lane through the jungle, the ground-growths worn through to the hard brown earth.

Mat-kai-no paused and looked in both directions, then turned to the right, walking in leisurely fashion toward the hills, idly swinging his lance in one hand, his ax and throwing-stick in the other, following the twists and turns of the trail as it led toward higher ground.

Steadily the trail climbed, and it was in the hunter's mind that this might show him a way through or over the hills, when suddenly, unexpectedly, and without the slightest warning, as he turned a corner, the earth caved under his feet. Instantly he twisted sidewise, grasping at the brush which lined the trail, but to no effect; he did indeed clutch a branch of a bush, but it tore through his hands, scraping the skin from the palms, and the ground still gave under him; with snapping and cracking of wood, amid a shower of earth, Mat-kai-no fell, pieces of wood and quantities of dirt falling with him, till he brought up, one leg twisted under him, at the bottom of a pit. He was jarred and dazed by the shock, and for some time lay still, gathering his wits; then got to his feet and looked about.

Mat-kai-no knew well what had happened—many a time had he set just such a trap along a game trail—and it was with little hope of escape that he examined his prison, his eyes gradually growing accustomed to the dim half-light that filtered, greenish, through the opening by which he had fallen.

The pit was some three or four paces in length, and twice the height of a tall man in depth, its width at the top being that of the trail in which it was dug, though at the bottom it was twice as wide, the sides as well as the ends sloping outward to make them more difficult to climb.

Upright in the earth at the bottom were set half a dozen stakes as thick as a man's arm and nearly as tall as Mat-kai-no, and he realized that had he fallen on the sharpened point of one of these stakes he would in all probability have died agonizingly, perhaps quickly, perhaps slowly—cases had been known where men, so impaled, had lived through two rounds of the sun.

Fortunately, however, he had escaped death, and indeed was uninjured save for a bad twist his leg had received, and for a trifle of skin scraped from his side by one of the stakes. Idly he wondered for what kind of beast the trap was set, and he thought to himself that should Snorr-m'rai-no, the lion, the gigantic Fear that Walks the Night, come tumbling in, he himself would be little better off than had he fallen on the stakes.

Spurred by this thought, Mat-kai-no set himself to find a way out. He could not scale the walls, that he knew, but he might be able to escape, none the less, and for some moments he studied his prison carefully.

He chose the longest and stoutest of the stakes, grasped the upper end, and worked it back and forth till the butt was loosened in the ground, then drew it forth, turned it upside down, and rested the butt against the end of the pit, the stake slanting, then scrambled up it, his injured leg paining him mightily.

It was his plan to place his foot on the butt of the stake, hoping that with a strong leap he might be able to grasp the edge of the pit and draw himself up, and he was about to spring when he bethought him that should the ground at the edge give way or should the branches which covered and hid the opening prevent him from getting a grip, he would fall back, and this time perhaps be impaled. He slid down the stake forthwith, loosened, and drew out the others and laid them down on the ground, then climbed up once more, steadied himself, and sprang.

As he had feared, the earth at the edge of the pit broke under his hands, and he fell heavily to the bottom, the loosened dirt getting into his eyes and mouth.

Cursing and spitting, he rose, shook himself, and was about to try again, when he heard excited voices above, and looked up to see a man's face peering down through the opening. There was some busy chatter in a language Mat-kai-no could not understand, the branches were hastily torn from the mouth of the pit, and half a dozen eager faces looked down at Mat-kai-no's upturned countenance, silence falling on the group of trappers as they gazed.

Presently one spoke in the language of the Ta-an, though slowly and with difficulty, and in such strange accents that the prisoner could hardly make out what was said till it had been repeated several times.

"Send up your weapons first," said the stranger, lowering a rawhide thong into the pit, and though Mat-kai-no hesitated to part with them, he realized that he was in no position to make a fight, and tied ax and lance, throwing-stick, and quiver of darts to the thong, which was drawn up out of sight. Presently a stout strand of a climbing vine came down, and the trapper said:

"Knot it about your body, beneath the arms," and Mat-kai-no, obeying, was in turn hoisted to the earth's surface, to find himself surrounded by a group of men who instantly fell on him, tied his arms behind his back, and then stood back, looking at him with interest.

"Your name? Your tribe?" asked the one who had spoken before, and the captive replied:

"Mat-kai-no, of the Ta-an," whereat there was much jabbering and gesticulating among the group, till Mat-kai-no broke in:

"And you?"

"Warriors and hunters of the Gra," was the answer, and Mat-kai-no's heart sank; there was no doubt whatever in his mind of the fate in store for him; he would be taken—if all the tales were true—before the chieftain of the Gra, he would be sacrificed on their altar, his body eaten, and his skin made into a robe for one of the priests.

He wondered whether his skin would be taken before the sacrifice or after—the tales differed—and there flashed across his mind the memory of the wolf whose sufferings had so enraged Nan-ai; he remembered the beast's writhings, and sick terror flooded over him—he flung himself on the ground at the feet of his captors, crying aloud, screaming, imploring mercy, offering them great rewards if they would free him.

They looked at him in astonishment; they were not accustomed to see a prisoner show such abject, mortal fear—most of their captives defied them! Wondering, they looked from one to another, and Mat-kai-no heard the one who spoke the language of the Ta-an say something to his comrades, whereat they laughed. Groveling, Mat-kai-no heard in his own tongue the words:

"Get up! Walk!" and the point of a spear jabbed into his back warned him to obey. Sick and reeling with terror, his knees weak, he scrambled up and marched in the direction indicated, away from the hills.

All the rest of the day the party traveled, passing the water to which the trail led shortly after the start, and turning eastward on the farther bank of the stream, for here the brush thinned out, evergreens taking its place, and they could walk easily. Mat-kai-no went first, and one of the Gra, armed with lance and ax, followed close at his heels lest he try to escape, though, his hands bound, he could not in any case have run fast.

At sunset they camped—a cold camp—and Mat-kai-no, his first terror somewhat abating, observed his captors carefully, for he had never seen one of their tribe, and tales of their ferocity and cruelty were rife among the Ta-an, who had more than once, in past years, met them in battle, the People of the Mountain Caves always, by reason of better weapons, greater personal strength, and better training, emerging victorious from the war.

The prisoner, then, examined the warriors of the Gra closely, finding them very different from the men of his own tribe. They were smaller in stature, the tallest being no higher than Mat-kai-no's shoulder, this difference being mainly due to the shortness of their legs, for their bodies were large and powerful. Their arms were long, the hands hanging almost to the knees, this being due in part to the fact that the men stooped somewhat, slouching the shoulders and bending forward at the waist, whereas the Ta-an stood straight, even the old men carrying themselves more erect than these warriors of the Gra.

And in countenance the men of the Gra differed even more from those of Mat-kai-no's people, for their foreheads were low, their eyes small and deeply set, their cheekbones prominent, their noses flat and broad, with outward turned nostrils—though not so flat as those of the negro tribes—their teeth large, set in powerful jaw-bones, and their beards thin and scanty, though their bodies were heavily thatched with hair.

Altogether, though white of skin, the Gra reminded Mat-kai-no in no small measure of certain great apes he had once seen while hunting, and their garments of skins as well as their weapons were crude and rough compared to those of the Ta-an, so that the captive began to feel a certain measure of contempt for the men who had taken him prisoner, and hoped that he might be able to escape through trickery if not by force.

When the men of the Gra had fed and were preparing

to sleep Mat-kai-no called the one who spoke the language of the Ta-an and asked that his hands might be unbound.

"Rest is far from me," he said. "The thongs are cutting my wrists, and I am in pain. Free me, I beg; a guard can be set that I may not flee."

But Jen—he had told Mat-kai-no his name—examined the bonds, grunted, and lay down to sleep, leaving the captive tied. When the men of the Gra slept, as Mat-kai-no could tell by their heavy, raucous breathing, the prisoner began to try to work loose.

His hands did indeed pain terribly, for the bonds had in some degree stopped the flow of blood, and, fastened behind him, they could not easily be moved to loosen the thongs. Still, he had noticed that one of the Gra, lying down, had laid his ax beside instead of under him, and toward this Mat-kai-no slowly edged his way, reaching it after an hour or more of cautious approach. With difficulty he managed to lift the weapon, propped the blade up, slanting, on a root, and slowly and carefully sawed the thongs back and forth across the sharp edge of the flint, feeling one after another, cut through, give way.

At length, free, he rubbed his numbed hands and wrists, noting dully that he had given himself three or four slight cuts in severing the thongs, and rose carefully to his feet, gazing upward to get his bearings by the moon and the stars.

A faint noise behind him struck his ears, he whirled about, and even as he turned the flat of an ax descended on his head, a million flaming sparks whirled and danced for an instant before his eyes, and he fell senseless.

When he came to himself again the men of the Gra

slept, and Mat-kai-no felt that not only his wrists but also his elbows and ankles and knees were bound. Helpless, his head aching terribly from the blow, he lay stretched on the ground and gave himself over to despair.

In the morning the men of the Gra, woke, and Jen, grinning at Mat-kai-no, remarked:

"Still here!" then ordered the captive's arms unbound that he might eat and drink, a guard standing with spear-point at Mat-kai-no's breast the while. Breakfast done, arms were bound once more, legs freed, and a lance-thrust in the thigh served as command, Mat-kai-no scrambling to his feet to resume the march; all he had gained by his effort at escape was an aching head.

And this day his lamed leg began to pain; the day before his fears had been too vivid for him to give it much attention, but now he felt it, and limped sadly, an occasional prod with a lance serving to speed him up when he lagged too much.

Altogether, the captive was in sorry plight, and it was a relief when, as the sun stood at its highest, the little troop stepped into an open space in the forest, ringed round with small, rude huts—hardly more than the merest shelters—and came to a halt, waiting while Jen went forward to the largest hut of all.

A crowd of men and women and children gathered quickly, jabbering excitedly with Mat-kai-no's captors, pinching and pulling at the prisoner, jeering and pointing, examining him with interest, and looking at his weapons with obvious admiration.

One old, old crone came close, carrying a skinning-knife of flint, and pretended to cut and strip a piece of skin from

Mat-kai-no's breast, whereat he, the terror returning, flinched and drew back, and the crowd howled with laughter, slapping their thighs in delight, but at that moment Jen, pushing through the group, struck the old woman violently alongside the head with his fist and gave a brief order, at which the guards prodded Mat-kai-no forward with lances.

Across the clearing they marched, the crowd following at a distance, and into the largest hut, where the men of the Gra prostrated themselves on the hard-packed earth. Mat-kai-no, peering about in the dim twilight of the interior, strove to make out what the hut contained, but a heavy blow between the shoulders sent him sprawling, and Jen's voice spoke:

"Your face to the ground when the Great Chief looks upon you!"

A deep, resonant, not unmusical voice said some words in the tongue of the Gra, and Jen spoke once more:

"Up, Mat-kai-no! The Great Chief would see your face."

Mat-kai-no rose, jerked to his feet by two of the guards, and, his eyes accustomed to the half-light, looked at Su, the Leopard, chieftain of the Gra, whom he found gazing at him with interest.

Su was a man of middle age, totally different from his followers in face and feature. Indeed, but for his eyes and hair, the former a light blue, the latter a bright yellow, he might have been in everything one of the Ta-an themselves; he was evidently of another race than the Gra, and Mat-kai-no found himself wondering how this man came to be chieftain of such a tribe—even his voice was different, for theirs were harsh and rough, like the croak of a raven, whereas the chieftain's was pleasant, with a vibrating, singing note.

Sleek, muscular, and lithe as the leopard of the forest, Su was seated on a tall chair, over which was thrown the hide of the beast from which the chieftain took his name, and he wore a garment of leopard's hide, tawny, spotted, magnificent. His bare feet rested on the back of a negro who, a human footstool, knelt on all-fours before the chieftain's seat, and ranged in a semicircle behind the chieftain were twelve women, young and—for the Gra—beautiful, evidently Su's wives. After some moments of inspection, Su spoke, Jen translating back and forth.

"Your name?"

"Mat-kai-no, Great Chief."

"Of the Ta-an?"

"In very truth."

"Why wanders your tribe so far from the Mountain Caves?"

"The Great Sickness has smitten us, O Chieftain, and the Great Father of the Ta-an, O-Ma-Ken, has bidden us seek a home in the Land of the Dying Sun, among the Little Hairy Men."

Su smiled and made some remark, whereat all present laughed quietly and with respect, and Mat-kai-no looked inquiringly at Jen, who said:

"The Great Chieftain says you shall find a long home nearer than the Land of the Dying Sun."

Mat-kai-no shrugged his shoulders, saying:

"It may be; also, it may not. Many times have the Gra attacked the Ta-an, but the Ta-an still live."

Jen translated this, and Su's eyes flashed; leaning forward, his face twisted with rage, so that Mat-kai-no shrank from the wrath and power of that stern face, he spoke rapidly, Jen translating to the captive:

"Never under the leadership of Su, the Leopard, have the Gra attacked the Ta-an. This will be the last time; death shall come upon the Ta-an in the night, swiftly and on silent feet."

Gradually Su relaxed, sinking back in his chair, the anger passing from his face, and spoke again, and the guards, placing their hands on Mat-kai-no's shoulders, turned him about and marched him from the hut. As they went, he asked of Jen:

"Whither now?" and Jen replied:

"To the place of sacrifice."

Mat-kai-no flinched, but braced himself, resolving to make the journey into the Long Dark as bravely as might be, and asked:

"How shall I die?"

"Pinned to the ground by a sharpened stake driven through the belly. Should you live through two days and two nights, your skin will be taken to make a robe for the chief priest; should you die sooner, you will be judged unworthy, and your carcass thrown to the beasts."

At the prospect of forty-eight hours of such frightful agony Mat-kai-no's knees gave way and he sank to the ground; jerked roughly upright, a sudden resolve gave him strength, and, breaking from the guards, he rushed, closely pursued, to Su's hut, where, flinging himself on his face, he poured forth a torrent of words, begging, imploring, promising. The guards were about to drag him forth when Su raised his hand, asking, contempt in his voice;

"What says the coward?"

"O, Great Chieftain," replied Jen, prostrating himself and beating his forehead on the ground, "he begs that you will spare his life, and says that in return he will deliver the Ta-an into your hands, that you may take them alive or slay them as you will, the Gra losing no warriors."

Su meditated for a time, then asked:

"How can he do this; how can he keep faith? Is he of such power among the Ta-an? Will warriors trust a man who, fears to die?"

Jen questioned Mat-kai-no, then turned once more to Su.

"He says that when on guard he will stand aside and let your warriors, pass to fall upon the Ta-an, they sleeping."

Su fell into deep thought, Mat-kai-no watching anxiously and in fear for signs of his decision, and at last the chieftain spoke again:

"Let him go free; show him the way to his tribe. Five moons from now must he be on guard—how to arrange it is his task—and when the Gra approach at dawn he will let us pass freely. Indeed, the word of a coward is a feeble staff on which to lean, but"—and here the chieftain's face grew stern, his brows bent, and his voice was slow and resonant—"should he fail me, I will give orders that he be taken alive when we fall upon the Ta-an, and the death that meets him will make the sharpened stake seem merciful!"

Mat-kai-no attempted to stammer forth his thanks; relieved from the fear of an awful death, gratitude filled him, but Su waved his hand, spat contemptuously, and said:

"Take him hence; the sight of a coward is poison to me! We may use a traitor, but love him we need not!"

The guards lifted Mat-kai-no, conducted him out, unbound him, gave him his weapons and food for the journey, and three of them led him, a march of five days through the forest, to within sight of the spot where the Ta-an were camped, but never once, during the five long days of travel, did one of them speak or look at the traitor, or by the slightest sign acknowledge his presence.

Only when the journey ended and the smoke from the fires of the Ta-an was in sight did Jen, touching Mat-kai-no on the shoulder, point toward the encampment and say:

"Five moons!"

And, turning, the men of the Gra were lost to sight in the forest.

5

A WOMAN'S INTUITION

WHILE MAT-KAI-NO WAS absent the other hunters, sent out to westward, had returned, bringing game, berries, and roots, and, more than all else, news of a pass through the mountains. A day's journey from where the Ta-an were camped the barrier hills were rent apart, and of great importance was the fact that in this pass were cliffs whence the tribesmen might get flints to renew their stock of darts and other weapons, worn or lost or broken during the long march from the Mountain Caves.

This was in truth needful, since no man might say what awaited them in the Land of the Dying Sun; food they would have to kill while traveling, and after reaching the home they sought—why, there were the Little Hairy Men, who might give battle. So the tribe moved to the pass, where Na-t'san, examining the place with care, gave orders to make camp for a few days, while the artisans labored with the flint they found.

The pass was a strange one, a cleft in the rocky hills, through which roared and brawled a mighty river that, broad and smooth to the north, narrowed to a width of perhaps twenty or thirty paces as it hurled itself between sheer cliffs hundreds of feet in height, to mingle, beyond the hills, with the Great Blue Water.

Tortured into vast waves that rolled and plunged, tossing their foamy crests high into the air, the water thundered through the chasm with deafening uproar, sending a chill of awe and dread even to the stout hearts of the warriors of the Ta-an.

No man could hope to live in that fearful, whirling rush; the stoutest swimmer could not win through. Indeed, one of the hunters, losing his balance—grown dizzy at the sight—had fallen from the path and had been swept away; an instant's view of him his companion had had as he was borne down the flood, a momentary glimpse of his anguished face as he was hurled aloft, arms tossing in despair, on the crest of a giant wave—and he was lost to them forever!

But still they pressed on, seeking, and at length finding, a pass, for the rocky path along the eastern edge of the cañon, rising with gradual slope, wide enough for four men to walk abreast, at length brought them, amazed, to a lovely meadow, level, and grown with thick, soft grass and small trees.

The rocky wall at their left as they mounted turned aside, the cañon widening out to a breadth of five hundred paces or more, and the meadow was some thousand or fifteen hundred paces in length—amply large enough for the tribe to camp.

On the eastern side of the meadow the rock rose sheer for ten times the height of a tall man, and to the west it dropped as sheerly, a still greater height, to the river. On the western side of the cañon the cliff rose straight from the river, towering above the opposite wall, smooth and impassable, and at the southern end the walls, drawing close once more, left a ledge of rock barely wide enough for two men, leading out from the chasm and opening beyond to the southern slope of the barrier hills.

Thus the Ta-an, marching along the narrow path, the rocky ledge that led up from the river, found themselves on this fair meadow, fenced in on the left by the rocky cliff, protected on the right by the river and the wall beyond it, behind them a path that four men could defend, and before them one narrower still.

Truly a safe and pleasant place, where they would be glad to rest while flints were chipped from the rock and shaped into tools and weapons! And much food was there in the pass as well, for wild cattle and sheep grazed over the meadow, no man having ever set foot there to frighten them, and the deep lush grass covered the earth with a green carpet, so that the Ta-an, approaching, were able to slay enough to keep them for many weeks ere the hunted animals escaped, some rushing along the narrow path at the southern end, some, more agile than others, stampeding around the tribesmen down the wider path by which these had come, and many, surging, frantic along the narrow ways, being-pushed and crowded over the edge of the cliff to die in the tossing, thunderous waters far beneath.

That night was there great feasting among the Ta-an, and much meat hung drying in the smoke of the fires, fires which were not altogether for safety but also in no small measure for warmth, for the pass was high up among the hills, far above the level of the Great Blue Water, and though the summer days were warm the nights were cool, and a fire was grateful.

By one of the fires sat Nan-ai, the Poplar, combing her thick brown hair with a comb that Ken-o-san had given her as a bethrothal gift, a comb carved from the tooth of Do-m'rai, the Hill that Walks, carved by Na-t'san, the Great Chieftain himself, and given by him to his grandson.

The hand of the Great Chieftain had lost none of its cunning since the days of his youth, when he was known among the tribe as the Carver of Tusks, and the comb was not merely shaped for use but was beautifully ornamented as well, bearing on one side an intaglio figure of the mammoth from which the ivory was taken, and on the other a deeply graven figure of a woman in the act of combing her hair.

As Nan-ai looked from time to time at the comb she thought of him who had given it to her, and tears came to her eyes—she bent her head to hide them from Ban-ku, who sat near—as she wondered where he might be this night, outcast from the tribe, the hand of every tribesman against him.

Did he still live? Or had he fallen prey to some savage beast? Or to still more savage men? Lower and lower bent the shining head, as the tears welled higher and, flooding over, trickled down the fair cheeks. Her mind full of Ken-o-san, she looked up eagerly as a step sounded—it might be her lover!—she drooped again; it was Mat-kai-no.

He was welcomed gravely by Ban-ku, told briefly the tale of his adventures, saying that he had been captured by the Gra, but had slain his guards and made good his escape; then went straight to Na-t'san to report his return. Presently he was back again, seating himself close to Nan-ai, and it was not long before Ban-ku, muttering: "The night air grows chill for old bones," wrapped himself in his wolfskin and, lying down, soon sent forth grunting, gasping snores.

Mat-kai-no sat quiet for a time, but at length moved closer to Nan-ai, who shivered as he approached, but kept her place.

"Nan-ai," said he, with a note of sadness in his voice, "I bring news."

The girl looked up, eager, and asked.

"Good news?"

Mat-kai-no shook his head, turning his eyes down, and replied:

"Nan-ai, though you love me not, yet I love you more than life itself, and it grieves me to wound you, to bring sarrow to your heart. Yet would it be more cruel to let you hope, Nan-ai, Ken-o-san is dead."

"How know you?" the girl flashed back—she could not believe it. "Did one tell you? Or do you know it of your own knowledge? Did you slay him from ambush? For the courage is not in you to stand before him in fight!"

Mat-kai-no glanced up at her with a hurt look on his face.

"Indeed, Nan-ai," said he, "you are bitter to me, who loves you! Not I slew Ken-o-san, but the Gra, ambushing him and his men, took them to sacrifice. I may not tell you how they died, yet is there no doubt. I myself had it from the men who took me captive, and, seeing the weapons and garments and—and—well, the weapons and garments of Ken-o-san and his men, I must believe. Ken-o-san, L'vu, and Sar-no-m'rai they took alive; Kan-to, Ser-va, and the others-died in the fight. Ken-o-san was stunned by the blow of a club, and ere he recovered was bound; he died with a—he died as a sacrifice."

Nan-ai, remembering the tales she had heard of the Gra, filled in the pauses of Mat-kai-no's words with horrors; her heart turned sick, but even in her misery she knew it was not the fault of Mat-kai-no—he had told her in all kindness, to spare her vain hope; better to know the worst than to wear out one's heart in longing and desire!

She felt more kindly toward the son of Ban-ku than for many years, and reaching out her hand she pressed his, then drew her long thick hair about her face, laid her hands over her eyes, and wept bitterly.

Long the relieving tears flowed, and her body shook with sobs, but at length she mastered herself and looked up, to find Mat-kai-no sitting silent, his grave face toward her. She tossed back her hair, choked down a last sob, and with a pretty gesture held out her hand to her cousin, he grasping it eagerly in both of his.

"Mat-kai-no," said the girl, "I give you thanks; it was kindly done. Better to know the worst than to hope and grieve for one who comes not! My thanks are yours, and—and—Mat-kai-no, this night do I feel a stronger friendship and a kindlier feeling than I have given you hitherto." And she pressed his hand once more, smiling at him as she spoke.

Mat-kai-no leaned forward, his face lighting with pleasure.

"Nana-mé, my cousin, my love," he exclaimed, giving her the pet name of childhood, "is there in your heart love for me? Oh, my sweetheart, can you look on me with favor—have I favor in your eyes? Be my bride, Nana-mé, and all my life will I cherish you. I will protect you from the—I will protect you even with my life, and you shall share my home and all that I have is yours!"

"No, my cousin," she answered, "it may not be! Not as a woman of the Ta-an should love her mate do I love you, but as a cousin, a friend, a sister. And—and—once more do I thank you for your kindness of this night. Sleep well!"

And, rising, she took her furs, wrapped herself in them, and lay down on the other side of the fire, Mat-kai-no stalking off, his head bent in dejection.

Sadness filled the young girl's heart, and for a long time sleep came not to her eyes; from side to side she turned, tossing wakefully, restless, trying in vain to find a comfortable spot, gazing at the myriad stars that shone and twinkled in the clear air, living over in memory the happy hours she had spent with Ken-o-san, calling to mind the thrill of delight and happiness, almost too great to bear, that had been hers when he first spoke to her of his love, and at times sobbing quietly to herself, her head wrapped in her furs, that Ban-ku might not hear.

But at last drowsiness fell upon her eyelids, and they closed sleepily; she was drifting off into dreams when suddenly a phrase of Mat-kai-no's came to her mind with a shock, and instantly she was wide awake, sitting up, remembering.

"I will protect you from the—" From what? What had he meant? Did some danger threaten? Had he secret knowledge of some peril? Or did he but mean the dangers that lurk always about?

Staring into the darkness, her brows wrinkled in thought, Nan-ai pondered deeply. Why had Mat-kai-no not looked at her when he told of Ken-o-san's death? Was it to spare her pain? To spare himself the sight of her suffering?

Her mind flew back to the tortured wolf—no, the pain of others held no fears for Mat-kai-no! But what *could* he mean? Why his furtive looks, his halting speech?

She resolved that the first gleams of dawn would see her before Na-t'san, to lay the matter before a wiser head than her own.

But it was broad day when she awoke; the stars had begun to pale before her racked and tortured mind had rested in sleep, nor would Ban-ku let her be wakened, and the Ta-an were afoot before she had eaten her morning meal. That done, however, she took her way to the southern end of the meadow, to where the Great Chieftain sat, and bowed before him, tracing in the grass the three propitiatory circles.

"Sit, Nan-ai," said Na-t'san, kindly, for he loved her, and she obeyed, then poured out her tale. But the chieftain shook his head, smiling.

"Nay, my child," said he, "it is not in my mind that Mat-kai-no is traitor to the Ta-an. In truth, he is not such a one as Ken-o-san; there was a man!"

A spasm of pain crossed the chieftain's face at the memory of his grandson, for Mat-kai-no had told his story of the death of Ken-o-san, but he went on:

"Had he but turned his face toward the welfare of the tribe he had gone far; few have I known, in the eight tens of years that I have lived, who were his equal. But Mat-kai-no, though not so brave or strong or skilful as Ken-o-san, is yet an honorable man, not one to turn his hand to treachery. A man in love speaks not straight on! It was but confusion, nor do I wonder"—and the chieftain's glance rested in admiration on the maiden—"for in truth, Nan-ai, your beauty might blind the eyes of wiser men than Mat-kai-no! Nay, dismiss these thoughts, my child; I have no fear of Mat-kai-no!"

Somewhat comforted, but not entirely at ease, Nan-ai bowed respectfully to the Great Chief, and returned to Ban-ku's fire, where she busied herself for the next four days in preparing meat; cutting it into strips and drying it in the smoke, that it might not spoil on the journey that lay before the tribe.

Mat-kai-no did not press his suit; he seemed inclined to accept her offer of a sister's love, and was unfailingly kind and thoughtful, doing little errands for the girl, helping her, and ever pleasant, with a smile when her eyes turned toward his.

But Nan-ai was far from happy. The memory of Ken-o-san was vivid; at times she thought to hear his voice in her ear, and turned quickly, to see only the broad meadow with busy folk moving to and fro over it, and to hear but the cries of the workers, bandying jests back and forth, and the ever-present roar of the tossing, hurrying river.

She slept ill, and at times rose from her bed of skins to wander over the meadow, endeavoring to weary herself into sleepfulness, or, seating herself on a fallen tree, wooed drowsiness by counting the stars. But ever her thougthts turned back to Ken-o-san, and often she wept bitterly, when none was near, keeping, however, a brave face before the Ta-an, who looked at her pityingly as she went back and forth about her daily duties; they had heard of the death of the man she loved.

One night some four days after the return of Mat-kai-no, Nan-ai, sleepless, rose from her place by the fire and wandered out along the brink of the river. Coming to the southern end of the meadow she turned back, following the base of the cliff that towered high above her, walking aimlessly, in utter misery. It seemed as though she could not bear the pain that filled her breast; something must happen, some relief must come, or she would surely die, and thinking thus she turned her eyes upward toward the blue dome that arched overhead.

It was in her mind to pray to the Star-Marked One, bride of O-Ma-Ken, the Great Father, and friend of lovers; to beg for mercy, for comfort, for forgetfulness, but even as her lips formed the first words of her prayer a movement along the edge of the overhanging cliff caught her eye, and she held her breath, watching. The figure of a man detached itself from the rock and came slowly down the face of the cliff—was it an enemy? Could it be a night attack?

Nan-ai shrank back into the shadow of a thorn-bush, and watched, ready to scream aloud and call the warriors to arms should another follow, but none came; alone the man climbed steadily down the sheer face of the rock, and Nan-ai, watching, trembled, for no living thing, wingless, could descend that glassy surface.

For a space the height of a man the figure was full in the moonlight, then passed into the shadow cast by the opposite cliff, and the girl could not easily keep him in sight; he was not a negro, at least, but a white man—or a spirit— or a sorcerer. On and on he came, and at last reached the ground not five paces from where the maiden crouched, trembling; she knew she had seen a deed beyond human power—this was one of the Devils of the Night.

Terror-stricken, bound fast to the spot by her shaking limbs, Nan-ai kept her eyes fastened on the approaching form, and as it passed within arm's reach she gasped, knowing it for a spirit for one returned from the dead:

"Ken-o-san!"

Instantly the figure stopped, turned toward the faint whisper, and stood listening tensely, looking. In a moment he spied the crouching girl, eyed her an instant, and with one swift motion stepped close and caught her in his arms.

For a moment she struggled in terror, striving to cry out, then realization came—this was no spirit, but a living man—he was warm to the touch! And with a happy cry, half-stifled, Nan-ai sank into her lover's grasp, her arms about his neck, her lips against his own, while he held her tight, so tight it hurt—a joyous hurt!

Again and again, he kissed her, pressing her close against him, then held her away that he might look into her eyes, shining now with love and gladness, and at length the two sat side by side on the grass, arms about each other, Nan-ai's long hair wrapping her lover like a mantle.

"My love, my love!" spoke Nan-ai after a time, gazing as though she could not see his face enough, and:

"Nana-mé!" he answered.

But presently other thoughts came to her, and she asked:

"How came you down the cliff? Smooth is its face, and slippery as the ice that locks the streams in the Long Cold!"

Ken-o-san chuckled softly, and replied:

"By the help of a thong of deer-hide, twisted of a dozen

thongs—braided, rather. Making it fast to a rock above, and placing my feet against the cliff, my hands holding fast the thong, it was an easy matter. Na-t'san has placed guards on the paths, and I might not come that way. L'vu and Sar-no-m'rai watch above."

"L'vu and Sar-no-m'rai?" echoed the girl, wondering. "Then they are not dead? And—and—oh, Ken-o-san, you also are not dead!"

Ken-o-san laughed.

"Has that thought but now come to you?" he asked.

"Why—why—yes!" exclaimed Nan-ai. "Mat-kai-no said the Gra had slain you! Though I knew when I felt your arms about me that you lived! Oh—oh—I cannot explain! I knew, yet did not know!"

"A solid spirit, I!" said Ken-o-san, "as I will yet prove on Mat-kai-no, who speaks with two tongues! Nay, my love, for weeks have I and my men followed the trail of the Ta-an, but the Gra we have not seen."

"But why did you come? It is death if the Ta-an find you!"

"Look in my eyes and see," Ken-o-san replied, and the girl, looking, drew him closer; raising her lips to his.

Then for an hour the two sat side by side, at times silent, thrilling with love and happiness, at times talking, and Ken-o-san told all that had befallen him since the day when, pursued by the Ta-an for the death of Ja-ko, he had gathered his warriors to him and had fled from the Mountain Caves. It was on the girl's lips to ask if he had indeed slain the chief priest, but she held the question back; whether or no, he was her lover, and she adored him—she would love him had he slain a dozen priests!

So the young warrior told her of the stockade he and his men had built, of the new weapon—"three times as far as one can hurl a dart will it shoot, and I have pierced a leopard through from side to side"—and of how, learning of the Great Sickness, they had followed the Ta-an.

And in return she told him of the story Mat-kai-no had brought back, and Ken-o-san's face grew stern as he listened. And over them the stars swam in the heavens, and the moon sank to her rest, and all about them came the soft noises of the night, the chirp of drowsy birds, the hum of insects, and the rustling of branches in the wind, and over all, steady, unfailing, the roar of the mighty river, hurling its waters onward, ever onward, to the sea.

After a time Nan-ai spoke, thoughtfully:

"My love, it is in my mind that Mai-kai-no plans treachery to the Ta-an."

"It may be," answered Ken-o-san, and the girl looked swiftly at him.

"Neither do you trust him?" she asked, and Ken-o-san replied, succinctly:

"He speaks with two tongues."

Then Nan-ai told her lover of the words of Mat-kai-no that had roused her suspicion—"I will protect you from the—"—and of his furtive manner, but Ken-o-san shook his head, saying:

"Naught does it prove, Nana-mé. And Mat-kai-no has honor among the Ta-an. Indeed, you go too far, sweet!"

The girl leaned forward, eagerly, insistently.

"Ken-o-san, by the love I bear you, I swear that Mat-kai-no plans treachery! How I know it I cannot tell; it is here!" And she laid her hand on her bosom. "He *is* a traitor! I swear it! It is known to me, even as it was known that you were not dead, that I should see you once more, that you still lived! Something within my breast tells me it is in very truth real! Oh, Ken-o-san, my love, can you do aught to keep this peril from the Ta-an?"

The young warrior was staggered by her earnestness, her sureness, and he sat silent, his thoughts turned inward, meditating. Suddenly, like a flash of lightning illuminating the night, there came to him the memory of the fires which Sar-no-m'rai had pointed out from the hilltop, and his eyes widened.

"The Gra!" he exclaimed, and Nan-ai cried:

"You have said! Oh, Ken-o-san, save the Ta-an!"

But a shadow of gloom passed over the young warrior's face as he replied:

"And why should I do aught for the Ta-an? Outlaw am I, nor is there one of the tribesmen who would not slay me could he do so! Fly with me, Nana-mé, and leave the People of the Mountain Caves to their doom, if doom it be!"

The girl's arm fell from Ken-o-san's shoulder, and drawing back, she looked at him in sadness and reproach.

"What words are these for Ken-o-san, son of the son of Na-t'san, the Great Chieftain? Are they not your people? Can their anger turn you from them? Is it not your duty, at the hands of the Great Father, to labor and battle ever for them? Oh, Ken-o-san, many a time and oft have I grieved at your wild ways; loving you, more than another have I grieved, as has also Na-t'san, yet have I never spoken of my sorrow, holding it the part of a maiden to let her lover choose the path that he will tread.

"But, Ken-o-san, fail me now, and I swear by the bright brow of the Star-Marked One that never again shall you see Nan-ai; the river that roars behind us shall carry my body to the Great Blue Water, to rest there forever and ever!"

Then, falling into entreaty, she begged, her arms once more about his neck:

"Oh, my dear love, I pray that you may do this for Nan-ai, whom you love so dearly that life itself is naught to you without her; so dearly that you will scale a cliff into the camp of death and danger for a sight of her! And besides—" her own voice fell to a whisper—"I have heard it whispered that Na-t'san himself was outlawed in his youth but was restored to his place in the tribe for his great services to the Ta-an; it might be—it might be—"wistfully her voice trailed off into silence as she gazed beseechingly at him.

Ken-o-san sat silent, his eyes bent on the earth, and in his soul there was a great struggle as conscience and hatred, duty and rage, fought for the mastery. Again and again his face was twisted and distorted as waves of emotion swept over it; again and again his whole body trembled and shook with the violence of his passions, so that to the girl, watching, it seemed that she could verily see the powers of good and evil contending for his soul.

But at last he grew calm, he raised his head, and in the dim light she could see his face, swept clear of hatred and the desire of revenge, his mouth set in a firm line, deep furrows graven on his countenance by the strength of his resolve.

"So be it, Nan-ai," he said. "You have your will. Ken-o-san and his men will follow after the People of the Mountain Caves, Watching ever for signs of danger—to protect those who have cast them out!" he added bitterly.

The girl flung her arms about him again—she had dropped them while he fought the fight within his soul—and kissed him again and again, he at first cold, but warming gradually to the warmth of her love.

"I knew you would not fail me!" she cried, then, softly, looking down, "and—and—Ken-o-san, if you may not win back into the tribe through service—I—will—go—with you—into the forest!" And she hid her face on his shoulder, while he clasped her close to him.

From the cliff above there came the shrill, insistent call of a bird, the harsh scream of a hawk, and Ken-o-san leaped to his feet, crying: "L'vu's signal!" and looking eagerly about for danger. Naught could he see that threatened, and, puzzled, he turned to Nan-ai, then, realizing that he could see her face clearly, he turned his eyes upward.

"Great Father!" he exclaimed, for the sky was light with the coming dawn; the stars had paled and disappeared long since, and the air was filled with chirpings and songs of birds.

"Great Father!" repeated the young warrior, and caught Nan-ai to him for one more kiss, then rushed to where the stout rope of braided deer-hide hung against the face of the cliff, grasped it tightly, and placing his feet against the rock, walked swiftly up, climbing hand over hand up the rope as his feet moved. Reaching the top, he swung himself over, turned to wave farewell to Nan-ai, and vanished.

Nan-ai, humming happily to herself, her heart full of joy, returned to the fire of her uncle, where she stirred the embers, heaped on more wood, and set about preparing the morning meal.

6

LORD OF THE WINGED DEATH

KEN-O-SAN RETURNED, SILENT and thoughtful, to his camp on the crest of the mountain, L'vu marching quietly beside him. Arriving, the young chief sent his lieutenant to summon Kan-to and Sar-no-m'rai, and when they had come he told the three of what Nan-ai had said, and of his own resolve as well.

"In truth, it may be," said Kan-to, meditatively. "It is well known to us all that Mat-kai-no speaks with two tongues; it was known long since. It may be that he plans treason, hoping to win your woman by force or guile if not by love. Let two men watch the paths, bringing you word should Mat-kai-no leave the camp, that he may be followed."

"The words of Kan-to are good," L'vu spoke. "And it is in my mind that Nan-ai has spoken well. It is true that the Great Chieftain was outlawed in youth; my father's father, who was also father to Ka-tem, knew Na-t'san well, and he it was who told me. And it is my mind that it were shame did we, even outlawed, stand aside and permit the Gra to triumph over the People of the Mountain Caves. I have been captive among the Gra, as you know well, and the tales are not false."

"So let it be," was the word of Ken-o-san. "Do you,

Kan-to, keep watch over the southern path, and you, Sar-no-m'rai, over the wider one to the north, since your eyes are the keener by night, and it is most like that Mat-kai-no, should he depart, would pass that way. Take each two men, that you may send a messenger. Go at once; L'vu remains with me. Watch day and night, and send word swiftly should you see aught of note. Watch from the cliffs above. Go!"

The watchers rose, bowed, and departed, Ken-o-san saying to L'vu:

"Pass the word among the men that ours is a cold camp till I say otherwise." Then stretching himself on the ground beneath a bush, he slept.

The camp where Ken-o-san and his men lay hidden was on the very top of the mountain, eastward from the pass where the Ta-an were encamped. During the day, while the sun shone, it was well enough, but at night the wind was chill, and, fireless, the men shivered, hardy though they were. Wrapped in skins of beasts, they sought the lee of bushes and rocks, eating cold food, drinking from a spring so small that, three men having drunk, the next must wait for the basin to fill.

But for all their discomfort, so devoted were they to their leader that none grumbled; they were sure that he, wisest of all, thought first of them and of himself last. Besides, word had got out and was passed from man to man that perchance the ban of outlawry might be lifted from them, and they were willing to endure; already had they felt the loneliness of outcasts, against whom the hands of all men were raised.

So they waited, sitting about under rock and bush,

polishing their weapons, chatting in low tones, and waiting, ever waiting.

On the second day a party of four, who had been hunting far off on the northern slope, returned in great excitement, bringing with them a captive, who was immediately haled before Ken-o-san, where L'vu recognized the man, by features and weapons, as one of the Gra, putting questions to him in his own tongue, as asked by Ken-o-san, for the burly lieutenant knew the language of these wild men. But the prisoner remained sullen and refused to speak, till Ken-o-san, losing patience, cried:

"Bind him hand and foot to that tree and stuff his mouth with fur that his yells may not be heard!"

It was done, and the leader continued:

"Bring a stout thong of tanned hide and tie it loosely about his temples and skull!"

The order was obeyed, and Ken-o-san said:

"Tell him, L'vu, that when he is ready to speak he shall give signal by closing his right eye, the other remaining open, then thrust the haft of your ax through the thong and twist!"

The chieftain's words were repeated to the captive, and as L'vu's great ax turned slowly the thong began to tighten about the man's head. Tighter and tighter it drew, cutting deep into the skin, which puffed up in ridges as the thong sank in, the veins swelling, the skin turning purple.

The prisoner writhed and groaned in his throat, straining at his bonds, twisting his head in futile effort to escape the agony, and tighter and tighter drew the thong, pressing on the skull, squeezing and crushing it. Fiercer and fiercer grew the pain, and harder and harder the efforts of the captive, but ever L'vu turned the ax, and ever the thong tightened.

In the silence the warriors could hear the roar of the river, and through occasional lulls in its noise there drifted to them cries and calls from the tribesmen camped on the meadow, as one shouted to another.

The young warriors, sick at the horrible sight, turned from the straining, purple face of the tortured man to their chieftain, but no sign of relenting showed on his countenance; stern and unflinching he watched the agonized victim writhing against his bonds, watched the bloodshot eyes starting from the head. Hardened though they were to battle and death, more than one of Ken-o-san's men turned away from the awful sight, shuddering, and one muttered to his neighbor:

"He will not give in; it is death!"

But the captive could bear no more; with an effort he drew the lid over his right eye, and instantly L'vu stopped, then turned the ax backward, loosening the thong, and the prisoner sank limp and helpless against his bonds. Ken-o-san, shuddering, passed the crook of his elbow upward over his face, wiping off the sweat that poured down it, and said:

"The Great Father be thanked! I could have borne but little more!"

Water was thrown on the prisoner's face, cold water from the spring, and he revived, then answered Ken-o-san's questions.

"It is for to-morrow at dawn," he said. "Mat-kai-no will be on guard and will allow the Gra to pass in silence, approaching up the northern path."

"Bind him to a tree," said Ken-o-san. "Give him food

and water and let one watch him. If he has spoken truly he shall go free, but if he has spoken with two tongues he shall die by the thong about the temples."

But the captive was not alarmed; he merely bowed, saying:

"I speak true words, master."

When the fires of the Ta-an had died down and the tribesmen were sleeping Ken-o-san lowered himself from the cliff a second time, moving stealthily about among the groups till he came to where Nan-ai lay. He touched her on the shoulder, and she woke, getting to her feet at once. The young warrior drew her to one side and spoke swiftly:

"To-morrow at dawn the Gra come. Be on the watch and give the alarm; I and my men will aid. Mat-kai-no is to allow them to pass; they come by the northern path."

"But my love, shall I not go to Na-t'san and warn him?"

Ken-o-san smiled grimly.

"Saying you had the word from me?" he asked. "Nay, Nana-mé, this is the only way. Be brave and watchful; so shall we win the fight. Now must I return; one kiss!"

He clasped her in his arms and kissed her, then turned and passed swiftly and silently across the meadow, flitting from shadow to shadow, and at length scaling the cliff down which he had come.

Back to his own camp went Ken-o-san, and lay down to snatch a few hours' rest, saying to the one who guarded the man of the Gra:

"Summon me when the stars show two hours yet to dawn."

At the appointed hour the guard aroused his chief, who leaped to his feet and woke his men. Kan-to and his two had come in the night before, and Ken-o-san, dividing his band into two parties, gave one in charge of L'vu, with careful instructions, taking the leadership of the other himself, Sar-mo-m'rai going with him, Kan-to with L'vu.

The two parties went to their appointed stations, Ken-o-san leading his men down the mountain and lying in ambush beside the beginning of the northern trail that led into the pass, where, hidden amid brush and tall grasses, they could watch without being themselves seen.

His warriors placed, Ken-o-san stretched himself on the ground, peeping out from behind a bush and waiting for the attack to come.

Never, it seemed to him, had the dawn approached so slowly; never had the stars moved in such languid course. About him the brush moved, rustling, in the night breeze; to his ears came the roar of the river, narrowing five hundred paces to the south into the funnel-mouth of the pass; to his nostrils came the cool, sweet scent of the dawn; occasionally a fish leaped from the surface of the water that flowed, smooth and black, before the chieftain's eyes.

Tense he lay, every nerve, every sense strained to catch the faintest sound, the least glimmer of marching forms, and in the east the stars paled to the first light of morning. Sar-no-m'rai's hand gripped Ken-o-san's arm, and Ken-o-san caught the words, faintly breathed in his ear:

"They come!" but no sign of the approaching enemy could he make out. Presently the sound of marching men came to his ears, and, shoulder to shoulder, in a compact mass, the warriors of the Gra came up the path, Su at their head. Ken-o-san, watching closely, counted twenty-six tens and three, and thought to himself:

"Coming on the Ta-an asleep, they might easily be victors; the Great Father surely sent us the warning!"

Up the path, around a slight turn, and out of sight passed the Gra, and Ken-o-san, after waiting a time for possible stragglers, spoke to his men, who rose and followed him up the path in the footsteps of the Gra.

Higher and higher they climbed, the pass narrowing in and the path growing narrower as well, till no more than four men might walk abreast. On their left the sheer wall towered, and on their right the cliff fell away, ever deeper and deeper, to the foaming flood below.

Onward they pressed, keeping back that they might not be seen, though the Gra were nearly a thousand paces ahead, when suddenly, ringing on the still air, echoing back and forth from the cliffs, they heard the shrill, piercing scream of a woman.

Instantly came a deep shout from the attackers, cries arose through the encampment, cries that Ken-o-san could faintly hear over the roar of the torrent, and the Gra, abandoning stealth, rushed forward.

Ken-o-san and his men sprang onward, making the best speed they could up the slope, but long ere they reached the spot the battle was joined. Wakened from sleep, the warriors of the Ta-an seized ax and lance and dagger and rushed to the defence, meeting the Gra on the narrow path above the river—the battle was joined!

Then followed a fierce and deadly fight, one of unnamed, unstoried thousands fought through all the ages, battles small in numbers of men engaged, but vast in their import, incalculable in their results, for here a higher race of men fought for their lives, for the life, the very existence, of the tribe, against men of lower race, doubly dangerous in that they were led by a renegade from a tribe the equal of the Ta-an.

Su, the Leopard, crafty, merciless, a born chieftain, outlawed for his many crimes, establishing himself as leader of the Gra, had trained his rude followers to battle, had taught them to fight in mass, one aiding another.

And it was this body of trained men that now hurled themselves upon the Ta-an, unsuspecting, surprised, and for a time bore them back by the very weight of attack, by the momentum of their rush. But swiftly the Ta-an gathered to the fight, running to the spot, drawn by the shouts, the yells, the noise of battle, and for a time the attackers were held.

Above, the sky grew brighter and brighter with the coming of day, flushing to a rosy pink in the east, while the hilltops, catching the first rays of the sun, sprang into gorgeous masses of green and gold; below, in the narrow defile, on the sloping path, Ta-an and Gra mingled in desperate death-struggle, filling the air with harsh battle-cries, with screams and groans of agony.

The advantage of surprise was with the Gra—the advantage of position with the Ta-an, for they fought down-hill; the advantage of individual strength lay with the Ta-an—the advantage of numbers with the Gra.

Ken-o-san, rushing up with his few men, saw, even in the short space of time he took to cover the distance between, two changes of the fight. First, the Gra, rushing, swept the Ta-an back; next, the Ta-an, gathering, pressed the Gra down the slope, and, finally, the Gra, rallying, held the battle firm.

Well Ken-o-san could picture that fight; pressed together by weight of numbers crowding behind, neither Ta-an nor Gra could give back—no space was there to swing an ax or wield a lance—foot to foot and hand to hand they fought, with tooth and fist and dagger—bodies of men, dead or dying, none cared, were hurled from the path, the splash of their fall lost in the rush and sweep of the mountain torrent that poured through the defile—grappled in deadly clutch, men gasped out their lives as the daggers rose and fell, or, prostrate on the ground, stabbed madly at the legs and bellies of those who trampled them.

In the forefront shone the yellow hair of Su, the Leopard, and before him men gave back—none might endure his strength and skill.

And now the warriors began to lose their footing—the path grew slippery with blood—and many fell, to fight, gripped in each other's arms, prone on the bodies of men—and now the Gra pressed forward, driving back the Ta-an, still struggling madly, toward the meadow.

Ken-o-san, as he and his men ran panting up the sloping ledge of rock, looked ever upward to the edge of the cliff, seeking, ever seeking.

"Where is L'vu?" he thought. "Oh, Great Father, speed his steps!"

And even as the prayer flashed through his mind, he caught a glimpse of the round face and broad shoulders of the man he sought, peeping over at the fight below. An arm waved, and the cliff was lined for thirty paces with L'vu's men—another signal, and from above there poured down on the backs of the Gra a deadly sleet of arrows. Above the tumult of battle rose the deep voice of L'vu, counting:

"Ho!" and in unison the arrows were drawn from the quivers;

"Ei!" they were laid to the bows;

"Na!" back to the ear each archer drew the string;

"Ku!" and as though sped by one hand the arrows flew, piercing flesh, smashing and splintering bone, burying themselves in the backs of the invaders. Again and again fell the storm, and naught might stand before it—the Gra, caught front and rear, wavered, turned, gave back, broke, and fled down the path, seeking in vain shelter from the death that smote them from above.

Ken-o-san, now within a hundred paces, saw them turn—he shouted an order—the four men in the lead dropped on one knee, the ones behind stood upright, and now Ken-o-san began to count, and as he counted a second storm of arrows met the Gra.

Flesh and blood might not face that fearful sleet of wood and stone; the Gra, assailed in front, behind, and from above, lost all order, all hope—they were no more than a band of sheep before the slayers. In scores they fell—so thick was the press that more than one arrow pierced and slew two men—and many, desperate, leaped into the river, to die, whirled down, battered against the rocks, tossed in that mighty stream. Many fell on their knees, and, hands uplifted, cried for mercy, but the streaming arrows silenced them as well, and so the work went on.

And now but three of the Gra still stood, tallest among them Su, their leader. But slightly wounded, he rushed down the path toward Ken-o-san, who, seeing him come, shouted aloud:

"Hold!" for the lust of battle leaped up and flamed in

his heart. The bowmen held their arrows on the strings, as Ken-o-san, flinging aside his bow, armed but with dagger of flint, sprang forward to meet the renegade chieftain. Small seemed the warrior of the Ta-an beside the great height of Su, and slight his limbs; a faint smile twisted the mouth of the Leopard as, halting, he surveyed his enemy, then, leaping forward, he attacked, feinting at the face of Ken-o-san, then sweeping his dagger upward at the young man's belly.

But with a swift motion Ken-o-san caught Su's wrist in his left hand and struck with his right—Su warded the blow with his forearm and caught Ken-o-san's wrist in his own left hand.

Thus, neither able to strike, they stood for an instant, breast to breast, panting—Ken-o-san with a quick twist freed his right hand, flung it over and down and up—the sharp flint dagger struck Su below the ribs, ranging upward—his grasp relaxed—and Ken-o-san, stooping, caught him about the thighs, lifted, hurled him—and Su flew clear of the path to fall in the river.

One glimpse of his face had Ken-o-san as it showed for an instant above the flood, washed clean of blood and grime; then the waves caught the chieftain of the Gra and swept him onward to the sea, and he vanished forever from the eyes of men.

And now, the battle won, the Ta-an ranged down the path, slaying the wounded, toppling the bodies into the stream, and Ken-o-san, signaling to his men, withdrew, going to his camp on the crest of the mountain. Here they stretched themselves on the ground to rest, for they were weary, though not one of them bore a wound.

He meant to let them rest for a time, then withdraw deeper into the forest and await tidings from the Ta-an, perchance sending a messenger to the tribe, later.

But they had hardly readied the camp and lain down before sounds were heard as of one approaching, and Ka-tem came through the brush, to stand before Ken-o-san. Instantly the latter was on his feet, an arrow fitted to his bow, the point toward Ka-tem's breast. But Ka-tem bore no weapons, and raised his hands in sign of peace, so the bow was lowered. And then Ka-tem spoke:

"Ken-o-san," he said, "Na-t'san, the Great Chieftain, bids me find you and bring you to him."

"My men?" asked Ken-o-san.

"Your men as well."

"In peace?"

"In peace."

Ken-o-san turned to his men and gave an order, and, rising, the band followed Ka-tem down the slope of the mountain and up the rocky path to the meadow, where they were met and followed by a number of the warriors, who escorted them to the Great Chieftain.

Ken-o-san faced the chief, bowed, and outlined on the grass the three circles of ceremony, then waited, humbly, for Na-t'san to speak. The Great Chieftain lay on a pile of skins of wolf and leopard and bear, his back propped against a log so that he half reclined. In his hand he held the ivory baton, mark of his rank, and around him stood a half-circle of warriors, full-armed, behind them women of the tribe, peering close, listening eagerly.

Close at the chieftain's side knelt Va-m'rai, his faithful wife, holding to his bosom a pad of fur, saturated with the blood that oozed from a slight wound in his chest, and in the silence—for none spoke—could be heard the slow breathing of the aged chief. At length his lips moved and from them came words welcome to the young warrior, his grandson:

"Ken-o-san, son of my son," he said, "this day have you served the Ta-an well; but for you and your strange new weapon had we been overborne, our warriors slain, our goods taken, our women and children carried into captivity. For this the Great Father, O-Ma-Ken, bids me say that if you will leave your evil ways and return to the tribe, dealing in all things as becomes the son of a chieftain, your sins shall be forgiven and the Ta-an shall receive you once more among their number. Your greatest sin, the death of Ja-ko the Chief Priest—Mat-kai-no, wounded unto death, confessed that he had traitorously slain that one, laying your dagger beside the body, that you might be outcast and he receive Nan-ai. The Ta-an awaits your reply."

"Oh, Na-t'san, Great Chieftain," answered Ken-o-san, "bitterly have I repented me of my evil deeds, and gladly would I return among the Ta-an. But my men, who followed at my word—I may not leave them. Does the Great Father permit that they also return?"

"If they, too, will turn from evil they may return; good service have they done."

"Their warrant will I be," said the young man, falling on his knees.

"Rise and draw near," said Na-t'san, and as the young man did so, "let me see and touch the new weapon."

Ken-o-san took his bow and an arrow and laid them in

the chieftain's hands, he examining them carefully, then, saying:

"Speed me a dart, that I may watch near at hand."

Ken-o-san looked about, caught sight of a vulture, gorged, perched in a tree some three hundred paces away, and indicated the bird, a murmur rising among the warriors—not one of them could hope to speed a dart from a throwing-stick so far, and as for striking a chosen mark— But Ken-o-san, bracing himself, drew back the arrow to the head, held it an instant, and loosed.

The bow twanged with a deep hum, and like a streak of light the arrow flew. The vulture flapped heavily once or twice, striving to rise, then fell to the ground dead, even as half a dozen young men raced forward to pick it up. One reached it before the others, and bore it swiftly back to Na-t'san, who looked it over with care and asked:

"But where is the dart?"

"Oh, Great Chieftain," replied Ken-o-san, "it has passed through and gone on its way!"

Na-t'san laid the dead bird on the ground and gazed at the sky, thinking deeply, then faced Ken-o-san once more.

"Son of my son," he said, "leader of men are you, fit chieftain to the Ta-an. This new weapon, the Winged Death, shall bring victory to the tribesmen, serving them well in peace and war. I grow old; years of strife and labor bear me down, and this wound, though slight, still further draws my strength. Take then this staff of ceremony, badge of the Great Chieftain of the Ta-an, and swear to me to lead the Ta-an, the People of the Mountain Caves, faithfully and well, serving them ever, thinking ever of them, placing them before yourself, in peace and in war. My race is run;

six tens of years have I led the Ta-an, and for the few years still left to me I desire rest and comfort. Swear this to me by the Great Father who rules above; then may Na-t'san give over his labors and have the rest his aged body craves."

Ken-o-san knelt, took from the chieftain's hand the staff, and said, firmly:

"As O-Ma-Ken, the Great Father sees me, I swear to serve and lead the Ta-an faithfully and well, to my own hurt if need be!"

"It is well!" said Na-t'san, "it is well, T'san-va-men, Lord of the Winged Death!" And he laid his hand on the bent head of the new chieftain, his eyes closed, and his lips moving in prayer.

One by one the warriors of the tribe had knelt before T'san-va-men, laying their hands between his and swearing fealty to him. When Ban-ku knelt, T'san-va-men stooped and whispered:

"Nan-ai; is she mine?" and Ban-ku replied:

"Yes, lord; and my heart is filled with joy, for in very truth have I always loved you, though I loved not your deeds!"

Whereat the young chieftain, laughing, slapped Ban-ku on the shoulder and bade him rise.

The ceremony ended, T'san-va-men called Nan-ai, and the two walked to the southern end of the valley, following along the narrow path to where it broadened out on the southern slope of the mountain. Here they turned and toiled far up the hillside to where a mighty cliff, outcropping from the earth, gave far view over the lowlands that lay beyond.

To the top of this cliff they climbed, skirting around behind it, so coming out from the forest almost on the verge of the sheer drop, and here they stood, looking, looking, over the vast expanse of forest and stream that lay spread out before them.

Far, far below the river twisted and turned, broadening out as it escaped from the defile, shining like silver, blue as the sky, under the warm sun of afternoon, and following its course with the eye the two could see, a faint line in the dim and hazy distance, hardly distinguishable from the overarching dome, the Great Blue Water.

The heart of the young chieftain thrilled as he thought of the change of fortune that had come upon him; yesterday an outlaw, a fugitive, before the wrath of the tribesmen, to-day Great Chieftain of the tribe, honored and obeyed by all, bound to lead them to the Land of the Dying Sun—and after. He drew the girl close to him and looked in her eyes, but she slipped from his arms and knelt before him, saying:

"Who am I that I should be bride of the Great Chieftain of the Ta-an?"

He laughed and raised her, replying:

"Nan-ai are you, whom the Great Chieftain loves! Is not that enough?" And he kissed her, holding her tight, her arms about his neck. At length she said:

"Come, my love; we must return. The feast will be set, and we not there! Come!"

He kissed her once more and then, hand in hand, they took their way down the mountain and back to where the tribesmen waited, drawn up in serried ranks with L'vu, Kan-to, and Sar-no-m'rai at their head, to greet Nan-ai, the Poplar, and T'san-va-men, Lord of the Winged Death, Great Chieftain of the Ta-an.

THE CAVE THAT SWIMS
ON THE WATER

1

FOR SACRIFICE

"**INTO YOUR HANDS**, then, shall she be delivered. Be you at the Great Rock by the river, two thousand paces downstream, to-morrow at sunset, and you shall see her come; by her yellow hair may you know her for the one you seek, though in truth no sign is needed, for alone will she come."

The speaker was Ta-nu-ko, chief priest of the Ta-an, and the one to whom he spoke was Gur, chieftain of the Little Hairy Men. Fifteen years before, led by T'san-va-men, Lord of the Winged Death, the Ta-an had come to the Land of the Dying Sun and had there made their homes, stretching for miles along a fair valley. During fifteen years had they warred with the Little Hairy Men, and now for the first had one of the Ta-an spoken in peace to one of the olden-time dwellers in that land.

A strange contrast the two made as they faced each other, concealed in a deep thicket that nestled high above the river, clinging to the face of the hill, for the chief priest was tall and straight, long of limb and smooth of face, with a noble head, albeit his countenance was somewhat marked with lines of selfishness and deceit, whereas Gur was short and squatty, with stooping shoulders and long arms, so that his hands, hanging half-closed, reached nearly to his knees.

The Cave That Swims on the Water

by Paul L. Anderson

His face, with broad, low forehead, flattened nose and outward-pointing nostrils, with retreating chin and prominent cheekbones, marked him as one of a race lower than the Ta-an—a race not too far removed from the great apes, the resemblance being heightened by the thin growth of hair that covered his features.

And even in the garments and weapons of the two men was an equal difference, for Ta-nu-ko, clad in finely worked clothing of leopard's hide, bore well-chipped ax and dagger of flint beside which those of the Little Hairy Men were rude and ill-formed, and carried also a bow and quiver of arrows, Gur's chief weapon being a long and heavy club of oak, air-dried and seasoned in the sun. Also, Gur's sole garment was roughly shaped from the hide of a wild horse, worked and dressed with little skill.

Seeing the two in converse, none could have doubted that they were of different race; his only wonder would have been that the priest of the Ta-an should be speaking in friendship with an enemy.

"At sunset, then, shall A-ta, the Girl of the Mountain Caves, daughter to Ban-tu-v'rai of the Ta-an, come to the Great Rock. Do with her as you will, save only that she must not live." Both spoke in the same tongue—that of the Little Hairy Men.

"May I not keep her as my slave, to do my bidding?"

"As I speak, so shall you do, else A-ta comes not!" flamed the priest, leaning forward with a hard stare, from which Gur shrank back, muttering:

"It shall be done!"

"It is well!" said Ta-nu-ko. "Slay her as you will; young and strong is she, and should make good sport ere her spirit passes into the Long Dark."

"It shall be done," repeated Gur, licking his lips with an evil grin. "I will bind her and flay thongs for my garments from her white skin; soft and tender are the thongs made from the hide of a maiden!"

And he grinned again in anticipation, while Ta-nu-ko looked at him with a shudder of repulsion, disgusted at the thought of such deliberate cruelty.

"But tell me, tall man," went on Gur, "why wish you death for the maiden? Why may I not keep her as a slave, binding her with thongs, watching her, or perchance hewing off her foot, that she may not flee?"

"Because," returned the priest, "none can say that she might not escape you, finding her way back to the Ta-an. Menzono-men, Slayer of Wolves, is vowed to the priesthood of the tribe by his parents, and he loves and is loved by A-ta. Should they marry, should he take her to his cave, then is he lost to the priest clan, for by the law of the Ta-an a priest may have no woman."

"And can you not claim him, in fulfilment of the vow?"

Ta-nu-ko shrugged his shoulders, replying:

"Were she other than A-ta, yes. But T'san-va-men,

Great Chieftain of the Ta-an, loves the maiden, to whom he is even as a father. In childhood did he save her from death in a swift stream, and indeed it is in my mind that she is even dearer to him than his own daughter, also that she loves him more than she loves her father. It is his joy to give her pleasure; should she desire Menzono-men she need but speak two words to the chieftain—and who may withstand the Lord of the Winged Death?"

"Straight are your words," answered Gur. "Your will shall be done: sweet will it be to torture a maiden of the Ta-an, watching her writhings and harkening to her screams!"

Ta-nu-ko shuddered again, but controlled himself, nodded, and turned away, saying:

"At sunset, then." And plunging into the bushes, he disappeared down the slope.

Gur stood looking after him, marking his progress by the waving of the brush, and as the priest drew farther and farther toward the river Gur's evil smile spread wider and wider. At length he chuckled, and muttered to himself:

"Sweet indeed would it be to torture a maiden of the Ta-an, but sweeter still to keep her as a slave! Then should she labor for me, carrying water, preparing my food, dressing, with her greater skill, the hides of beasts which I slay—perchance even teaching me to bring to life the Red God, that he might warm me in cold and dry me in wet! Also, thus could I beat her each day! And who shall tell this traitor priest that Gur has not obeyed him? And could he harm me did he know? In truth, I will keep the maiden alive!"

And grunting and chuckling, shaking his head in glee at the prospect, Gur took his way down the hill in turn, swinging south, then west along the river-bank to a point opposite the Great Rock, where, after gorging himself on a lump of raw meat, afterward drinking deep from the river, he stretched out in the shadow of an overarching tree to sleep away the long hours between noon and sunset.

The Ta-an had made their homes along a winding stream, dwelling in the caves and grottoes of steep cliffs that overhung the water, these home; stretching for some six or eight hundred paces along the twists and turns of the river-bed, and to one of the largest and finest of the caves the chief priest made his way, climbing to the entrance, some ten or fifteen feet above the ground, by means of a rude ladder—the stout trunk of a tree, with footholds chopped deep into the wood on each side.

Reaching his home he seated himself on the rocky floor at the cavern's mouth, squatting where he could overlook the broad river and the path which led along the bank. Here he sat for an hour or more, meditating upon the fate of A-ta, for the priest was not by nature cruel.

But he could see naught else that he might have done; jealous of the power of the priesthood, believing firmly that in the priest clan was bound up the welfare of the tribe, it behooved him to secure for that clan the finest and best of the young men.

And such a one was Menzono-men; tall and strong and handsome, well formed, young, filled with high ideals, he would be a ministrant most acceptable to O-Ma-Ken, Great Father of the Ta-an. And the priests of the tribe might not marry! In very truth, A-ta was a stumbling-block in the way of the priesthood!

But was there not some other way? Even yet it was not

too late; it were easy to let Gur go balked of his victim! And for the hundredth time Ta-nu-ko turned over in his mind plan after plan.

To slay the maiden himself, in secret; to betray her into some pitfall; anything to bring her a more merciful death. But no; the trackers of the Ta-an were skilled and crafty; Sar-no-m'rai, The Eyes That Walk By Night, friend and boyhood companion of the Great Chieftain—keener was he than a hunting wolf; no man might hope to elude his wondrous vision, to move without leaving traces that he could see and read.

No, this was the only way; for the hundredth time Ta-nu-ko reached this decision, now final, and, rising, he made his way down the ladder and turned his steps eastward along the shore of the river.

Five hundred paces had he gone when he was aware of a movement, a rustling of the bushes ahead, and he stopped in his tracks, unslinging his powerful bow from his shoulders and fitting an arrow to the string—none might tell when some beast of prey would attack! But he lowered the bow and replaced the arrow as a girl of nineteen rounded a turn of the path and came toward him, smiling, and he smiled in response, feeling a twinge of pain in his bosom as he did so, for it was A-ta.

And once again the priest sensed a regret that so fair a one must die, for indeed A-ta was fair, fit bride for such as Menzono-men. Tall she was, so that her eyes looked level into Ta-nu-ko's; long of limb, and slim yet round, the muscles playing under the smooth, sleek skin; brown of hair and of eye, as beseemed a maiden of the People of the Mountain Caves, and so beautiful of feature that in the tribal songs her name was coupled with that of the half-fabled A-ai, the Dawn, bride of Snorr, the Great Chieftain of olden time.

As she stood in the patches of sunlight that filtered through the trees, clad in a scanty garment of leopard's hide that left bare her arms and right shoulder and breast, and reached but to the middle of her thighs, Ta-nu-ko wondered not that Ro-su, Carver of Statues, had cut from the tusk of a mammoth a figure which he named A-ta; not fairer was its surface than the velvet roundness of the living form!

A-ta drew near, smiling, for she was friend to every man and to every woman of the Ta-an, and the Chief Priest turned sick, closed his eyes, and swayed where he stood as a vision rose before him of that lovely form, bound and writhing in agony as the savage chieftain of the Little Hairy Men stripped thongs of skin from the tortured flesh.

Instantly A-ta was at his side, her arm about his waist, supporting him, as she said, anxiously:

"Ta-nu-ko! You are sick? Has illness overtaken you?"

He recovered himself with an effort, thinking silently:

"It is for the Ta-an!" Aloud he answered: "It is but a passing weakness; not since dawn of yesterday have I tasted food." Then, once more erect and firm:

"A-ta, we are well met; I sought a messenger, and you will serve. It is for the Ta-an!"

"Speak!" answered the girl. "In what way can I serve the Ta-an?"

"To-morrow is the Great Sacrifice of the Hunt; it is for that I fast. Go you to the Great Rock that overhangs the water, two thousand paces to the south from here, where the Smaller Water joins this our stream. The place is known to you?"

The girl nodded silently, and the priest went on.

"Take with you this sacred basket of woven reeds, bathe your hands and arms even to the shoulders seven times in the water, bathing also the basket. As the sun sinks to rest in the Great Water, pluck from the rock three handfuls of the moss that grows there, returning swiftly to the Place of Sacrifice, where I will take the moss, needed for the sacrifice to-morrow. Let no sound pass your lips from now till it is in my hands, and see that the moss is touched by naught save only your fingers and the basket in which you bring it. And fail not to pray in silence to the Great Father that you may be worthy to render this service. Go in peace!"

The girl bowed, then hesitated as she turned away, raising her left hand and her eyebrows in inquiry.

"Speak!" said Ta-nu-ko.

"Think not that I seek to avoid serving," spoke A-ta, "but did not the son of Sen-va bring the sacred moss but yesterday?"

"It has been defiled. One of the children of the tribe, meaning no harm, laid a hand upon it as it was carried from the young man's hands to the altar. Go in peace, omitting not to pray to the Great Father."

The girl bowed, and kneeling before the chief priest, said: "Your blessing on my errand, Ta-nu-ko!"

Once more Ta-nu-ko shuddered, but laid his hands on the girl's head, moving his lips silently—words would not come!

Satisfied, A-ta rose and continued along the path, the

priest watching her till she was hidden in the bushes, when he covered his face with his hands and bent his head.

"Great Father," he prayed, "accept the sacrifice of my honor! In thy service has a priest of the Ta-an spoken with two tongues and sent to her death the noblest maiden of the tribe. May the sacrifice find favor in thy sight!"

Rousing himself, he passed on to the cave of T'san-va-men, Great Chieftain of the Ta-an, where the two sat long, planning the Great Hunt, when the tribe would move, men and women and children, ten days' journey to the north and west, to make a camp where they would hunt, storing meat, dried in the smoke of the fires, to keep them through the Long Cold.

The plans made, Ta-nu-ko returned along the river to his own cave, where he wrapped himself in skins of wolf and leopard and lay down to sleep.

He slept ill, being troubled much by dreams, and on awaking, he caught sight of a man hurrying along the path by the water's edge.

Nearer and nearer drew the figure, and soon Ta-nu-ko recognized it for the burly form of L'vu, friend and right-hand man to the Great Chieftain. Coming near, L'vu looked upward, and, seeing the chief priest above, halted and raised his left hand. Ta-nu-ko nodded and beckoned, clenching his right fist and moving it back and forth across his body, knuckles upward, and L'vu climbed the ladder, bowing deeply before the priest.

"Ta-nu-ko, Chief Priest," he said, "T'san-va-men, Lord of the Winged Death, Great Chieftain of the Ta-an, sends me to pray you come to him swiftly."

Ta-nu-ko leaped to his feet. "Trouble is come upon the Ta-an?" he asked.

"Nay," answered L'vu, "upon the Great Chieftain. A-ta, whom he loves as a daughter, returned not to her home, and he fears misfortune may have come upon her. Savage beasts are abroad."

"I come!" And quickly the two climbed down the ladder, making their way in haste to the cave of T'san-va-men. Arrived there, the priest bowed before the chieftain, who motioned him to sit, L'vu, Sar-no-m'rai, and others standing respectfully.

"Ta-nu-ko," spoke the chieftain, "A-ta returned not to the cave of her father yesternight. She was seen to speak with you by the river, and by none has she been seen since. Can you perchance tell us aught of what has overtaken her?"

"Nay, naught is known to me, save only that by me was she sent to bring the sacred moss for the Great Sacrifice of the Hunt, going to the Great Rock to gather it."

"Did not the son of Sen-va bring moss?"

"By chance was it defiled."

T'san-va-men turned to Sar-no-m'rai.

"Sar-no-m'rai," he said, "most skilful of all the trackers of the Ta-an are you. Go swiftly to the Great Rock and bring news of what you read there."

The famous hunter bowed in silence, examined his weapons—ax and dagger of flint, bow and arrows—and, turning, left the cave, proceeding on a jog-trot down the river. In silence he went, and in silence he returned.

Straight to the chieftain's cave he came, bowing before T'san-va-men and starting to draw in the dust the three circles of ceremony without which none dared address the Great Chieftain of the Ta-an. But T'san-va-men waved his hand impatiently, saying:

"That another time! Speak quickly!"

"Oh, Great Chieftain," said Sar-no-m'rai, "to the Great Rock went A-ta. There knelt she by the stream, bathing hands and arms; her knees had pressed deeply into the grass by the river's edge. Rising, she went to the Great Rock and took from it some moss. While doing so, she was seized from behind by one of the Little Hairy Men, who crept close and sprang upon her; the tracks were clear. Bitterly she fought, but was overpowered and carried away. Also, I found where the Little Hairy Man had lain and slept. Also, I bring the basket of woven reeds given A-ta by Ta-nu-ko, thus proving his words."

And he laid down the basket at the chieftain's feet, drawing back and bowing as he took once more his place in the circle.

The chieftain's face grew red with anger and his brows drew together as he leaped to his feet, clenching his fists. But his eye fell on Ta-nu-ko, who sat with his face buried in his hands, muttering:

"And I sent her to death! It is I who am to blame!"

The Great Chieftain eyed the priest askance for a moment, for he had no strong love for the priesthood, but Ta-nu-ko's grief and self-reproach were evident, and his face softened. Stepping near, he laid his hand on the shoulder of the chief priest, saying gently:

"Nay, Ta-nu-ko, blame not yourself! One or another must bring the moss, and who so fit as A-ta, purest of the pure? And it is not known that she is dead; it may be that the Little Hairy Men but hold her captive. Blame not yourself, Ta-nu-ko! If she lives, rescue will find her—and if not, the Little Hairy Men shall journey into the Long Dark!" He turned to L'vu.

"L'vu," he said, "take Kan-to, Sar-no-m'rai, and Sen-va, also others, as you may see fit. Go swiftly up the river and down, also up the Smaller Water; summon the warriors of the Ta-an, bidding them come armed and with food, prepared for war, for by the Great Father above I swear to rescue A-ta whole and unharmed from the hands of the Little Hairy Men, or to carry swift death and destruction to all their tribe, from the Snow-Crowned Mountains on the east to the Great Water on the west; from the Great Blue Water on the south to the farthest north that the foot of man has trod. Go swiftly; summon the tribesmen to war! Go!"

2

AT THE ROCK OF COUNCIL

THE FOLLOWING MORNING as the chieftain, with Nan-ai, his wife, arose, and the two stepped to the mouth of the cave, they stopped, smiling, for their son, a lad of fourteen, squatted in the sunlight polishing and testing his boyish weapons.

"Oh, Great Chieftain, my father," greeted the youth instantly, "take me, I pray, with you into battle! Beasts have I fought and slain, but never armed foes. Strong am I, and skilled in the use of weapons, even as you yourself have said; let me then go with you, I beg, that I may learn to meet the shock of battle, as beseems a chieftain's son of the Ta-an!"

T'san-va-men looked with pride at the youth, then turned to his wife, saying:

"Your son is he also; shall his prayer be heard?"

Nan-ai clung to her husband's arm, mingled pride and fear showing on her face as she answered, doubtfully:

"Our only son is he, and I fear for him! Yet—yet—Tsu-ven must learn! Only—I beg—watch over him in battle, my husband!"

The chieftain's eyes glowed proudly, but he controlled himself, saying only:

"L'vu and Sar-no-m'rai shall keep near him. Better teachers could he not have; craft and skill, skill and strength—he will return to you, bearing the weapons of his foes!" Then turning to his son he nodded, saying: "Your wish is granted; you shall go."

The youth's face glowed, and his eyes shone, but he said, quietly and soberly:

"I thank you, my father; and you also, my mother." Then rising, he took his weapons and left the cave, turning into the forest, while the chieftain turned to his wife, speaking gently, laughing a little:

"Nay, put fear from your heart, Nan-ai; even such a one was I in my youth—yet I still live!"

"L'vu comes," said Nan-ai, and T'san-va-men turned to greet his messenger, who drew near, hurrying along the river-bank. Reaching the cave, L'vu knelt before the chieftain, drew in the dust with his finger, and said:

"Great chieftain, the men of the eastern caves are at the Rock of Council."

"It is well," replied T'san-va-men. "And Sar-no-m'rai approaches from the north!"

Even as he spoke Sar-no-m'rai came, reporting as had L'vu, and swift on his heels Kan-to from the west and Sen-va from the south.

"To the Rock of Council," said T'san-va-men, and stepped within the cave, to gather his weapons when, striding along the path by the river, hurrying, appeared a young man of some twenty years of age, tall and handsome, slim of build, but wiry and muscular.

Approaching the cave, he knelt before the chieftain, drawing in the dust the interlocking circles of ceremony. By his unmutilated hands, which bore all the fingers intact, the youth might have been an artist, but he carried only the lance and dagger of boyhood, and by the absence of ax and bow it might be recognized that he had not yet been inducted into any of the clans, either priestly, artist, or warrior.

"Speak, Menzono-men!" said the chieftain, and the young man began, doubtfully and hesitatingly:

"Oh, T'san-va-men, Great Chieftain of the Ta-an," he said, "it is known to you that from childhood my parents have destined me to the priestly clan?" He looked up questioningly, and the chieftain nodded, whereat the youth continued:

"I crave a boon—I—I—" and he stopped, seeking words.

"Speak! I can but refuse," said T'san-va-men.

"I—I—O Great Chieftain, let me be one of the warriors rather than the priests!" said the Slayer of Wolves. "I—I love A-ta; to give her up—I could not endure to see her another's! And—and—to slay a bound and helpless victim on the altar—I cannot do it! My heart sickens, my hand weakens at the thought! To slay in battle, in defense of my life and of the tribe, yes, but at the altar I cannot! Let me be of the warrior clan and go with you to seek A-ta!"

T'san-va-men turned on his companions a look which they understood, for though it was not seemly that the chieftain should oppose the priests, yet to his boyhood companions, men who had stood by him in outlawry and had been with him received again into the tribe, it was well known that the Great Chieftain had no love for the priest clan.

His enmity was perhaps natural; Ja-ko, then chief priest, had endeavored to have him slain, but though Ja-ko had long since gone into the Long Dark, yet still it pleased the chieftain could he draw the best of the young men to the warrior clan.

But he turned a stern face to the kneeling youth.

"Menzono-men," said the chieftain, "this is a great thing you ask. It does not become a chieftain of the Ta-an to oppose the priests, taking from them one vowed to them from childhood! Nor has your training been that of a warrior; how, then, shall you handle weapons and endure the hardships of war?"

"Oh, Great Chieftain," spoke the Slayer of Wolves eagerly, "long have I trained myself in the use of weapons, and to endure the long march and the cold camp! Ever in my mind has been the thought that perchance I might be a warrior. And for the rest—if a priest I must be—my lance will set me free!"

"Speak not thus!" said the chieftain sternly. "It is to serve the Great Father that you are vowed to the priest clan! He will not receive with favor one who shuns his service! Your body to the beast and your soul to the Place of Evil should you thus avoid your duty! Only by favor of the priest clan, only with their consent, can you be a warrior. But go we now to the Rock of Council; do you follow, and this matter shall be laid before the tribe."

So saying, the chieftain and his men bent their steps to the north, fording the river and taking the shortest way across a neck of land, formed by a loop in the stream, Menzono-men following submissively, head bent.

This short-cut saved perhaps some three thousand paces in distance, but made necessary the fording of the river a second time, and this at a dangerous place, where the water, narrowing below a little island, and made swift by the shallow bottom which alone made possible the ford, foamed and boiled waist deep over a rough, rocky, and uneven bed.

More than one man, daring this passage, had been swept from his uncertain footing and whirled and tumbled down-stream until, battered and bruised by the sharp and jagged stones which thrust up from the rapids below, his lifeless body was spewed ashore from some eddy far down the river.

But the chieftain and his men, confident of their strength and skill—and not unwilling to test Menzono-men—strode along the narrow path toward the river.

Reaching the river-bank, the chieftain plunged unhesitating into the water, and after him L'vu.

Then followed Sen-va, and after him came Sar-no-m'rai, and last Kan-to, Menzono-men—who had never dared the ford—watching, awestruck, at the careless manner in which these men flung themselves to what seemed certain death.

At length the young man's turn was come, T'san-va-men, who had reached the farther bank, swinging about to see the manner of the young man's coming. But at that instant the chieftain's eye was caught by Kan-to, who slipped on the wet rock, staggered, caught at his balance, poised wavering, flung up his arms, fell, and was carried away by the rushing water, his form now appearing, now lost to view as he was swept down the flood.

Among the Ta-an it was, if not a disgrace, at least unusual, for man or woman to be unable to swim. By force of long tradition, the mothers took their children, while yet infants, to a shallow pool in some near-by stream, there letting them sport and play in the smooth water, so that often indeed a child could swim before he was able to walk.

But it had so chanced that Kan-to when young, had had his right leg broken by a falling rock, and although he had, by long and arduous training, overcome this handicap, and was known as a warrior of especial strength and skill, he had not learned to swim as well as most of his tribe.

But even as the chieftain turned to run, a white form rose from the farther bank, curved downward, plunged, and Menzono-men, like a swooping bird, cleft the water in one magnificent dive, disappearing with scarce a splash, and rising to the surface at once, his arms and legs flashing in the long, sweeping overhand stroke that carries a swimmer with utmost speed.

T'san-va-men, running, eyed the water anxiously; five hundred paces below the rocks broke the surface in those rapids where no man might live. Could Menzono-men bring Kan-to to shore ere the flood carried them there?

Faster and faster the swimmer closed on the drowning man, flashing through the boiling, surging water even as the salmon darts. No spray flew from those gleaming arms; in smooth, even strokes they broke the water, and gently if swiftly they clove it again—only the arms showed above the surface; body and head buried, save only that at times the head was raised for breath or for a quick glance ahead.

Thus Menzono-men bore down on the older man—half-way to the rapids he overtook him—dove—came up behind—passed his right arm through the crook of Kan-to's elbows, drawing Kan-to's arms behind him—turned on his left side, bringing Kan-to's face above the water—and, swimming with legs and left arm alone, made his way slowly toward the shore, where the others waited his coming.

Still the river swept them down, and doubt was in the minds of T'san-va-men and his followers—could he make it? Nearer and nearer drew the rapids—but now Menzono-men was close at hand—into the water plunged T'san-va-men, grasping the hand of Sar-no-m'rai, he holding to Sen-va, the burly L'vu, as anchor, gripping tight an overhanging limb of a tree.

Out into the stream stretched the living chain, and as Menzono-men bore down on them the out-thrust hand of the chieftain caught the wrist of the young man, and the two were hauled ashore, where they lay gasping, exhausted by the struggle. Kan-to recovered first—he had but rested while Menzono-men swam with him—and staggering to his feet he spoke:

"Ours must he be; not for such a one the bound and helpless victim on the altar!"

"In very truth!" answered the chieftain, and L'vu and Sen'va echoed his words: "In very truth!" while Sar-no-m'rai, ever silent unless speech were needed, nodded his head in agreement.

Presently Menzono-men, too, rose, and the six—though now more slowly—resumed their march to the Rock of Council, some four hundred paces from the ford, where were gathered the warriors and priests from the neighboring caves both up and down the river, and from the caves and shelters along both sides of the Smaller Water.

The Rock of Council, flat-topped like a table, and some ten paces in diameter, rose two-thirds the height of a man above the level of the plain, and grouped in a semicircle about it—for the river flowed under one side—were four or five hundred armed men, strong, active, and eager of face, each dressed in a single scanty garment of hide, each bearing ax and dagger and lance, bow and quiver of arrows.

On the rock sat, or rather squatted, five men, Ta-nu-ko, and four lesser priests, for among the Ta-an the priest clan had equal voice with the warrior clan in all deliberations concerning the welfare of the tribe.

Toward this rock the Great Chieftain strode, followed by his four trusted lieutenants, and Menzono-men, and the crowd opened before them, closing in again behind, each warrior raising his lance erect, full length, above his head, while a mighty shout rose to the sky:

"Comes T'san-va-men! Hail, Lord of the Winged Death, Great Chieftain of the Ta-an!"

Reaching the Rock of Council, T'san-va-men took two quick steps and, burdened as he was with weapons, leaped full and free to its surface, landing erect. Followed L'vu, Sar-no-m'rai, and Sen-va; last Kan-to, though for him, weakened from the river, the effort was great.

Menzono-men halted at the foot of the rock, kneeling as became one who had a gift to crave, but T'san-va-men, turning, beckoned him, using the clenched fist moved back and forth across the body, breast-high, and the Slayer of Wolves, rising, leaped also upon the rock, while a murmur of astonishment ran through the crowd—an unfledged youth, not yet admitted to either warrior or priest clan, standing on the Rock of Council! But swinging about on the edge of the rock, his men beside him and the priests behind, rising to their feet, the chieftain spoke:

"Warriors of the Ta-an, too bold grow the Little Hairy

Men! To all of you is known A-ta—but yesternight was she, going to the Great Rock for the sacred moss, attacked and carried to death or captivity by one of their tribe. Shall this be? Shall one of the noblest of the Ta-an be slave to a savage people, a people who command not the Red God, but, losing him, go cold till they can beg a spark? * Or shall she be victim to a people who torture captives, slaying them through long days, and even, it is told, devouring the bodies of those slain in battle or upon their vile altars? Shall not the warriors of the Ta-an move to the rescue, punishing this base people, driving them far from our homes, and—it may be—sending them into the Long Dark? How say you, men of the Ta-an? Speak!"

Then from the crowding warriors rose a great shout:

"Lead us, O chieftain! Lead us against the Little Hairy Men, that we may destroy them! Lead us! Lead us!"

The chieftain turned to the priests.

"And you, Ta-nu-ko—how say you? For your word also must we have ere we go to battle!"

Now, Ta-nu-ko would gladly have opposed; hoping for the death of A-ta, and fearing the capture of Gur, willingly would he have negatived the proposal to war—yet dared not! No reason could he give that would not betray him, and he bowed, saying:

"Lead, T'san-va-men! The Great Father will send victory!"

Then rose a greater shout than before, and weapons were tossed on high, but the chieftain raised his hand.

---

* Even at the present day there are savage tribes who are familiar with the use of fire, but cannot generate it, depending on keeping alive a spark, or, if this be lost, on fortuitous origins, such as lightning—AUTHOR.

"Yet one thing, men of the Ta-an! Here stands before you Menzono-men, Slayer of Wolves, a youth vowed to the priesthood, who yet craves admittance to the warrior clan, that he may go with us to seek A-ta, beloved by him. Also, he craves not the service of the altar, slaying the bound victim, but rather the shock of battle. How say you, warriors and priests; shall his prayer be heard?"

This was a serious matter; diverting from a clan one vowed thereto; and the warriors stood thoughtful, a murmur rippling through the ranks. Aghast stood Ta-nu-ko; should this be granted, his crime had gone for naught! Useless his betrayal of A-ta, useless his lies, useless his sacrifice of honor! He leaped forward, throwing out his hands.

"Warriors and priests of the Ta-an!" he cried, "this may not be! From birth is Menzono-men vowed to the priesthood; not for us now to turn aside that vow! The wrath of the Great Father would lie heavy on us did we thus! This may not be! Further, untrained is the youth to war; no skill has he in the use of weapons; no warrior, he, but a priest, to serve at the altar!"

Again the chieftain spoke:

"Not an hour since did this youth save the life of Kan-to, who stands beside me now, plunging of his own free will into the Ford of Death to bring to shore Kan-to, swept down the flood! Is it for such a one to serve at the altar or to fight shoulder to shoulder with other warriors in battle?"

Once more a murmur spread through the ranks, this time of astonishment, and all looked with respect on the youth who had dared, swimming, the Ford of Death. Then forward stepped Sar-no-m'rai, raising his hand, and the crowd was still, listening with attention, for Sar-no-m'rai was known as one who, usually silent, spoke, when he spoke at all, with the tongue of wisdom.

"Men of the Ta-an!" he said, "this youth has courage. Also, strength has he, his deed proving well my words. Yet the chief priest says he knows not the use of weapons as a warrior should, nor can he endure hardships as beseems a warrior. Let us then put this to the proof.

"Let Menzono-men lie, fasting, for seven days and seven nights on the Rock of Council, unsheltered from the sun and from the storm. Let him then bring to the Rock of Council—still fasting—the skin of Menzono the wolf, the horn of the Beast that Wears a Horn on His Nose, and the Poisoned Slayer—this last living, and borne in the naked hand. So shall he prove his skill with weapons, his craft, his courage, and his endurance. Is the word good?"

"The word is good! The word is good!" shouted the warriors, and Sar-no-m'rai turned to the chief priest, asking directly:

"Is the word good?"

Ta-nu-ko, confident that the youth could not meet the test, and sure also that A-ta, for all her strength and spirit, would be dead long ere the test was ended and the warriors should move—in his heart pleased with the proposal, yet feigning reluctance, answered:

"The word is good!"

"Do you accept the test?" asked the chieftain of Menzono-men, and the youth bowed, replying:

"Gladly, Great Chieftain!"

"It is said!" spoke T'san-va-men, turning to the group. "Go you now to your homes; prepare for war, taking food, making ready your weapons, each man carrying five tens of arrows, for perchance is this a long war. On the twelfth day be here once more, to greet Menzono-men, and thereafter we march. Go, prepare! It is said!"

He waved his hand and leaped from the rock, and the crowd melted swiftly away, the warriors going to hunt beasts for food, that the flesh might be smoked over the fires, going to make new stores of arrows, to look over their weapons, and to make ready in all things.

There remained the chieftain and his followers, the priests under Ta-nu-ko, and Menzono-men. To the last the chieftain turned, saying: "You have heard! Water will be brought you daily. The Great Father aid you!"

And the ten strode off into the forest, T'san-va-men taking one path, Ta-nu-ko another, and the young man was left alone to his vigil on the Rock of Council.

3

THE CAVE THAT SWIMS ON THE WATER

AND NOW FOR a time we turn to A-ta, the Girl of the Mountain Caves. Trusting the words of Ta-nu-ko, fearing naught, and rejoicing to be entrusted with so holy a mission, she followed her instructions with care, going duly to the Great Rock, bathing herself and the basket, and repairing to the rock to gather the sacred moss for the sacrifice.

While kneeling before the rock, A-ta caught a slight sound, the rustling of a dry stick, perhaps, and turned swiftly, fearing some beast of prey, but even as she turned, as she had a glimpse of a squat, hairy form, there descended on her head a club, a million lights flashed and whirled before her eyes, and she sank back, dazed.

But deep within her breast a voice seemed to say: "Fight! Fight!" and with all her powers she struggled to rise. Her limbs seemed weighted down, and but slowly and with infinite effort could she stir, yet she stood upright and as Gur advanced, grinning, she closed, grappling him, biting, scratching, striking with fist and knee, so that the chieftain of the Little Hairy Men gave back, amazed.

Closely A-ta followed, for it was the tradition and training of the Ta-an—and A-ta was a warrior's child—ever to carry the fight forward, not standing on defense, but ever attacking, and closing with Gur once more she sank her teeth deep in his upper arm, so that the blood gushed forth and the man howled with pain. But he wrenched free, leaped back, and as A-ta came forward again his club fell—once more the lights whirled and danced before her eyes—and all was black.

When she regained consciousness she was being carried over Gur's shoulder, belly down, her legs in front tight clasped in his muscular left arm, her face, behind, bumping against the small of his back as he proceeded at a shambling trot through the darkening forest. Her feet were tied together with a thong, her hands were tied behind her back, but as soon as A-ta was fully conscious she began once more to struggle.

Gur stopped, leaned his club against his body, reached around with his right hand, and caught the girl's long hair, which was flowing loose. He twisted it about his forearm, pulling it taut and drawing her head over to one side, picked up his club, and resumed his swinging trot, and A-ta, now helpless and tortured, again lost consciousness.

All during that long night Gur proceeded thus, never once stopping to rest, but keeping on, on, ever on. At times A-ta came out of her swoon and realized what was happening, at times all was black and she knew but vaguely the pain of the regular jerk, jerk, jerk on her imprisoned hair.

Once the slap of cold water on her face roused her to full consciousness as Gur forded a river, and A-ta wondered dully at the marvelous strength and endurance in the ungainly, almost grotesque body of the chieftain who could carry a grown woman thus tirelessly through the midnight dark of the forest, but as the water grew deeper she swooned once more, half strangled by the flood that swept over her face.

A-ta never knew how long Gur carried her (it was, in fact, for several days, with intervals for rest), nor had she any slightest notion of the route he followed. When next her senses came to her it was late afternoon—the sun was just setting—and she lay, still bound, on the floor of a rude cave, the home of her captor.

At first A-ta did not move; indeed, she could not, for every bone and muscle ached fiercely from the terrible ride, and her head throbbed agonizingly—she had been carried head downward for long hours. So she lay still, looking about, examining what came within range of her eyes, for the cave fronted the west, and the last rays of the sun struck brilliantly into it.

The roof of the cave was not ornamented with drawings and paintings of bison and mammoth, as were the caves of the Ta-an, nor had any slightest effort been made to shape the grotto into a better home; the floor was not swept, nor was the daily litter removed; gnawed bones, scraps of fur, weapons, tools, and other objects mingling in heaps about the place, so that A-ta felt a wave of disgust as she saw the filthy way her captor lived.

"Even the beasts thrust offal from their dens!" she thought, and her disgust grew as she watched Gur, squatting before a fire, cook and eat his evening meal, for he tore the meat like a tiger, grunting and growling and snarling over it, nor, to A-ta's amazement, did he allow it to cook through; instead, he roasted the outside over the flames, gnawed off that layer, cooked it a little more, gnawed off the next layer in turn, and so on, cooking and eating alternately.

A-ta gave an exclamation of disgust, and Gur rose, coming to stand by her side, grinning down at her and saying something which was unintelligible to the girl, for he spoke in the tongue of the Little Hairy Men.

Turning, he apparently called some one, and four women of the tribe entered, to stand watching the captive, jabbering excitedly, whereupon the girl, exhausted, overwrought, tortured, and in an agony of fear, swooned again.

Then for many days A-ta, a prisoner, labored for Gur, carrying wood and water, curing hides, preparing food, doing the work of the chieftain's household, beaten if she failed to do it, beaten if she did it, but ever borne up by the hope of escape. So A-ta labored for Gur, seeking ever her chance, watchful always, thinking ever of some way to get back to the Ta-an.

Gradually, day by day, she made her plans for escape, deciding finally that by water, if at all, could she win back to the home caves of the Ta-an. Could she make the journey, beset as it was by nameless terrors?

So thinking, that very night A-ta made up her mind to the attempt, but it was an attempt foredoomed to failure. Gur following hard on her trail, and recapturing her, despite her desperate resistance. Then followed fresh indignities, until she resolved to plan more fully, to see if it were not possible to devise some means which would enable her to evade pursuit, and the thought came that she might follow the stream *in* rather than *beside* the water, for then she would leave no trail, no scent would lie, and the sweep of the river itself would carry her on her way.

But she could not hope to swim any such distance—would it be possible to float on a log? No, a log would roll under her; she could not sleep on it, nor could she carry food, for any least little wavelet would sweep it away.

Day after day she pondered over the matter, turning it over and over in her mind as she worked for Gur, and at last the solution came. She would travel on a log, beaching it at night—taking the risk of discovery—and would hollow out a place for her food—instantly there flashed across her mind the thought: "Why not hollow out a place for myself, too? Lying down, I could draw leaves and branches over myself, and the Little Hairy Men, passing, would think it but a stranded tree!"

The more she thought it over, the more this idea pleased her, and she set about to accomplish her purpose.

The first thing that occurred to her was that she must work at night, for during the day she was too cleverly watched, so night after night she slipped from the cave to work in the forest, it being, fortunately, full moon, so that there was light enough to see.

Each night, as Gur placed the bonds on her ankles and wrists, A-ta craftily set her muscles—a trick she had learned from Sar-no-m'rai—so that when she relaxed the thongs might fall slack and her hands and feet, slim and flexible, be drawn through, nor did Gur, dull of brain and slow of wit, but, trusting the bonds, and sleeping soundly, once notice the deception. But for all her care it was no simple matter to escape nightly from the cave, nor was it easy to force her tired limbs, worn and exhausted by the labor of the day, to struggle with the task she had set herself.

But night after night she persevered, first burning with a slow fire—the coals stolen from Gur's hearth—the wood from the surface of the great tree she had chosen.

It was a long task for a young girl, but at length it was finished; and then the thought occurred to her; how was she to propel her log?

Down-stream the current would carry it, but she must travel against the current after reaching the junction of the rivers.

Long she pondered this matter, and finally cut a pole, trusting that she might be able to push her craft along, striking the pole against the bed of the stream; then, ready to start, she placed in the hollowed-out space her provisions, stolen, little by little, from her captor; dried flesh of deer and wild horse, roots and berries, and a bundle of salt, wrapped in a fragment of skin. As she was doing this her eye fell on her adze, and she thought:

"A dull tool cuts not well; will not a sharpened log cut the water better than a dull?" And down she sat to debate this new question.

All that day this question was in her mind, and when night came she had decided to sharpen one end of the log to a cutting edge—speed might be needed on the journey! This held her back three days—the longest three since she had begun her toil!—but at length the task was finally done and all was ready for the start.

Provisions stowed, adze beside them, pole ready, she prepared to slide the craft to the water—and could not move it!

A-ta was no heroine of romance, she was a poor, tired girl, worn out by her frantic labors, tortured and tried by the cruelty of Gur and his wives, borne up by the hope of escape; the dream of seeing her home and friends once more—she dropped full length on the ground and wept as though her heart would break.

Long she lay there, sobbing, thinking of the bitter contrast between her present fate and her happiness of a few short weeks before, when, of a sudden there flashed into her mind the humorous quirk of the chieftain's mouth and the gleam of his eyes as once he said, in time of famine:

"If the prey comes not to the hunter, then must the hunter go to the prey!"

Raising her head, A-ta stared intently into the forest, thinking hard; she rose, stepped to the waters' edge, looked long at the river, then:

"Perchance can I bring the river to the log!"

She looked up at the stars and saw that scarce three hours remained till dawn, then seized her adze and frantically began to scoop a canal, barely big enough to pass the log, from the river to the craft. Long and desperately she labored, until, when she was beginning to despair, she broke down the last barrier, in rushed the water—A-ta held her breath, watching—the log was afloat! About to step into the hollowed log, A-ta heard behind her a rustle, a gasp of astonishment, and whirled quickly, to see Boh, oldest and ugliest and most cruel of the wives of Gur.

Boh's mouth was open to yell, to call for help, but in that instant, before the sound came, A-ta's pole, driven by her strong young arms, the hatred engendered by weeks of torture urging, plunged, butt-first, into the woman's stomach.

Eyes goggling, mouth lolling, Boh doubled up and fell

slowly forward; as she fell the pole swept up and down, striking full on the back of her neck, and, the chief of Gur's wives pitched forward, dead. A-ta watched a moment, pole ready, but Boh did not stir, and the girl, stepping into her craft, sat down and pushed off from the bank, turning the bow down-stream.

Then followed days of comparative ease for A-ta. Once in her slow progress a band of the Little Hairy Men appeared on the southern bank, shouting and gesticulating, but after that no human being did she see, but many animals; Snorr-m'rai-no, Fear That Walks the Night; Do-m'rai, the Hill That Walks; Ven-su, the Beaver; Va-m'rai, the Swift Runner, trooping daintily down to the water's edge, his does and fawns following; Kzen, the Rat who lives in the water, and once, chancing to look up, she saw, depending from a spreading branch, the green and glistening form and evil, beady, black eyes of Sen-zo the Poisoned Slayer.

At length the mouth of the great river, as large almost as that on which she was, came in sight, and A-ta, poling her craft ashore, beached it at dusk to sleep one full night and in the morning take up the long struggle against the current that must be hers before she could win once more to the homes of the Ta-an.

4

A WARRIOR'S METTLE

MEANWHILE, MENZONO-MEN fasted on the Great Rock of Council, finding the task, indeed, more severe by far than he had expected it to prove. A fast of seven days and seven nights was naught to the young man, glorying in the strength of youth, nor—after the first day—did the wolf in his belly gnaw, but from the fierce sun Menzono-men sheltered himself as much as might be, following the shade while it lasted, and covering his bowed head with his hands; but for all he could do it seemed at times as though the blood seethed and bubbled within him, and more than once he felt, during the hottest hours, as though worms and maggots and grubs crawled and writhed within his skull.

And at night the coolness brought a chill from which he shivered.

Twice daily, at dawn and at sunset, water was brought by Ta-nu-ko and Kan-to, for neither priest nor warrior clan would trust the other to deal fairly, and the two made each trip in company.

So the weary days wore on, and on the fifth came the worst torment of all Menzono-men endured.

On the fifth day the wind had blown all morning, hot

and searing, his scanty allowance of water was exhausted long since, and he huddled, bent over, clasping his head in his hands and moaning slightly from time to time.

Once more Menzono-men groaned, and, stripping his scanty garment of hide from his loins, he wrapped it tightly about his head. Hot and suffering before, he was now half suffocated, yet he knew it was his only salvation, so he endured. Presently, little puffs of yet hotter wind came, bringing with them faint, sifting dust, which touched his skin almost caressingly, then faster and faster they came, till the dust, wind-borne, struck against him continuously, like rain, but no longer caressing; it burned and cut and stung, it dried yet further his already parched skin, it sifted through the covering about his head, it clogged his eyes, it filled his ears, it drove into his nostrils, it scorched his lips, till Menzono-men, tortured, could scarce restrain himself from leaping from the rock and running to the river, that, plunging in, he might find relief from his agony. One thought only held him back, and over and over he repeated to himself:

"A-ta! A-ta!" grinding his teeth and clenching his fists till the nails, cutting into the flesh, brought a new pain which in some measure diverted his mind from the old.

So for three long hours he held on, till the storm had blown itself out, and with the coming of the shade came Kan-to and Ta-nu-ko, bearing the precious water.

Menzono-men, knowing his haggard looks from the shocked expression of the warrior's face, yet contrived a twisted smile of greeting, winning thus a nod and smile of approval from Kan-to, who loved brave men.

"Endure yet two days," said Kan-to. "And it is permitted

to say to you that the Ta-an march not till your test is done, the Great Chieftain, Lord of the Winged Death, having sworn that should you succeed it shall be yours to seek out and slay the one who has taken A-ta captive."

Menzono-men, glancing from Kan-to to Ta-nu-ko, surprised a curious look on the latter's face, but thought little of it, taking it merely for disappointment at the favor shown. Rinsing his mouth, he took a long swallow of the life-bringing water, and after a vain effort spoke in a harsh, rasping croak:

"Bear my thanks to the Great Chieftain, I pray, and tell him I will endure; the suffering is great, but so likewise, and greater, is the reward!"

Kan-to nodded approvingly, and said:

"Good! Your words shall go to him." Then, turning, the two left Menzono-men to the last stretch of his fasting.

The worst was now past; there came no more dust-storms, and cooler weather made more endurable the days, the chill of night being less hard to bear than the heat of the day. Still, Menzono-men suffered, and was rejoiced when, at sunrise of the eighth day, there came to the Rock of Council T'san-va-men and Ta-nu-ko, none others being with them.

"Descend, Slayer of Wolves!" said the Great Chieftain, and the priest nodded, whereat the youth, gathering his strength, leaped from the rock and knelt before them.

"Menzono-men," said the chieftain gravely and solemnly, "the first part of the test have you passed. It remains now to pass the second. From this day forth water is yours where you shall find it, but not food. Swear now, by your honor as one of the Ta-an, by your worship as a child of O-Ma-Ken, the Great Father, and by your hope that after this life you may be with the spirits of your fathers in the Place of Good, that no food shall pass your lips till you come once more to the Rock of Council; bearing the horn of the great beast, the hide of the wolf, and the Poisoned Slayer; for none goes with you into the forest."

"As you have said, so do I swear," answered Menzono-men, solemnly and reverently.

"It is well!" said T'san-va-men. "Take now these weapons, a gift from me to you. Bear them into the forest and use them well, that your prayer may be granted! Go!"

And T'san-va-men dropped over the youth's shoulders the thong of a quiver of arrows and the string of a bow, placed in his girdle a beautiful dagger of flint, with handle of oak, and in his hands ax and lance. He touched the young man lightly on the shoulder, repeated: "Go!" and, turning, disappeared into the forest, followed by Ta-nu-ko.

Menzono-men remained kneeling while he uttered a prayer for aid, then, taking his way to the river, luxuriated in a quiet pool, whence, when he had bathed, he set out in search of a trail along which he might place a trap for the Beast that Wears a Horn on His Nose.

All that morning he tramped, till the sun was high overhead, when he rested for a time, and again took up the search, walking along the bank of the river and examining carefully and with attention the grass and brush which grew close down to the stream. Many game trails he passed, but none which bore the mark of the huge foot he sought, till about the middle of the afternoon he found the desired track. Casting a glance at the sun, the young man decided it was too late to set his trap; so, climbing a tree, he made a rude platform of branches wattled across two great limbs, and lay down to watch the trail.

At length, grunting and rolling his little piggish eyes, the prey he sought, the Beast that Wears a Horn on His Nose, came to the river to drink and then went away. This done, Menzono-men climbed cautiously down from the tree and with all possible speed—for it was at best a long task—selected a heavy tree, from which with infinite labor, he made a deadfall.

Presently came the first of the beasts, a troop of wild sheep, but they passed in safety, unalarmed—Menzono-men had cleared away, as well as might be, all signs of his labor, and had strewed the ground with strong-scented leaves plucked near the river." Next came a dozen wild cattle, and at last the chosen prey of the hunter.

Slowly he walked down the trail, grunting and snorting, his huge, ungainly bulk looming large in the dusk of the forest. On and on he came, and Menzono-men's heart beat fast—never had he hunted such mighty game! On and on, and Menzono-men, lips parted, watching closely, gathered tight the end of the vine—nearer and nearer came the beast—Menzono-men's eyes glowed—his muscles drew slowly taut—one step more—a strong jerk—the upright pole snapped—the great log, gathering speed, swept crashing down, striking the prey just behind the shoulders—and Menzono-men, after watching a moment, climbed down his tree and, taking his ax, began to cut away, the horn; the deadfall had broken the beast's spine and it had died instantly.

The following day saw Menzono-men returning toward the homes of the Ta-an, for while searching for the Beast that Wears a Horn on His Nose he had marked down a wolf's den, a cave in a pile of tumbled rocks, and here he planned to take the hide of Menzono the Slayer.

Here the young man lay in wait, and late in the afternoon his vigil was rewarded, for there suddenly appeared, without warning, like a magic trick, the head of a great gray wolf, framed in the black mouth of the den.

For some moments the wolf looked about, seeking danger, seeking to know whether or not he could safely leave his home, and the young man silently rose to one knee, lifting his bow, an arrow fitted to the string.

Slowly, silently rose the Slayer of Wolves, drew back the arrow to his ear, and sped the shaft—the wolf dodged back, catching sound of the twang of string, and Menzono-men dashed the bow furiously to the ground, cursing—the arrow had flown wild! Again he cursed, and stood a moment in thought, then looked at the sun, now low down toward the horizon, reflected a moment more, and with a reckless air dropped his weapons on the ground, all but his dagger, fell on all fours, and crawled head first into the wolf's den!

The dagger Menzono-men carried was a large one, the flint blade alone being half the length of the young man's forearm, from elbow to finger-tip.

Menzono-men had no fear, could he but reach the wolf with this, and on he crawled, down a little slope, the smell of the dank earth, mixed with the strong animal reek, in his nostrils as he went.

The entrance to the den pitched slightly downward, and the passage was at first barely wide enough for him to travel, but presently it widened slightly, giving more elbow-room, and became higher, so that he could walk, crouching. His feet struck against a few bones as he progressed, but for the most part the hard-packed earth underfoot was bare and clean.

And now there came to his nostrils another scent, that of blood, whereby he knew that some partly devoured prey of the wolf still lay in the den; lifting his head to sniff, his eyes caught the gleam of two greenish eyes ahead—the eyes of Menzono—his hand tightened on the dagger—in that instant there sounded a ferocious snarl—the eyes moved—the wolf sprang—and Menzono-men struck!

Twice he struck, even as the sharp teeth gashed his left arm, out-thrown, from elbow to wrist—again—again!—and all was still, save for his own hard breathing. Cautiously Menzono-men reached out and felt before him a warm, furry body; he was conscious of the hot blood gushing down his wounded arm; seizing the carcass, he backed from the den, dragging it after him, and, reaching the open air once more, flung himself down on the grass, panting, the great beast a huddled heap beside him.

Presently he rose, sought healing leaves, and bound them tightly about his arm, first bruising them between his hands that the soothing juices, entering the wounds, might allay the pain and prevent stiffening, then set to work to strip the hide from the wolf.

This was no slight task, weakened as he was by fasting, wearied by his labors at the deadfall, and further weakened by loss of blood; but he persisted, though the work was not finished till after nightfall, and Menzono-men saw scores of eyes gleaming about him, and heard rustlings in the brush.

At length, the hide taken, the young man thought of rest, and as he cast about for a safe place his eye lit with a sudden glint of humor; he would sleep in the wolf's den! No fear of the wolf's mate returning; this was the season of young, and there were none in the den, so this was a lone beast, unmated, and Menzono-men, pushing the rolled-up skin before him, crept into the den, curled up, faced the opening, and slept.

In the morning he woke, crawled from the den, finding the bones of the wolf picked bare of flesh by hyenas who had feasted during the night, and took up the third and most perilous part of his task, the search for the Poisoned Slayer. For this he struck inland, away from the river, for only seldom and by chance did the reptile come down to the water; he preferred the higher ground, where piled rocks offered many dens and lurking-places, and where, stretched out on their hot surface, he could sun himself through the long, unshaded days.

So Menzono-men turned his face away from the stream, climbing the slope of the gently rising ground to a place he knew, where were many tumbled rock masses, the chosen home of his third prey. All that morning he tramped, the forest gradually thinning out, till toward noon he came to the crest of a low hill and saw before him a little open space, rock-floored, where lay in twisted, interwined piles the green and shining bodies of thousands of snakes.

Snakes big and little, snakes young and old, lay in the hot sun, their unwinking eyes staring like black jewels in their evil, flattened heads. Menzono-men, drawing near, was conscious of a strong, sickening odor that rose from the deadly reptile, and he hesitated—the snakes, at sight of a man, lifting their heads and weaving them back and forth, darting their forked tongues in and out, while from the mass rose a low, prolonged hissing sound.

Menzono-men was no coward—none save a man of proved courage could crawl into a wolf's den to slay the beast!—but he was smitten with sick horror at the dreadful sight before him; instinctive fear, racial, from his ancestors, came upon him, and he retreated a few steps, shuddering; he leaned against a tree, shaking from head to foot, his empty stomach retching agonizingly as he strove vainly to vomit.

For some time he stood thus, then, calling up all his forces, he cut from a tree a straight branch some six feet in length, and with this in his hand approached once more the heap of snakes. Thrice he drew near and thrice recoiled, as there rose before him the memory of one he had seen die from the bite of the Poisoned Slayer—as there rang again in his ears the screams of the dying man, and his cries: "I burn! I burn! In pity, slay me!"

Menzono-men feared not death, but torture he feared! At last, with bitten lip and blood therefrom trickling down his chin, he stepped forward and extended the stick toward the nearest snake, which instantly flung itself into a coil and struck, recoiling swift as a flash of light. Still Menzono-men held out the stick, and again and again the snake struck till, exhausted or sullen, it refused to strike again.

Immediately the young man pressed the stick down firmly on the back of the snake's neck, and, despite its writhings, held it down while he gripped it tight with his right hand, clasping three fingers about its neck and pressing hard with thumb and forefinger against the sides of its jaw. He rose erect, the reptile twisting itself about his arm and wrenching in its efforts to reach him with its fangs, but Menzono-men held fast and turned once more toward the river.

Suddenly a thought struck him—how was he to carry the snake?

For a time the young man was puzzled, and was minded to slay this snake and capture another, but there came to him a recollection of what an old man of the Ta-an had told him; that should he press firmly on a certain spot on the snake's neck the reptile would sleep for a time. He tried, using his left hand, and to his amazement the snake ceased its struggles, became utterly rigid, stiff as the haft of an ax, and so remained.

He laid it down, took a thong of rawhide, made in it a slip-knot, fastened the other end to a long stick, slipped the loop over the snake's neck, drawing it snug, lifted his prey, and made his way to where he had left the hide of the wolf and the horn of the Beast that Wears a Horn on His Nose. These he lifted, and with them and his weapons set his face again toward the homes of the Ta-an and the Great Rock of Council.

5

TO THE DEATH

DOWN THE BANK of the river marched T'san-va-men, Great Chieftain of the Ta-an, followed by more than four hundred armed warriors of the tribe, each bearing ax and dagger, lance and bow, and a quiver of arrows.

A magnificent body of men were they, each man stepping proudly in the company to which he belonged.

Menzono-men, a full-fledged warrior, had knelt at the altar while Ta-nu-ko, the chief priest, with the adze and hammer of ceremony, struck off the little finger of his left hand, thus proving his induction into the clan, and he now strode forth proudly in the Company of the Wolf, following directly behind L'vu, Sar-no-m'rai, Kan-to, and Sen-va, these in turn stepping in the footprints of their chieftain, while beside Menzono-men walked Tsu-ven, son of the chief, claiming fulfilment of his father's promise.

The chieftain had sent out scouts, seeking a passage directly overland to the homes of the Little Hairy Men, but these had returned, confirming his belief that the Farther River was impassable, and he had resolved to march down the river on which he was to the junction of that with the one on which lived the Little Hairy Men, to cross the broad water by swimming, and make his way up the confluent branch along the southern shore.

Now, for seven days had the warriors marched, pressing on through forest and brush, fording or swimming small streams, and sleeping where night overtook them. Five days of rest and feeding had Menzono-men received, then three of fasting and prayer before the ceremony of induction, so it was now the twenty-eighth day since the disappearance of A-ta, and Menzono-men feared greatly, though L'vu oft reassured him, saying:

"Did she not die forthwith, she still lives, a slave." On the evening of the twenty-eighth day, as the warriors were preparing to camp, came one to T'san-va-men, greatly excited, begging speech with the chieftain. This granted, he knelt and drew on the grass the three circles of ceremony, saying:

"Oh, T'san-va-men, Lord of the Winged Death, Great Chieftain of the Ta-an, an omen!"

"Speak!" answered T'san-va-men, and the warrior replied:

"There comes a log toward us, moving against the stream!"

At these words there was a stir among those near the chief, and Tsu-ven broke out:

"Oh, father—Great Chieftain, rather—is the omen of good?"

T'san-va-men smiled at the boy's eagerness, answering gently:

"Go we forthwith to learn." And, rising from where he sat on a fallen tree, he led the way the few steps to the bank, where the crowd of warriors, eagerly peering, made way respectfully.

In very truth, far down the stream, there appeared a log, and in very truth was it making its way against the current. T'san-va-men looked for a time, then turned to him who stood at his left, saying:

"Sar-no-m'rai, keenest of all is your sight; look now and tell us if the omen be of good or of evil!"

Long Sar-no-m'rai looked, shading his eyes with his hand against the glare from the sky, then, smiling, he turned to the chieftain, replying:

"Good, in very truth! It is A-ta who comes!"

At these astounding words a buzz of wonder ran through the crowd, and T'san-va-men looked keenly at the most skilful tracker among the Ta-an.

"A-ta!" he cried. "Sar-no-m'rai, is this indeed sooth?"

"I speak not with two tongues," replied Sar-no-m'rai, and the chieftain answered:

"Indeed, that is known to me. It is A-ta!"

Forthwith a great shout broke from the warriors, and crying: "A-ta! A-ta!" they rushed along the bank till opposite the strange craft, which swung inshore to meet them. Amid much buzz of talk it was dragged up on dry land, and A-ta, half led, half carried, was taken to where the chieftain had resumed his seat on the log, over which had been thrown a lion's hide.

As she drew near he rose, and when she knelt he lifted her, pressing her in his arms and seating her near him on a smaller log which was quickly brought. Menzono-men was sent for, and food and drink were brought, and when the girl had rested and eaten she told her tale, showing the scars of the beatings she had received from Gur and his wives, and showing also her limbs, gaunt from starvation.

Frequent and loud were the curses as the tale was told, for A-ta was loved of all the tribe, and many were the demands to be led at once, without delay, against the Little Hairy Men, but T'san-va-men, thoughtful, asked:

"Was it chance, think you, A-ta, that Gur waited at the Great Rock? Or was it appointed?"

"Nay, Great Chieftain," replied A-ta, "he boasted that the chief priest of the Ta-an had sent me to him!"

"Gur speaks then the tongue of the Ta-an?"

"Nay, he did but point to me and to himself, saying: 'Ta-nu-ko! Ta-nu-ko!' and laughing."

For a long time the chieftain sat silent, thinking, remembering various trifles which at the time had made no impression, then, rising, he said:

"L'vu, Kan-to, Sen-va, take you the trail to the homes of the Ta-an. Reaching there, tell Ta-nu-ko I require his presence here. Tell him no other word, and in especial speak to none of the return of A-ta. Should he refuse—though it is not in my mind that he will—bring him by force, but unharmed. Go!"

The three bowed and took their departure, and T'san-va-men spoke to Sar-no-m'rai.

"A-ta being once more among us, the Little Hairy Men may wait our pleasure. Here we camp till these return with Ta-nu-ko; see to it!"

So camp was made, and for ten days the warriors of the Ta-an busied themselves with hunting and with drying over fires the flesh of the animals slain, adding thus to their store of food, to the supplies they carried with them to the war. On the eleventh day, at about the middle hour of the morning, appeared the messengers, and with them the chief priest, coming of his own will, though wondering.

Straight to T'san-va-men they went, bowing before him where he sat on his skin-covered log at the edge of a little glade in the forest, L'vu—having drawn the ceremonial sign—saying:

"Oh, Great Chieftain, the errand is accomplished; before you stands Ta-nu-ko, chief priest of the Ta-an!"

"It is well done," answered T'san-va-men. "Call now the warriors."

Presently, full-panoplied, the warriors of the Ta-an came hurrying, and grouped themselves in a semicircle about where sat the chieftain, none speaking; Ta-nu-ko standing alone three paces from him, and facing him. When all were placed T'san-va-men, closely watching Ta-nu-ko, said:

"L'vu, go you and bring A-ta," and he saw that Ta-nu-ko, for all his self-control, started and looked about quickly as though seeking escape. Quickly came A-ta, led by the burly lieutenant of the chieftain, and the circle parted to let her pass.

"A-ta," said T'san-va-men, "you have said that this priest betrayed you into the hands of Gur; tell now once more, that all may hear, what happened, that all may judge of the guilt of Ta-nu-ko, sending to death or slavery one of the Ta-an!"

But as A-ta was about to speak, Ta-nu-ko, who had recovered his self-possession, broke in:

"It needs not; the maiden speaks truly. I it was who sent her to the Great Rock, knowing that Gur awaited her coming. And this I did that Menzono-men, losing her whom he loved, might keep the vows made for him, following the path of the priestly clan, to the glory and honor of the Great Father of the Ta-an. The sin is mine, if sin there be; for the welfare of the tribe did I thus, sacrificing my honor to the glory of the Great Father, and mine is the punishment, if punishment there be!"

And he looked about him proudly and bravely—defiantly, even—at the throng of threatening faces, for from the warriors there rose a fierce growl, and a murmur of:

"Death to the traitor! Slay! Slay!"

But the chieftain raised his hand for silence, and in the hush that followed whispered briefly with L'vu and Sar-no-m'rai, both of these nodding. Then, addressing Ta-nu-ko, he spoke:

"Ta-nu-ko, chief priest of the People of the Mountain Caves, it is in my mind that you have done ill; betraying a maiden of the tribe into the hands of savages, to death or worse, false have you been to the Ta-an, nor does it seem that the Great Father approves your act, since before you stand A-ta, escaped from slavery, and Menzono-men, no priest, but a warrior, your plot a failure.

"Yet, since to your twisted mind it seemed a worthy act, since you hoped thus to add to the glory of the Great Father, it is not in my mind to slay you forthwith, even though by the law of the tribe treachery is so punished.

"Therefore make now your choice; either to die on the Great Altar, at the hands of the priests, in sacrifice, that the Great Father, seeing your death, may accept this in expiation; or taking bow and arrows, to seek Menzono-men in the forest, fighting with him. Should you slay him against whom you have plotted, then may the Ta-an take it as a sign that O-Ma-Ken approves your act, and you shall go free, returning once more to the priestly office. Choose!"

Now it chanced that Ta-nu-ko, unlike the most of the priests, was skilled in the use of the bow; with him it was a diversion, an amusement, and often had he practised it in hours of leisure from his duties at the altar. Therefore, when T'san-va-men offered the alternative, the priest's eyes lit up, and not doubting that he could conquer, he answered:

"I accept the trial; let bows be given, and set us to seek each other deep in the forest!"

"So be it," said the chieftain. "L'vu and Sen-va, let the bows be brought; give each man three arrows; conduct the priest a thousand paces into the forest thither"—and he pointed northwest—"and Menzono-men a thousand paces there"—and he pointed northeast. "Then let them seek each other. It is said; go!"

L'vu and Sen-va, each with a bow and three arrows, stepped forward to lead the duelists to their places, Menzono-men casting a last look at A-ta as he followed the steps of Sen-va. Then the warriors of the Ta-an settled themselves to wait the outcome, squatting about the little glade and speaking in hushed voices.

A-ta, knowing the chief priest's skill with the bow, crouched, shivering with fear for her lover, behind the log where sat the chieftain, impassive as a rock. Presently was heard the long-drawn, quavering call of L'vu, announcing that his man was placed, and that of Sen-va replying, and the warriors knew the hunt was on; that one or both of the duelists would fall—the die was cast. At length Sen-va returned, to take his place in the group about the chieftain, and soon L'vu also stepped from the forest.

All that long afternoon the Great Chieftain and his men sat in the little glade, and behind him crouched A-ta, clenching and unclenching her hands; and so the slow day dragged on.

And now the chieftain began to cast anxious glances at the sun, which was drawing low down in the western sky; no sign of either of the two had appeared, and sunset was near. But as the sun touched the tops of the western trees and the long shadows crept across the grass a sudden sound broke the hush of afternoon; one long, shuddering scream, the scream of a man in agony, rang through the forest—and once more all was still.

The Winged Death had found one—but which? A-ta's heart swelled till it seemed as though it would burst, then the blood swept away from it, leaving her cold. Which would return, which would step from the forest? It seemed long hours ere a step sounded, a rustling in the brush as a man passed through, drawing nearer and nearer the little glade—which?

A long-drawn sigh from the eagerly watching warriors, a joyful cry from A-ta—and Menzono-men, blood trickling from a wound on his shoulder, staggered forth to kneel at the feet of T'san-va-men! The Great Chieftain rose, grim and stern.

"Menzono-men," he said, "you have returned; what of Ta-nu-ko? Is he in very truth wrapped in death? Has his soul gone into the Long Dark? Or does he lie wounded in the forest? Speak!"

The young man strove to answer, but, exhausted from the hunt, pitched forward at the chieftain's feet. T'san-va-men motioned to the warriors to lift him up, but at that moment

Sar-no-m'rai touched his leader on the shoulder, pointing upward. Far above the tree-tops showed a speck in the sky, growing swiftly larger and larger, till presently, clearly seen of all, a vulture, wide and black of wing, dropped from the blue, falling, falling, like a plummet, straight to the forest. Another followed—another—another—

NEXT MORNING T'SAN-VA-MEN called his warriors together, and when all were assembled he spoke to them, saying:

"Men of the Ta-an, A-ta, escaped from the Little Hairy Men, has given counsel. At one spot only can we ford the Farther River, on the southern bank of which the Little Hairy Men make their homes. This ford they guard well, it being further guarded by the high bank of the stream. Therefore, says A-ta—and the counsel seems good—let us pass this river on which we have made our camp, betake ourselves through the forest to the Farther River, and there make for ourselves many of the Cave That Swims On the Water, such as that in which A-ta returned.

"Thus shall we pass the river that guards the Little Hairy Men on the north, avoiding also the morass which—A-ta tells—guards their homes on the south and west. Thus may we cross, falling upon the Little Hairy Men from the east, the up-stream side of their camp, the side unprotected save by themselves. Is the counsel good?"

"It is good! It is good!" cried the warriors. "Let us go! Lead on, Great Chieftain!"

"One other thing," spoke T'san-va-men. "It is against the law of the Ta-an that a woman go with us to war, yet would I have A-ta, that she may show us the manner of making the Cave That Swims On the Water. What say you, tribesmen?"

A silence followed, each man eying his neighbor doubtfully; the word of the chieftain was strong, yet strong also was the law and the respect due the law. At length spoke Sar-no-m'rai, he who spoke but seldom:

"Men of the Ta-an," he said, "who makes the law? Is it not ourselves? Can we not then unmake the law, even as an artisan can destroy the bow that he has made, or an artist the carving? If then it is our desire that A-ta go with us, shall she not do so? Who is there to gainsay us? It is *our* law!"

A murmur sounded among the warriors, growing in strength and at last breaking into words:

"It is our law! A-ta shall go! It is we who make the law; let the girl go with us to war!"

And the acclamation swelled till the Great Chieftain held up his hand, saying:

"It is enough; A-ta goes with us! Cross we now the river that lies before us and take we our way through the forest, to fall upon the Little Hairy Men!"

And taking their weapons and falling into formation in their various companies, the warriors of the Ta-an marched some two thousand paces back up-stream to where the river, broad and shallow, offered easy passage, and, fording the stream, plunged into the depths of the thick forest, T'san-va-men, accompanied by L'vu, Sar-no-m'rai, Kan-to, and Sen-va, leading, and with them A-ta, first of the women of the Ta-an to march with the men to war.

6

THE SWAMP OF FEAR

FIFTEEN DAYS LATER the Great Chieftain sent for Menzono-men, and the latter accompanied Kan-to, the messenger, to their leader. During those fifteen days the Ta-an had pressed through the forest, crossing the broad "V" of land, five days' journey in width, that here separated the river of the Ta-an from the Farther River, and had established their camp several thousand paces up-stream from the homes of the Little Hairy Men and half a day's travel inland.

They had sent out scouts—sentries, rather—to guard against wandering individuals from Gur's tribe who might chance to discover them, and under this protection the artists and craftsmen of the tribe, aided by the warriors, had set to work to fell trees and make canoes, instructed by A-ta, inventor of the Cave That Swims On The Water.

It was, indeed, somewhat unusual for the artists and artisans of the Ta-an to accompany the fighting-men to war, but in such a case as this, when the call went out for the full man-power of the tribe, they did so, and in this instance it was well that they were there, for the warriors, trained to battle and in the hunt, could not handle tools so well as men trained from infancy in their use.

At suggestion of L'vu the canoes were made of the largest logs, capable, when hollowed out, of holding twenty men, and Sar-no-m'rai also had come forward with advice. To this genius of the trail may be credited the invention of the paddle, fashioned from a tree limb, as a result of which each man of the tribe was furnished with this implement of progress, in more senses than one.

By now three canoes had been completed, and the tribesmen were looking forward eagerly to the day, not far off, when they should make the projected descent upon the Little Hairy Men, the tribe that acknowledged Gur's leadership.

Menzono-men, summoned, followed Kan-to, wondering at the chieftain's sending for him, and questioning Kan-to, who, however, knew naught of the purpose. Coming to where the leader sat, calm and dignified, on his skin-covered log, the young man bowed, tracing with his finger on the grass. T'san-va-men's face relaxed and he smiled at the youth, then said:

"Menzono-men, you being now a warrior, and A-ta being once more among us, doubtless you desire to wed her as soon as may be?"

"In very truth, Great Chieftain!" replied Menzono-men.

"Your endurance have you proven in the test laid upon you; likewise your courage in face of peril. But A-ta, foster-daughter to T'san-va-men, Lord of the Winged Death, is one to mate with the highest. Therefore still further proof must you give, of craft and skill and courage in face of an enemy, even greater proof than in the fight with the Chief Priest. Take, therefore, twenty men, full-armed; take also a Cave That Swims On The Water; cross the Farther River; march secretly upon the Little Hairy Men, spying out their camp on all sides and bringing word to me of where and when and how we may best attack. It is said; go!"

Menzono-men bowed respectfully and asked:

"Great Chieftain, may I take with me Sar-no-m'rai as one of the twenty?"

The corners of T'san-va-men's mouth twitched slightly at this crafty request, but he suppressed a smile and answered:

"No; nor L'vu nor Kan-to nor Sen-va. Leader are you of the party, and upon yourself must you depend."

The young warrior bowed once more and withdrew, going among the party and choosing his men, instructing each to take weapons and food and join him. Soon they set out, plunging in single file into the trees, and all the rest of the day Menzono-men led his party through the forest, reaching the river about sunset and making camp—a cold camp, lest the fires be seen by any of the Little Hairy Men—a few yards from the shore, where he allowed his men to rest and eat while he waited for dark. Shortly before the woods were utterly dark he sent his followers to bring the canoe and paddles, he himself remaining oh guard. Behind him the woods were hushed save for the cries and chirping of nesting birds, and before him the broad river flowed smooth and black in the dusk, its surface broken at times as a fish leaped with silvery flash.

Beyond the stream the forest stretched black and impenetrable to the eye as Menzono-men peered across, seeking any slightest movement which might betray the presence of an enemy on the farther shore. But nothing appeared, and the solitude was unbroken till his men returned bearing the great canoe, when he bade them set it down by the water's edge that he might speak a few words. They did so, gathering in a compact group about him, and he addressed them:

"Men of the Ta-an, great honor has our chieftain done us, in thus sending us to spy out the land of the Little Hairy Men, for on us may hinge the outcome of the war; whether failure or success meets the arms of the People of the Mountain Caves, whether we return victorious or leave our bones to whiten by the Farther River. Be ye then swift and silent, following one who, younger in warfare than yourselves, has yet been named by the Great Chieftain for this work. Cross we now the river, treading softly down the farther bank till we reach the homes of the Little Hairy Men, seeking to leave no trail, seeking to learn of their camp, slaying but at need, and slaying, if slay we must, in silence. It is said!"

Crossing the river, dawn found Menzono-men and his scouts strung out in a long line, belly-down on the grass, peering through screening brush at the open space which lay before the caves of those whom they sought.

This open space, three hundred paces in width and a thousand in length, had on its northern side the broad surface of the Farther River, which here flowed almost due west; on the eastern end—where lay Menzono-men—the ground rose somewhat steeply to a terrace ten times the height of a tall man, and this terrace, curving round to the southern side of the flat below, showed the rude caves and shelters of the tribe of the Little Hairy Men over whom Gur held the chieftainship.

Farther south the hill sloped gradually down into a broad morass, which, turning the western end of the hill, protected Gur's camp on the down-stream end.

Thus the camp, guarded on the north by the river, on the west by the morass, and on the south by morass and hill, lay open to attack only from the east. Part of this the leader of the scouts knew from A-ta's words, part he could see from where he lay, and part was yet hidden from him, to become known at a later time.

As Menzono-men lay watching, there appeared at the mouths of the various caves numerous women, who stirred and made up the fires, then set about preparing the morning meal, and Menzono-men was astonished to see no warriors come forth; the food cooked, it was eaten by the women, companied only by certain youths and old men, and even while Menzono-men wondered over this there rose in the forest behind him a sound as of men approaching.

He whispered quickly to the man nearest, and as the word was passed, the warriors of the Ta-an, grasping their weapons, faced about and waited what might come.

Nearer and nearer came the rustling, and presently, with a shout, there burst forth a great crowd of the Little Hairy Men, who, returning from a hunt, had chanced on the trail of the scouts of the Ta-an and had followed swiftly to attack.

Taken by surprise, Menzono-men and his followers fought desperately, but, outnumbered, were swept back by the very weight of the swarming savages and were rushed down the slope which lay at their backs. Cornered, it seemed as though annihilation waited them, and they fought like men resolved to sell their lives as dearly as might be, but Menzono-men, struck by a sudden thought, shouted above the noise of battle:

"To the caves, men of the Ta-an! To the caves!" and led the way. No room was there to draw bow or use lance; swarming, surging, the men of Gur pressed close; knee to knee and breast to breast the tribesmen fought, using dagger or swinging the deadly ax.

Onward through the circling masses the Ta-an cut their way, moving forward step by step, feeling in their faces the hot breath of the savages, against their bodies the rough and sweaty skin of the Little Hairy Men; treading on still bodies or on men who groaned and writhed; panting, with contorted faces and snarling lips, shoulder to shoulder, cutting, striking, stabbing, they held their way till at length the caves were reached and a last desperate push cleared the path—into the largest cave—half held the opening while the others swung their bows—a storm of arrows swept the Little Hairy Men back—great stones were piled in the opening—and for the time the warriors of the Ta-an were safe.

Safe! As a wolf is safe in a trap! The heart of the leader sank as he realized, given space for thought, that there was no escape. But one way out, and that through the swarming foes! For a time he could hold them at bay, but in the end hunger must have its way with him and his men—the Little Hairy People need but sit and wait!

No aid could he hope for from T'san-va-men; the Great Chieftain would not move till his scouts returned—or till it was too late! And how long could he hold out? Two or three days at most; but sixteen remained of his twenty men—three had fallen in the fight, and one, snatched from the ranks, had been torn in pieces before his comrades' eyes. Yet, tortured, he had died as became a warrior; no sound had issued from his lips while the savages wrenched his limbs apart.

And another thing, worse than hunger, worse than wounds—thirst! No water had the men of the Ta-an, and all but two bore wounds; and all began to feel the thirst that comes from battle, of effort, and of loss of blood.

Quickly Menzono-men took count of these things, quickly he formed his decision, and called his men to him.

"Men of the Ta-an," he said, "not long can we hold out here; the Little Hairy Men have hunger and thirst to aid. Word must be carried to the Great Chieftain. Through the morass to the west can one slip out, swimming the river, and mine is it to take this task, since it offers the greatest peril. Ku-ten, yours it is to command in my absence; this night I go, seeking to pass the guards. If I return not, the leadership is yours."

"Nay, Slayer of Wolves," spoke Ku-ten, "rather it be mine to go; yours is it to lead. Further, A-ta awaits you, and none waits me; let me then go, for it is in my mind that he who goes is like to take the last journey—that into the Long Dark!"

Others spoke, each seeking the more perilous task, till at length Menzono-men lost patience and exclaimed, his eyes flashing:

"Am I not leader? Yours is it to obey! To-night I go!" and opposition ceased.

Three times that day the Little Hairy Men, forming in a compact though irregular body, swept up the slope and tried to storm the defenses, and each time, met by a deadly arrow-sleet, they were driven back, broken, fleeing before that storm of wood and stone. At last came night, drawing its kindly mantle over the death and torment that changed that pleasant place to a hell of agony and hate, and with the sinking of the sun Menzono-men prepared.

Drawing a little apart, he prayed to the Great Father for aid, then, rising, cast aside all weapons save only his dagger and flint, long and keen. In a sack hung from his quiver he carried a little stock of grease to keep his bow-string from wetting, and with this he rubbed himself from crown to toe, afterward rubbing the earth, that his white skin might not betray him. He pressed the hands of his comrades, one by one, and then, it being fully dark, the watch-fires not yet lit, slid like a snake over the rocks which formed a breastwork at the entrance, and, turning, crawled, belly to the earth, up the slope of the hill which lay behind the cave.

It was his plan to cross the hill and skirt along its base to the western end, there plunging into the swamp, for he knew that the Little Hairy Men would have a cordon of guards drawn about the cave, nor, indeed, had he reached the crest of the hill when, looking up, he saw, outlined against the sky, a savage form, not twenty paces before him the brush here growing thin and low.

Menzono-men lay silently as a sentinel passed along the crest, pacing slowly back and forth, meeting at each end of his travel another who also paced his round. Menzono-men's first thought was to creep near and, leaping on the man, slay him, but an instant's reflection told him that this would not do, and he crept toward the right, to the meeting-place of the two.

Silent, scarce breathing, he hugged the ground till they met, exchanged a few words, and parted, when Menzono-men, waiting till they were some paces off, wriggled swiftly past and down the southern slope of the hill. Reaching the bottom, he lay still and rested a few moments, then rose to a crouching posture and turned west. From bush to bush he flitted, keeping ever hidden; at times, where no cover offered, crawling once more, till at length he reached the swamp.

Here he halted for a time, considering. He dared not strike in close to the base of the hill, lest he be seen, nor, on the other hand, could he travel far to the west for fear that, mired, he should be lost, even as he had once seen the mighty bulk of a mammoth sink, wallowing and struggling beneath the mud and slime.

And now the great morass grew lighter, and he could see faint details as the moon peered over the tree-tops, pouring a cold light down upon the swamp—the home of reptiles, of miasma, of lurking death.

Menzono-men cursed to himself, drew a long breath, and crept into the morass. Deeper and deeper he went, the water rising to his waist as his feet sank into the ooze from which bubbles gurgled upward as from the lungs of a drowning man. The reeds blocked his way, and the sharp-edged swordgrass stabbed and cut at his naked body; swarming millions of mosquitoes, disturbed by his passage, rose in clouds about his head, singing their high-pitched song, biting, stinging, till the blood streamed down his face and chest and back, and, frantic from the torment, he plunged beneath the water. But the relief was momentary; when he emerged they settled once more about him, and through all that dreadful night his myriad torturers followed close.

The moon now gleamed on the swamp, lighting it up with steady glow, as on and on he pressed.

And now he began to grow weak from loss of blood; it seemed to him that mocking faces rose before him, among them the face of Ta-nu-ko, twisted, agonized, as the arrow pierced his vitals; the face of Gur, exulting; unknown, inhuman faces, half man, half beast; and Menzono-men, cursing, struck at them with his dagger, when they fled away, and only the never-ending swamp lay before him, glittering under the now waning moon.

On and on he struggled, the chill of night striking his limbs, numbing and paralyzing, and presently the moon had sunk, and a faint glow in the sky proclaimed the coming of the dawn.

Eagerly he pressed on, catching at times fugitive glimpses of the water, oily in its smoothness—of a sudden he stopped, arrested in mid-stride, for a momentary thinning of the mist, which closed again at once, had shown him the form of a man, one of his enemies, resting on his knees, his head thrown forward as if listening.

Was he to be halted now? Pulling himself together, calling up his failing strength, slowly, silently, more cautiously than ever, Menzono-men crept forward, dagger in hand—he drew near the spot where the closing mist had hid the foe—nearer—nearer—he could make out the form—nearer—he drew back his arm to strike—one step—he held the blow, staring in amazement—the man was dead!

A deep wound in the chest showed whence the life had fled; stricken to death in the fight of the day before, the

Little Hairy Man had rolled into the river; carried down, he had struggled ashore, had made his way to this spot of firmer ground, and here had died, resting against the bush that now upheld his lifeless form.

Menzono-men drew a deep breath, skirted around the body of the foe, and slipped into the river, pushing his way through the sedge till deeper water was reached, then, secure from chance vision, hidden under the fog wreaths of early morning, the cool water bringing new life to his wearied limbs, he struck out for the farther shore.

LATE THAT AFTERNOON the Great Chieftain, directing, deep in the forest, the making of the canoes, was startled at the appearance of a horrible figure that struggled through the brush into the clearing where the trees had been felled. Plastered and caked with mud and gore, blood still trickling from the newly opened wound in his shoulder, green slime from the swamp clinging in his hair, his head and arms and body blotched and swollen and distorted from the venom of the mosquitoes, Menzono-men, exhausted, reeled into the clearing.

Dropping their tools, the warriors crowded about him till L'vu and Sar-no-m'rai, pushing through the throng, caught him under the arms and led him before the chieftain. Summoning his failing strength, Menzono-men straightened up, speaking through swollen lips, his voice thick and blurred, mumbling:

"Surrounded—ambush—in the caves—fighting—Ku-ten commands—four slain—through the swamp—mosquitoes—devils—the river—" His voice trailed off into an unintelligible mutter, his head dropped forward, his knees sagged, his body slumped against the arms of the two who held him, and gently they eased him to the ground at the feet of the Great Chieftain.

For the space of ten breaths the chieftain stood in thought, while all watched, none moving, and then he spoke, his orders rattling like hail, his voice harsh with the note of authority:

"Take weapons, form ranks; leave these logs—those at the river will serve. L'vu, Kan-to, Sar-no-m'rai, with me; Sen-va and A-ta here; you, and you, and you"—with pointing finger he chose five from among the warriors—"here as a guard. Care for this man; bathe and feed him; give him to drink and let him rest; he has done well. To the rescue, men of the Ta-an! Forward!"

By midnight the warriors of the Ta-an had reached the river, bringing down to the shore the two canoes left by Menzono-men and three others since completed and hidden, in readiness for the attack. But now there rose in the mind of the chieftain a question, a doubt. Would it be better to cross far up-stream, making several trips to ferry across the four or five hundred warriors, then march down upon the Little Hairy Men, forcing their defenses, or to take a hundred men in the canoes and thrust straight across the river, trusting to surprise, to terrify, the enemy by their first sight of the Cave That Swims On The Water? He called his counselors to him and laid the matter before them, and, as usual, it was Sar-no-m'rai, the silent, who found the answer:

"Let the men cross straight," he said, "and to each log let as many as may find place cling fast, their bodies in the stream. Thus the logs will not be overweighted, yet may the warriors cross nor tire themselves with swimming.

Coming within bow-shot or nearer, let them loose their hold of the logs and swim ashore, those in the Caves That Swim On The Water covering them meanwhile with flight after flight of arrows. Landing, they will make good their footing till the others reach the bank."

"Well is it spoken," said the chieftain. "Thus shall we bring all to the attack, on the least guarded side."

And so was it ordered and so was it done. A hundred warriors, each with his strung bow and a quiver of arrows beside him, manned the canoes, and the rest, armed with ax and dagger for hand-to-hand combat, trailed in the water, hands on the gunwales of the craft, and thus, propelled by the silent paddles, the men of the Ta-an swept down on their foes.

It was a cloudy night; behind great masses of dark wind-driven clouds the moon shone, but little light did it cast on the river and the shore. From time to time fitful gleams broke through as the skyey rack was torn apart by hurtling gusts, which bent and swayed the trees and roughened the surface of the mighty river, making the passage to the unaccustomed paddlers of the Ta-an, doubly, trebly hard.

Yet was the wind an aid; the noise of its rush and sweep among the trees drowned all sounds of the passage, and the rough water was far less likely to show strange sights than had it been as glass. Further, the cloudy darkness helped, since the Little Hairy Men, blinded by their own watch-fires, could not well see the stream. Also, they trusted the river; none could cross it—to their minds—save by swimming, and warriors who swam that broad water would not come to shore with strength to fight. So it was that the men of the Ta-an were within fifty paces of the shore ere Gur, chancing to cast an eye toward the stream at the very moment that the moon peered from behind a cloud, caught sight of armed men coming in strange fashion on the bosom of the water. The Great Chieftain heard Gur's warning shout, and answered it with an order to his own men.

"Now, swimmers! Bowmen, make ready! To the shore!"

The swimmers loosed their grip and with the long, sweeping overhand stroke rushed for the bank, but the canoes, driven by strong arms, bade fair to overtake them, and on the instant T'san-va-men changed his plan. Loud above the roar of the wind and the cries of the gathering enemy sounded his voice:

"Bowmen, ashore! Make good the landing! Forward!" and the canoes crept on, passing the swimming warriors, rushing to the bank, driving high on the sloping ground, and from them sprang the warriors. In open order they knelt, speeding their arrows, holding back the rush of the enemy, till the axmen, landing, ranged themselves in line.

Then followed a dreadful fight, fought by the ruddy light of the leaping fires and the cold gleams that from time to time broke through the clouds. No quarter was asked on either side, nor was any given; falling, a man died where he fell, from blow of ax or club or from dagger-thrust. Thrice the swarming hordes of the Little Hairy Men fell back, but the fourth time, rallying to Gur's call, they pressed on and closed with the men of the Ta-an.

Ax and dagger and club rose and fell, the camp resounded with the shrieks and groans of wounded men, with the battle-cries of the Little Hairy Men, with the screams of the women, who watched from the slope of the hill. Backward and forward swayed the battle, the Ta-an at times hurled back toward the river-bank by press of numbers, then, rallying, driving their foes before them toward the caves.

In the heat of the fight met Gur and T'san-va-men, and the battle paused about them as they closed. Snarling like a beast, Gur rushed on his foe, his great war-club raised high for the downward sweep, but like the panther of the forest the Great Chieftain waited—the club swept down—the leader of the Ta-an sprang back—the club crashed on the earth, and ere Gur, overbalanced, could catch himself, T'san-va-men leaped.

"This for A-ta!" he cried, and his long, keen dagger flashed in the moonlight; Gur fell, and the Little Hairy Men, disheartened, gave back. At that instant the scouts of Menzono-men, rushing down the hill, fell on the foe in the rear, and the battle swiftly became a rout; some few of the Little Hairy Men escaped, passing over the hill to the east and losing themselves in the forest ere overtaken by the men of the Ta-an; some few, fleeing to the west, won through the morass, but most who chose that route were bogged and mired in the swamp and drowned.

And when the pale light of morning struggled through the clouds even T'san-va-men, stern chieftain that he was, shuddered as he looked about him on the havoc the night had brought. Above, on the hill, the wailing women; nearer, before the caves, three row of dead, where the Little Hairy Men had broken before the arrows of the Ta-an; still nearer, on the shore, a ghastly tangled mass of dead and dying, friend and foe mingled in strange, unnatural postures, the sands beneath them red. T'san-va-men sighed deeply and turned to the shore, shaking his head. Across the chieftain's shoulders L'vu, his giant friend, laid an arm.

"Nay, Lord of the Winged Death," he spoke, "it had to be; no other way lay open before us. Not safe were the lives of the Ta-an while the Little Hairy Men held sway in the forest."

"You speak the words of truth, friend of mine," answered the Great Chieftain. "Yet is my soul sick within me. Let us go."

The warriors crossed once more the river, ferried by twenties, and again back in the forest, a litter was made for Menzono-men, two poles being laid side by side and branches wattled across, leaves laid on these making soft the bed. Eight scout warriors lifted it, the young man resting thereon, for the return to the homes of the Ta-an, A-ta walking beside and holding the hand of her lover.

Gradually, as the days passed, Menzono-men recovered his strength, helped thereto in no small measure by the pressure of that soft hand in his and the looks bent on him by those bright eyes, ever turned in love toward his face, toward his contented smile, and the day before the homes of the Ta-an were reached he begged to be set down, that he might return, marching on his own feet, not carried on the shoulders of others.

His request was granted, and so the entry into the camp was made, when the young man saw admiring crowds pressing around him, to touch his hand—the chieftain had sent messengers ahead, to tell of the victory and of the part A-ta and Menzono-men had played. None ventured to touch the hand of A-ta; Menzono-men was a hero, but she was something more; he had crossed the Swamp of

Death, but she had made the Cave That Swims On The Water, and the women and children and old men of the Ta-an gazed on her with awe, pressing close, bowing, but not daring to lay hand on hers. Even her own father bent respectfully before her, whereat A-ta was mightily amused and wished to laugh, but did not.

Reaching the camp, the Great Chieftain sent out a call for all the tribe to assemble next midday at the Rock of Council, sending messengers in all directions, that none might be absent, and when the sun stood overhead on the following day came the throngs, with much buzz of thought, crowding about the Rock.

Presently came T'san-va-men, his own personal followers with him, also Menzono-men and A-ta, and the crowd parted to let them pass. Mounting the Rock, the Great Chieftain waited till silence spread over the multitude, then he spoke, his strong voice carrying to all parts of the clearing:

"People of the Ta-an," he said, "by now is it known to you, from the lips of others, how we fought and won; you have heard of the death of the traitorous Chief Priest at the hands of Menzono-men, in fair fight; you have heard of how Menzono-men, winning through the deadly swamp, brought news of the ambush; and you have heard of how the victory came, in no small measure, through A-ta, first maker of the Cave That Swims On The Water. Well indeed has Menzono-men proven himself, and great shall be his reward, for A-ta shall he have to wife.

"Remains then the reward of A-ta. People of the Mountain Caves, by old tradition, by the law of the tribe, handed down from ere the time of Snorr, Great Chieftain of the,

Ta-an, each chieftain is one who has aided the tribe. My service, the Winged Death, is known to you, likewise that of him who went before, Na-t'san, Son of the Red God, who first brought the gift of fire to the tribesmen.

"But to you here gathered do I say that the service of this maiden is as great as his or mine; in years to come the Cave That Swims On The Water is destined to bring aid and comfort, food and safety and help to the People of the Mountain Caves. Therefore should she be chieftain in my place when it is mine to make the journey into the Long Dark.

"But since no woman, by the law of the tribe, may rule over us, may hold the baton of the chieftain, this may not be. Yet reward must she have, and a great one, and therefore, calling to witness the Great Father who rules us all, in his name do I swear, and call upon you to see that the oath is kept, that the first-born son of A-ta shall take my place, ruling over the Ta-an in my stead when I am gone. I have sworn."

Waving his hand, the Great Chieftain stepped down from the Rock of Council, and a mighty shout rose swelling from the crowd:

"Hail, A-ta, Girl of the Mountain Caves! Hail to her who gives us the Cave That Swims On The Water! Hail and long life to her and to her husband, who passed through the Swamp of Death to bring word to the Great Chieftain! Long life and honor and joy be theirs!"

GREAT FEASTING WAS there at the wedding of Menzo-no-men and A-ta, great feasting and many songs. Wild cattle and horses were roasted whole, in great pits, together with sweet roots and fruit and berries from the forest.

Dances also were there, and beating of drums, for had not the Great Chieftain himself ordered that all honor should be paid these two? And when at last the feasting was done, the songs sung, and the dancers wearied, when the Great Chieftain, as became his dignity, had withdrawn to his own cave, torches were seized, and the People of the Mountain Caves, a compact body, escorted the young couple to the cave that was to be their home.

There in the mouth of the cave halted Menzono-men and A-ta, their eyes shining with happiness, she pressing close to him, his arm about her shoulders, while the crowd, a little down the slope, shouted and waved the flaring torches. Thrice Menzono-men strove to speak, but his heart was too full, and at last he merely flung out his arm in sign of greeting and thanks.

And so may we also take leave of them, of Menzono-men, Slayer of Wolves, the man who passed the Swamp of Death, and A-ta, the Girl of the Mountain Caves, who gave to her people the Cave That Swims On The Water.

Printed in the USA
CPSIA information can be obtained
at www.ICGtesting.com
JSHW020056071223
53156JS00001B/36